When the Mourning Dove Cries

BY

Madgelyn Hawk

This book is a work of fiction. Places, events, and situations in this story are purely fictional. Any resemblance to actual persons, living or dead, is coincidental. Although Part 3 is a true story.

ISBN: 1-4107-3449-8 (e-book)
ISBN: 1-4107-4000-5 (Paperback)

Library of Congress Control Number: 2003092170

This book is printed on acid free paper.

Printed in the United States of America
Bloomington, IN

1stBooks - rev. 05/05/03

Dedication

I dedicate this book first and most to my
dear Dale who told me over one hundred
years ago that he would take care of me for
all eternity and second to my most
treasured loves my children and family.

Maggie's story -Part 1

1835, is that the year or is that what the man paid for us? I hold Julie's hand as she stands on the auction block along side me. I was a dark skinned, skinny little girl about five years old named Maggie. My big brown eyes showed fright but I was determined that I would not act scared. After all, I needed to be brave. I stuck my chin out and held up my little head and looked directly into the many faces looking up at me.

My attention fell on a large burly man wearing a brown hat. He seemed to be motioning for me and Julie to join him As we stepped down off the platform I heard him say to his three companions 'Come on, get those gals ready to go. "Where?" I asked Julie. "Where are we going?" Julie just looks sad and holds my hand tighter. "We've been bought by that man over there, and we gotta get ready to go," she explains. "Lord only knows where to, but you remember don't tell nary a soul that I am not your momma gal, or they will sell you again with out me." I think, Julie is right, I just better hold her hand and go along without a fight. I heard the people auction man say that I am only five this year and I could get lost. I pick up my little bundle which contains my only doll that Fanny had made for me. I also have in my bundle a pretty rock that glitters in the sun. These are the only possessions that I had acquired in my short little life.

I watch as a big man walks toward Julie holding a big ugly chain. The man smiles at Julie and me as he places it around her ankle and says," This won't be so bad if you don't pull against it. Don't need one on the little one," he says. "She won't run." Why does he think I won't run, I wonder. He don't know nothin about me. Aint no one know nothin about me but the Lord in the sky. I knows all about the Lord in the sky because Fanny had told me daily about him.

Fanny was the lady that had taken care of me my whole life. It was from this woman's breast that I had received my nourishment.

I look at Julie and notice that she tries to smile even though she is as frightened as I am. I feel so bad for her as she is chained to the other people. These other dear people had been bought as we had been. I grab for Julie's hand as the line of people start walking behind a big wagon. Some of the fat women get to ride in the wagons as well as do some of the children. The man in the brown hat offers to help me into the wagon. I hold up my head and say, "No thank you, I will walk." He responds by shouting, "Hey, we got us a little lady here; maybe she will do good in the big house."

As I walk beside Julie I find myself wishing that I had gotten on the wagon with the other children because by now my feet had started to bleed.

1

I had not been given shoes, as Julie had, and my tender little feet hurt. I endure my discomfort quietly because no one will see that I am not lady enough to "do good in the big house", whatever that means. As we walk forever it seems, I feel so tired and I think my feet will never be the same again. As the sun starts to go over the hill we come to a stop under some big shade trees. I sit down with Julie and the others on the green cool grass. "Man, look at your feet gal." Julie exclaims, as she holds my little brown, dusty, sore foot up so she can examine it more closely. "It's all right I am O.K..," I tell her as I squirm to get away from her grasp. I am squirming not only to get away from Julie but I have an urgent need. "Julie I have to pee right now, can you walk with me over behind that tree?" Julie tells me to go by myself because she is still chained to the others and can't go with me. "Where do you pee?" I asked. Julie answered, "Well, I have to pee where I am at and then I kinda move over so as I don't sit in it." "Well, I'll just pee where I am at too." As I pee where I'm at I feel the grass beneath my sore feet become wet and my own urine soothes my tired, little, aching feet. I move over to sit down by my new momma, Julie. The man in the brown hat brings us our evening meal. It was only dried bread and some water but I was hungry and ate it without complaining. The fat women get something that looked like dried meat with their bread. I asked Julie, "Why do they get more to eat than we do? Is it because they are fat and they can eat more?" Julie smiled as she answered, "No, it because they are going to have babies and they need more to eat than we do." "Well," I said." If I ever get hungry I'll just have a baby." This made Julie laugh and I noticed how her big brown eyes took on a little sparkle and her laughter sounded like the cry of a small child.

As I finish eating my bread and drinking my little cupful of water I notice the people lying down, and I do also. As I lay down to rest my thoughts run over the events of the few last days. I see in my mind the place that I have called home since birth. In the large room where I spent my days there were other children that I called my friends. The walls of the room are bare wood as well as the floor. If I wasn't careful I could get a nasty splinter from the floor. Along one wall there are pallets where I slept along side other children all under the age of five. In the center of the room there is a long wooden table where we received our meals. At the far end of the room there is a big black fire place used for heat as well as for cooking. The only clothing I have is a little brown dress and when Fanny washes it I have to go naked until it dries. The babies wear a thin cloth for a diaper and when you don't need one anymore you only wear a dress. The boys wear the same thing.

I gather with the other children to visit with a man called Master Dave. Often when he visits us he brings candy and we are always excited to see him. I notice he keeps looking at me as he talks with Fanny. Fanny looks as if she is about to cry as she and Master Dave approach me. I smile my biggest smile in order to collect my candy. "Get her ready to go Fanny; she is old enough this year." I wonder where I am going, but I've learned by now not to ask questions, nor do I dare to talk when Master Dave is in the room. I look up at Fanny and I see tears in her loving brown eyes. She takes my hand and walks with me to the group of other people waiting outside. I am delighted when I am given a new dress to wear on my special adventure to somewhere. I look around to see if Fanny likes my new dress and I can't find her. There were other children gathered with me, many I had never seen before and they had on new dresses like mine. I now am getting a little frightened because I don't see a familiar face. I walk over to a young woman standing with a man over by a huge wagon. "Have you seen Fanny?" I asked. "No, we haven't honey", the woman replies. I notice that they are sad and I wonder what everyone is so sad about.

I start to walk over to the cabin where I live to find Fanny and the man in the brown hat stops me. "Where do you think you are going little missy?" he asked. "I'm going to find Fanny so that I can show her my new dress", I tell him. "Oh, is that right now? Well, you just march yourself back over to where you were put and I'll tell Fanny all about your new dress." "No, I don't like that," I tell him. "I will tell her myself." He stooped to my level, and his breath was so bad that I felt as if I couldn't breathe. He said in a low tone that frightened me, "You better get yourself back over with the others or I'll take that new dress away from you. I cried for Fanny and started to run. He grabbed me and carried me under his arm like a sack of flour to the others that had gathered by the wagon. He sat me down by the young woman I had talked to earlier. "This is Julie and she is your new momma." He said in a gruff voice. Now you don't tell anyone that she aint." I look up at the woman named Julie and I see that she is crying. "Where are we going?" asked her. Julie shrugs her shoulders and takes my hand. We are standing by the wagon with a lot of other people. As I look at the faces I see that some are crying and some are not showing any expressions at all. I hear my name called and I see Fanny running toward the wagon. She approaches and hands me a bundle. "This is a doll I made for you Maggie; you hug this doll when you feel scared." Fanny knew that thunder storms scared me and I would run to her in the night to be held tight." I also put your pretty rock in there, now you be a good girl and remember that I will always love you no matter where you are." "But, where am I going Fanny?" I cried. "I want to stay with you." "You can't baby," she said. "You just hold your little head up and be a brave little girl. Don't forget your Bible stories I told you and remember to say your prayers. God listens." I reach for Fanny but she just

3

shakes her head and walks away from me. I call her name but she keeps walking with her head down. I know that she is crying and I can't hold her.

I look at Julie and she too is crying. I see her smile through her tears as a young man approaches the wagon. He is yelling Julie's name as he runs to the wagon. I hear Master Dave yell, "Sug, you stop right there and go back to your house. You don't have any reason to be here!" The man called Sug stops in his tracks and says, "That is my woman and you aint gonna sell her, as long as I am alive I'll keep you from it!" He bellowed. "I love her and she loves me." The man in the brown hat walks over to the man called Sug and says, "Now why don't you just go home and mind your own business, everything is being handled here just the way it's supposed to be." At this time Sug took a wide swing and hit the man on the jaw. The man in the brown hat jumped on Sug. The man's companions jump Sug as well. I thought they were killing him.

I watched them throw him to the ground. I couldn't see the fight as others had gathered around them. I heard Sug's cries and as they finished their beating I could see Sug lying on the ground calling out Julie's name. He was bleeding so badly that I couldn't make out his face any longer. Julie was screaming and started to run to him. She was screaming out Sug's name and was in a fit of hysteria as the men grabbed her and tossed her to the ground. I had never seen anyone grown up have a temper tantrum so violently. I felt as though I should be able to do something, as I had helped Fanny with the babies in the nursery many times. I felt so helpless, lost and scared. As we walk away with Julie still screaming and others crying loudly I look up to the sky to see if Jesus is looking down at us, or even coming down to help but I can't see him anywhere. I once again look at others that are not crying and see a blank stare in their dark eyes. I wonder what kind of a place this is and where are we going. As I ponder this question I once again look back at the beautiful beaten man lying on the ground and I also cry.

Later in life I am told that Julie was only nineteen years old and I was sold with her to give the illusion that she was a fertile woman. I had no mother as I was born on a breeding farm. The children were placed in a nursery with wet nurses and when they were five they were sold.

I hear Julie call," Maggie, it's time to get up and get moving now," I wake with a start still sleepy, having fallen asleep just moments earlier. The sun was coming up and my world smelled new. I relieve myself where I stand only to find that this time my urine stings my feet. I vow not to cry out and start to walk with the others. Julie is crying again, and I feel as if she needs me so I'll walk on these little hurting feet with her. We walk for three more sunrises before we see a house that the drivers get excited about. Julie tells me that this is the place where she thinks we will stop. "I hope so," I say. "I don't think I can walk another day."

The Big house was built of wood and set back a lane hidden from view in the trees. As we draw nearer to the house I notice a lot of activity. I see people of all sizes working together and over all I hear laughter. I had never heard this much laughter nor had I ever seen this many people working together with smiles on their faces. I think to myself, that this might not be a bad place to stay. I look up at Julie's face and she seems to be a little more at ease than she had been just a few hours ago. I put my little hand under hers and feel her squeeze. As our wagon approaches, several people with shouts and smiles run to greet us. Many follow as the wagon travels to the back of the big house. I notice many small log cabins in rows. "I wonder if this is where we will be living." Julie speaks softly to me. "Oh no," I reply. "We will be living in the big house. Remember that man said so?" "Well now little girl, don't you go counting your chickens before they are hatched". Julie said. On that remark I looked around for the chickens thinking that just maybe I could help gather eggs and hold new fuzzy chicks. I couldn't help but feel the excitement in the air. My eyes were so big I couldn't see everything at once. When we got off the wagon I saw men, women, boys, and girls of all sizes gathering around us. I held Julie's hand tighter and smiled what I thought was my prettiest smile. One boy who looked about full grown to me offered me a piece of candy. I tried to bite it and couldn't so I held it in my jaw. I had never tasted anything as good as this candy and I wanted it to last forever. I couldn't help but notice that this half grown boy just kept staring at me. Later I am to learn that his name is Tad. The man in the brown hat unchains Julie along with the others and tells us to form a line. A stern looking man walks toward us. He is the tallest man I have ever seen and everyone becomes quiet when he approaches. The tall man looks at us and says, "I am your new Master and you will call me Master William. Things here run real smooth and easy when we all work together, but if you want to be happy you must live by the rules." He turned to the man in the brown hat and said, "Let's go inside so we can settle up." "Settle up what?" I asked Julie. Julie didn't answer as she had started once more to cry. I just hated it when she cried I felt so helpless because I couldn't do anything for her to ease her pain. We were shown where to go to relieve ourselves. I was glad to see that it was an outhouse hidden behind the small cabins. It smelled awful, but then again it was a place where I could sit down and keep my feet dry. We were given a wooden plate with food on it and I thought that it looked nasty. The meat and potatoes were all mixed together and I turned up my nose. "You better eat that little gal." Julie said. "I know you have to be very hungry and I'm not sure when you will get something else to eat." "What is it?" I asked. "It's some sort of stew, I think." Julie answered. I tasted it to find that it was good and I ate all that I had on my plate. We were told that we could sit on the ground and rest for the remainder of the day. The green grass felt comfortable and the afternoon warm breeze made me sleepy. I could smell honeysuckle so thick it was as if the flies carried it on their wings. The field behind me was a beautiful purple and I could hear the bees constant buzzing as they went to and fro from each delicate clover blossom. I had taken my candy out of my mouth in order to eat and still held it tightly in my hand. As I rested back on the grass I replaced it in my jaw and noticed that as I sucked on this delicious treat my little feet felt better. As I drifted off to sleep I was well aware of the fact that Julie was at my side. As I held on to her I knew that I had to take care of her.

The morning came with sunshine, chickens clucking, dogs barking, and people some laughing and some singing. I even heard the distant tune of a harmonica. I sat up with excitement and saw through my big brown eyes a beautiful summer morning. I knew that this was a nice place to be and even thought that I would like it even if Fanny wasn't here. A tall man wearing a white starched shirt and black pants approached us and said, Time to rise and shine you two, follow me." We followed him to the big house after we visited the Johnny. When we entered the kitchen I once again was overwhelmed by the smells the wafted by my nose. The morning aroma of breakfast entered my nostrils and I became very eager to find another wooden plate. As I looked around hoping to spot a plate for myself I was ordered to look into the face of a light tan skinned woman dressed better than anyone I had ever seen. She wore a beautiful highly starched black dress with a tiny tatted lace color. She had a snow white apron that nearly touched the floor. As I stared at her I allowed my eyes to follow her entire stature and as my gaze fell to the floor I took a short gasp. I had never seen anyone wear such highly polished shoes that reflected the light. As my little eyes traveled back up to her face I saw a smile as she looked at me and Julie. She spoke, "My name is Susanna, and I run this here kitchen. I have been waiting for you so as I can get on with my duties. No matter what others might tell you, you take your orders only from me. I will show you what needs to be done around here and your little one can help." I was pleased that this very important person had noticed me and I was determined to do just what I was told. Another woman who worked in the house came to meet us. She was a large lady dressed in a very colorful dress. The flowers on her long skirt danced with each step she took. She wore a headscarf of the same bright flowered fabric. She had a beautiful smile that lit up her entire face. The thing I liked about her the most was that she smelled like cooking vanilla. "My name is Birdie and when you get ready to make up your new clothes, I will help. I do all the sewing around here and I will even teach the little one how to sew, if I have the time. I will even teach you if you want to learn," she said to Julie. Birdie and Julie liked each other immediately and a close bond soon developed between them that would span decades of time. My duties were to fetch things for Susanna and Julie as they went about their chores of cooking and cleaning the kitchen. Julie and I cleaning more than the actual cooking. We quickly learned the many duties that it took to help run a plantation. The best chore I had was gathering the eggs.

As the busy days passed into months I became familiar with the family as well as the others who worked and ran the plantation. 'OL Master John was the head of the family but we were to answer to his son William and his wife Selena. John was a strong willed, and a very honorable man. Due to his

7

age he led a quiet life. William was a graduate from a prestigious college. With this knowledge he was a very business minded individual and ran the plantation smoothly. Selena was a frail, small, fair skinned, blue eyed woman who required much care. She gave birth to two healthy sons but had lost two others at birth. Selena grew weaker with the loss of each child. Her two children, John and Nathaniel were four and two when I arrived at their home. I often spent many nights watching these two children even though I was only a year older than John. Many times visitors would leave their children in my charge. I often wondered when I grew older just what they were thinking when they would entrust me with their children. I didn't know any more than the children I was caring for. I played more than I watched but this seemed to be all that was required of me as long as I was with the children.

When I was seven years old I had a "funny" feeling when I looked at Mrs. Selena. I was serving her at the dinner table when I had a very disturbing thought. I found myself thinking that I hoped she likes this dinner of fried chicken and mashed potatoes because this is the last dinner she will eat. I stopped dead in my tracks when I looked at her and saw a gray fog surrounding her entire body. She was smiling at Nathaniel and all seemed fine. I knew that these thoughts were not nice so I quickly dismissed them from my mind. The dinner went well and as usual I cleared the dining table and had proceeded to help Julie with the dishes. The dishes were a chore that I did not look forward to do but I couldn't escape this duty. The pots and pans were the worst part. The big old back pots were iron and food was always stuck in the bottom. If there was any food left stuck on the bottom I would get a scolding from Susanna. We had a pot scrubber made of small chains fastened to a wooden knob and with this tool the scrubbing was a little easier. Julie was a small woman but she sure could handle those big iron pots with ease. After the kitchen chores were completed we sat down and enjoyed a cup of brewed hot tea flavored with honey. I told Julie of my thought about Mrs. Selena and how it had frightened me. "Oh Maggie, we all have those thoughts now and again. Don't worry about it. When you find yourself thinking thoughts like that just don't pay them any mind dear. "Julie assured me. We were enjoying our final sip of tea when Birdie came running into the kitchen. She cried. "Oh my God, Mrs Selena done just fell over and she can't breathe." Birdie was wringing her plump hands and tears were streaming down her pretty round face. We all ran to the dining room just as Master William was carrying her upstairs. We heard someone say that she was again with child.

A large black wreath was placed on the front door and Julie and I were kept busy serving and feeding what seemed like hundreds of people. Mrs. Selena was laid out in the parlor with a large black net over the coffin. She looked so tiny but even in death she was the fairest woman I had ever seen. The kitchen help as well as the house staff had to keep a twenty four hour shift in able to feed and care for the mourners. I thought that the people would never stop eating and making an endless pile of dirty dishes. The family crypt was on the grounds and Julie and I were told to join the others in the forming of a line leading to the dark opening of the grave site. The line stood just behind the family and the visiting mourners. I looked up at the people's faces and noticed that the line of family and visitors were openly crying. I looked at the faces in my line and had to look very hard to see even one tear. A few were crying, but most of the dark faces I saw were just blank. As Mrs. Selena's coffin was carried to the crypt I heard the most beautiful sounds that to seemed to arise from the deep recesses of the ground itself. I listened and realized that I was hearing singing. All the second row of people were joining voices in song. I reached for Julie's hand and as we clasp hands I saw everyone else in my row join hands. I felt bad that Mrs. Selena was dead but underneath I felt real good.

The day was Sunday and after the many dishes were washed, dried and put away and all other chores completed Julie and I joined the others. Many had come from surrounding plantations with their Masters. Men and children had gathered in the yard and some women settled in the kitchen. This was a fun time for everyone even though it was a funeral. Julie and I joined women in the kitchen to discuss child rearing, sewing, cooking and of course gossip of other plantations. This was the main means we had to learn gossip and news from other folks living on the other plantations.

As the grown ups gathered and put their heads together I went to the back yard to join the other children at play. I joined a group of girls and entered into what has been known for years as girl talk. As always there was a little girl that was never included into our little klatch. Her name was Susie and she was different than us. Susie was the offspring of a woman named Rose which was very light complexioned. Rose's mother was owned by a man that took liberties with his slave women and as a result Rose had entered the world very light complexioned. Rose, as rumor had it, was the lover of her Master and from their union Susie was born. Susie had beautiful large green eyes and the softest hair one could only dream of. Her hair was always in long curls and hung well below her waist. I had black course hair that Julie kept cut close to my scalp. Julie cut my hair regularly by using the razor that was kept in the medicine cabinet in the kitchen pantry. I was well aware of where it was kept because I often had to fetch the razor strap for Julie when she thought I needed stern discipline.

I thought I looked real good on this particular day until I saw Susie. She had no need for the kerchief that matched her dress as I did. Each new dress Birdie made for me had a matching kerchief made from left over scraps.

Julie also had matching kerchiefs as well as most women that wore their best at this gathering. At this time I hated my hair and my matching kerchief. I gathered the girls around and told them of my scheme. We all giggled as we approached Susie as she sat by herself under the shade tree. "Oh Susie, we have started a club and we would like for you to join us," I said. Susie was delighted that we had approached her and even more delighted that we were asking her to join our new formed club. I said, "There is one thing that is required in order to join us though." Little Susie was eager to do anything in order to be included in our girl talk sessions. "Wait here, I'll be right back," I explained. I ran to the kitchen to discover that the adults didn't even notice me as I boldly walked to the pantry and took the razor out of the medicine cabinet. I hid the razor into the folds of my skirt and walked back to the yard. I explained to Susie as I approached her," In order to join our club you must have short hair like ours." Susie, being only a child of eight years of age, did not object. The girls and I ran with Susie to the back of the barn where the boys were playing and I cut her beautiful hair off to the scalp. I reached up and removed my kerchief and placed it on her head. "Now you can play with us". I said with authority. I felt real proud of myself. After we had played for a while I saw that the women had come out of the kitchen and was sitting under the cool shade of a large tree. It all at once seemed as if my world went into slow motion as I saw Rose point to a young lad named Benny. Benny had obtained some twine from the barn and had tied Susie's discarded hair into a pony tail. Benny was on all fours playing horsey with Susie's hair tied to his behind. I saw Rose grab for her throat and it appeared as if she was trying to swallow a boiled egg. The other women looked at Benny, looked at Rose as she swooned, and worst of all looked at me. Julie leaped to her feet, grabbed me and drug me to the kitchen where the dreaded razor strap was kept. I never knew how Julie or the others knew that it was my idea to cut off Susie's beautiful hair. I never forgot the beating but most of all I never forgot poor little Susie.

My childhood days went very fast due to the fact that I watched Little John and Nathaniel on a daily basis. The chores were still a major part of my full days but they seemed a little easier as I grew. The boys were always requiring my attention and I was really glad when Master William brought home his new wife. Her name was Elizabeth and she and I took an immediate dislike to each other. Even though I was only ten she seemed to act like I was her rival around Master William. I was not aware of my blossoming body that was filling out before it's time. I took it as approval from Master William when he would pinch me in my blossoming places. I once spoke to Julie about Mrs. Elizabeth's dislike of me and her reply was, "Well, you can't blame her, God seemed to forget her when it came to good looks." We both giggled about this and shared this as one of our little secrets when we would have to wait upon her daily, with a smile

Little John and Nathaniel seemed to be afraid of her and I often would have to dry their tears when she would grab one of them and slap him for doing natural things that all little boys did. I was real worried about Nathaniel because he seemed so frail and blonde just like his mother had been. He reminded me of Mrs. Selena and I watched him a little closer than I watched John. I thought that to many slappings would hurt him much more than they would hurt John. And I thought John needed more slappings than he got anyway. It was just a few short months after Mrs. Elizabeth moved in that Julie, Birdie and I were sitting in the kitchen watching Susanna knead bread dough. Susanna said to Birdie," You better get out your flannel material; looks as if we are gonna have another mouth to feed 'fore long." I looked at Julie's and Birdie's smile and asked. "Who is coming and why do we need flannel material?" Julie answered," looks to me that Mrs. Elizabeth is going to have a baby." I groaned. I was far to busy to add another kid to my babysitting chores but I knew that would be the plan. "Well," I said. "Maybe we will be lucky and it won't live." Julie, Birdie and Susanna gasp and I didn't duck fast enough to miss the sharp sting of Julie's hand on my face. I held my stinging cheek as Julie said. "I don't want to hear your thoughts. If you have these kind of thoughts keep them to yourself. Thoughts like that spoken out loud will get you in a heap of big trouble. Master William doesn't sell too many folks, but if he hears you talking like that you will be sold for sure." I ask what the flannel was for and Birdie hugged me and said," I have to make baby clothes with it, wanna help?"

Mrs. Elizabeth's pregnancy went well even though it made her more demanding I was able to keep up with her demands and attend to my daily schedule. The time for the birth arrived and all was a bustle in the house. A neighbor lady called a midwife arrived and attended to Mrs. Elizabeth. I was told to take John and Nathaniel to the creek to swim. As the boys were enjoying their swimming I sat on the edge of the water and daydreamed. I looked at the green fern and listened to the beautiful birds in the trees. I wish I could fly, I thought, I would just fly away from here and feel the breeze as it blew me along. I didn't know where I would fly away to but I knew one place I would go. I would stop and visit my friend Fanny. I often closed my eyes and I could still see her beautiful face. As I was halfway dreaming I heard someone rustle the tree limbs in the large weeping willow that I had sat under. I turned around to see the half grown man called Tad standing behind me. Tad was the one who gave me a piece of candy when I arrived on the plantation. "Hi Maggie," Tad spoke. "What'cha doin?" "Oh, I'm just watching the boys". I answered. "They seem to be just fine right now", he said. "Take a little walk with me." Tad was a lad that was next in line as overseer as his father was now acting overseer on the plantation. I had heard that Tad was real smart and when someone needed something read Tad was the one to read it for you. He had been taught to read at an early age and this was a special talent in many of the others eyes. Tad was fifteen years old and already had the build of a full grown man. He was dark complexioned and was quite handsome. I stood up and walked a short way with him into the woods. I could still hear the boys playing so I knew that they would be O.K. Tad sat down on the ground and took my hand to pull me down with him. As I sat with him he said." How old are you now Maggie?" I replied. I am eleven this year; see how long my legs have grown?" Tad's eyes lit up as he looked at my legs and I felt real proud of myself showing off what I thought was my best feature. Tad said, "Looks like other parts have grown to". I saw that he was looking at my breasts and for the first time I noticed that they indeed were a lot bigger than I had thought they were. I grasp the front of my thin blouse and tried to hide from his gaze. I realized that Tad was making me feel uncomfortable. Tad spoke in a low tone. "Maggie, do you know why boys and girls are made different?" I smirked. "Of course I do." I answered. Boys work in the fields all day and when they have to pee they can just stand in the field and pee. Girls do the house work and they can't pee in the house so they have to sit down on a johnny. That's why silly." Tad threw back his head and laughed and I drew down my eyebrows and looked at him like he was out of his mind. "What's so funny?" I asked. "Oh, Maggie you are so funny", he laughed. I didn't think that this was funny and I realized that I didn't need to feel uncomfortable anymore so I stood up ready to go back to my daydreaming spot beside the creek. I don't even like Tad, I thought, he laughed at me and I know that I'm not stupid. "Where you going?" Tad laughed. I tossed my head in the air and said. "Back to the creek edge to watch my boys. I don't need you to laugh at me." He grabbed my hand and pulled me back down with such a force and started kissing me right on the mouth. I couldn't move and I tried to fight him off but he was a big young man. I felt his hand under my skirt but I couldn't protest because his mouth was on mine the entire time. I felt a sharp pain that brought tears to my eyes and became real still as I felt him move on top of me. Tad completed his gyrations and fell off me. I scrambled to my feet and screamed at him. "What the hell did you stick me with you bastard?" I realized that I hated him as I heard him break into another loud laugh. "Now missy Maggie," He laughed, "You know now why boys and girls are made different". I straighted my clothes and noticed that he had even tore a button off of my blouse. I looked around for the button, found it and ran over to collect the boys from the water. "Come on boys. Let's go back to the house." I shouted. I took an arm of each child and started walking with them. I glanced back to see Tad looking at me and I saw him throw his hand up in a wave as I hurried out of the woods.

When we arrived back in the house I noticed that everyone was real quiet. "What did Mrs. Elizabeth have?"I asked. Julie looked up from her floor sweeping and said, "Please be quiet Maggie. Mrs Elizabeth had a little girl but she would not breathe." I felt as if I had been punched in the stomach. "You mean she died?" I cried. "Yes, Maggie the little girl was born dead." I turned pale and asked. "Julie, do you think my thoughts killed her? I said that maybe she will die but I didn't mean it". Julie pulled me close to her and said, "No dear, your thoughts didn't kill the baby. You have a special gift that allows you to see the future. The baby would have died even if you had not had those thoughts." I asked. What kind of gift do I have and what can I do with it?" Maggie you are a special child of God that will help many people if you learn to use your gift wisely." Julie answered. "I have seen you predict twice and each time you have been right." The next time you have such a thought please share it with me and I will help you in understanding your special gift." I didn't understand anything about my gift but I knew that I was from here on out going to watch my thoughts and not speak them aloud.

The small casket was constructed and the new still born little girl was placed inside. Not many came to the graveside service but still it was a sad occassion.

Things at the plantation went back to running normal again. I noticed that Mrs. Elizabeth was now rougher than ever on little John and Nathaniel. I tried to keep them out of her way as much as I could

One morning I was polishing the front hallway when I heard Nathaniel scream. I ran to see what wrath Mrs. Elizabeth had doled out to him. When I arrived to the back stairwell Mrs. Elizabeth scowled at me, entered her bedroom and slammed the door. I then rushed down the stairs to find small frail little Nathaniel lying in a crumpled heap at the foot of the stairs. "Julie, Birdie, someone help me!" I screamed. Everyone came running and Bill, Master William's man, picked Nathaniel up and carried him to his bedroom. We all followed and feared the worst. I couldn't help but notice that Nathaniel's little head was hanging at an odd angle. Master William came running in just as Bill laid Nathaniel on the bed. That great big tall man fell to his knees and uttered a cry that chilled my bones. I knew then that my little Nathaniel had gone to live with his momma in Heaven. I was so mad at Mrs. Elizabeth as I found myself shouting. "Master William, it was Mrs. Elizabeth who killed him. I saw it and I heard it!" The room went still and all I heard was the pine tree out the open window whispering my name. Master William looked up from his fractured son, just nine years old this year, and said. "Maggie if I ever hear you speak another word such as that, I promise you, you will wish when I finish with you that I had sold you." I felt the tears sting my eyes as I stood there with my head down. I felt all eyes on me and I had no way to express my anger nor to make Master William understand what I had just witnessed.

The family and friends arrived once again to attend another funeral. That precious little boy was laying in the parlor right in the very same place that his momma had laid just a few short years before. I was overwhelmed with grief and wanted to explain that Mrs. Elizabeth had killed little Nathaniel. Every time I tried to speak with Julie about it she would tell me to keep what I knew to myself. I was very busy serving and earring for guests and in my later years I supposed that this busy activity is what got me through seeing that blond small child placed next to his momma in the family crypt.

A full summer passed and I attend to my duties in silence. I found myself hating Mrs. Elizabeth more each day but I had to attend to her wants and needs. She allows me full say so in the caring of John the remaining son of Master William. I and Julie are preparing hams to hang in the smoke house when I see Tad approaching. "Oh Lordy, here comes that Tad." I say in a low voice to Julie. "Well Maggie," Julie says. "What's going on between you and Tad?" I threw back my head and answered, "Just what makes you think that something is going on?" "Well it seems like that every time he comes near you, you head in the other direction. Why?" As I open my mouth to speak Tad enters the kitchen. He always has a stupid smirk on his face when he looks at me. I remain busy at the table and don't look up from my work. Tad says in a cheerful voice, "Hi ladies, need some of those hams hung up yet? I will do it for you when you're ready." "O.K." Julie answers." It will be a little while yet, but I will send Maggie out for you when they are ready to be hung". Tad walked out the door and headed back to the barn. "Oh Julie, please don't make me fetch him for you". I pleaded. "O.K, lets hear it". Julie said. "What is going on between you two?" I told Julie of the incident that happened by the creek and how I didn't want to be alone with him again. "I still can't figure out just what he did to me but I didn't like it", I told Julie. I was so confused when Julie threw back her head with laughter. "What's so funny?" I asked, almost getting angry with her. "Oh Maggie, your so dumb. What Tad did was make you a woman. You're not a little girl anymore. I thought your hips looked fuller. Now I know why they really are fuller." I was getting a little perturbed with her just as Birdie came in the kitchen. "What's so funny you two?" she asked. "Guess what Birdie?" Julie said. "Remember just the other day we were talking about Maggie's hips? Well guess whose been helping her fill out?" Birdie answered. "Tad?" Well I was really mad now and still confused as to how my hips had anything to do with Tad stabbing me with something by the creek. I stomped my foot and said. "You better stop laughing at me and explain how my hips have anything to do with Tad." Julie and Birdie stopped dead in their tracks and looked at me with their mouths open. "You don't know?" Julie asked. "Know what?" I said." All I know is that Tad held me down and poked me with a stick now how can that make my hips any bigger?" I was really mad by this time and they knew it. "Sit down dear child." Birdie said. "We need to talk." As Julie and Birdie explained to me the birds and bees I felt really stupid. I also felt anger and disgust towards Tad. "Are those hams ready to hang yet?" I asked. I got up from my chair, straightened my skirt, and picked up a small ham. "Where you going?" Julie and Birdie asked in unison. "I'm going to fetch Tad". I answered. "I thought you didn't want to be around him again". Julie said. I found myself feeling really important as I turned to walk to the barn." Humph, if Tad wants what I got then by God I'm gonna learn to read!" And with a toss of my head I put the ham under my arm and walk towards the barn "OhTaaad."

As Tad and I were having our weekly "reading" sessions, Julie had started seeing Bill. Bill was the man who assisted Master William. If Master William needed a bath Bill was the one to carry the water and empty it when his bath was complete. Bill always smelled clean and fresh. Julie said it was because when Master William was done with his bath Bill could use the water. Bill was a pleasant man and everyone liked him. His main focus was tending to Master and other than this he had no other interest, besides Julie. I thought that Bill was a handsome man in his black pants and white shirt. I asked Julie," Do you love Bill?" "Oh, no Maggie I could never love anyone ever again. I will love my Sug until the day I die." Julie answered." I don't love Tad either." I said." But I am sure learning to read." Julie laughed; it was the kind of laugh that I loved to hear from her. She always seemed so sad to me. Not to many days after our talk about our love life I noticed that Julie was gaining a lot of weight. I just figured it was from all the cooking and eating that we did and I payed it no mind.

It was an early morning in winter that Julie took sick. When I went down the stairs to start my morning chores Julie wasn't in the kitchen." Where is Julie?" I ask Susanna and Birdie. I looked up just as Bill entered the kitchen. "Well, well now little Miss don't you go a worrying about my Julie. I am about to be a poppa". He said with a huge grin. "A poppa! I shrieked. Where is she?" Birdie said, "She's out in the birthin cabin. As soon as you finish cuttin that bacon and gathering the eggs you can go out there with her." I ran to the hen house, gathered the eggs, a chore I usually enjoyed, but this morning I gathered as fast as I could. I carried them in plopped them down on the table and started to slice the morning bacon. I didn't even notice the small cut I suffered on my finger as I hurried through my chores. When the bacon was sufficiently sliced I ran out to the cabin known as the birthing cabin. The cabin was located behind the smaller cabins that housed the slaves. I was glad that I was living in the big house over the kitchen. Julie, Birdie, and I shared a room that was for the house servants. When I entered the birthing cabin I heard and saw several women lying on cots. They all were in various stages of childbirth and all of them were moaning loudly. I saw Julie on one cot and I had not noticed her looking as fat as she did now. As I approached her she smiled at me and grasps my hand. Between her moans she said, "Sit down here beside me Maggie, I am scared." What are you scared about?" I asked." I have seen lots of babies around here so it must not be too hard to have one." Julie answered between her cries. "Oh. I've been carrying babies before I just never got this far with having one though. Seems like when I been with child two times before this one, I lose them before they are born. I ain't never got this far and I afraid that I'll lose this one to. That's why I am so scared." As I started to answer she took me to the ground twisting my hand.

As I lifted myself up and sat back down beside her on the cot I noticed the midwife in the room. She was attending to the lady we called Nessy giving birth in the next cot. As Nessy screamed the midwife said. "Here Nessy put this wet rag in your mouth and bite down on it. "My ears perked up when I heard Nessy scream." That damn Tad I'm going to kill him if he ever touches me again!" Julie looked at me to see if I was concerned and saw that I was not. I heard one more scream from Nessy and saw a tiny little girl emerge from between her legs. I was amazed to see that perfect little baby girl enter the world crying. She was so beautiful and was the color of fall grapes covered with a shimmering mist of morning frost. She glistened in the morning sun that was coming through the window.

I was so involved in looking at Nessy's new baby that I forgot Julie. "Maggie", she screamed. "Help me!" I didn't know what to do so I just let her twist my poor little hand until it was purple. The midwife came over to Julie's cot and put the same wet rag in her mouth and said." Julie push." Julie gave one final push and out popped another perfect little girl. Again I was amazed to see this all over again. Now I was getting scared that I might be next, I had gained a little weight. As Julie cradled her new little bundle the baby hardly cried at all, nor would she nurse when Julie put her to her breast. Nessy had already placed her new little one to her breast and they were both drifting off to sleep. The midwife was attending to another lady and her screams soon stopped when once again I heard the mewing cries of another new one.

"Julie she is so pretty", I exclaimed. "What are you gonna name her?" Julie answered, "I don't know yet. I will have to talk to Bill about it will you go tell him and Birdie that they can come see me now?" I ran to the kitchen with my good news. "What did she have? And is everything alright? Birdie asked with a worried expression. "Julie and little miss what's her name is fine, "I said. "She wants Bill and you to go see her." I was exhausted and I hadn't done anything I was glad that Julie was resting. I went about the rest of my daily routine of polishing and cleaning the house.

I let my thoughts run away with me as I cleaned. I thought about how lucky I was that Master William let us keep our children and allowed us to establish families. On many other plantations, like the one I was born on children were separated from their mothers at birth. Not here I thought, this is the best place to be living. If I ever have children I was going to be awful glad that I could keep them and love them forever.

The day gave way into evening and I had seen to it that John was in his room and settled down for the night. He was now such a big young man he resented me attending to him. On the other hand he really enjoyed my attentions. I was the main female figure in his life as Mrs. Elizabeth ignored him. She was once again soon to have another child and I was certain I was not thinking about whether it would live or die.

I went out in the brisk night air and walked toward the birthing cabin. When I entered I found Julie sitting up holding her new little girl. "Oh Maggie I am so worried." she said. "She won't nurse, and all she wants to do is sleep. I wonder if that is normal?" I shrugged my shoulders and looked at the pretty sleeping baby in Julie's arms. "May I hold her?" I asked. "Sure just be careful you don't drop her." Julie answered. As I took the baby I noticed that her tiny body felt so lifeless but she was sleeping and breathing just fine. She also felt very warm. "Julie?" I asked. "Is she supposed to feel so warm?" Julie said," I guess so, 1 don't know. What I am concerned about is she hasn't eaten yet." Nessy's baby has eaten twice and I can't get her to wake up enough to eat." "Well" I said in my fourteen year old wisdom. Maybe that's what some new babies do". Julie takes the baby back in to her arms and says, I am so tired I think I will sleep awhile. If you want to you can go," I had a funny feeling about leaving her so I said. I'll sit here beside you on the foot of the cot for a little while. You just go to sleep and she will be hungry before you know it." Julie and her baby slept soundly and I drifted off as I lay down at the bottom of the cot. The other women in the room were sleeping comfortably with their new little ones at their sides. I was awakened by Nessy's baby crying and watched as she attended to her. They soon were back to sleep. Not long after I again was awakened because Julie was stirring and she seemed to have a problem. I whispered." What's wrong?" I saw her face was a mask of horror. "She's not breathing and she won't move!" Julie cried in a horse whisper. "Oh my God she's dead", Julie stifled her cry as she held her hand over her mouth. "Don't say anything at all", she told me. I watched as she arose from her cot with her still infant in her arms. She walked softly to Nessy's cot and with one steady quiet motion she lifted Nessy's baby off the cot and replaced hers in its place. Nessy's baby started to whimper but Julie quickly sat down with it and placed it to her breast. I watched in shock and said in a low whisper. "What are you doing with Nessy's baby?" Julie drew down her eyebrows and answered. This is now my baby and don't you ever breathe a word to anyone about it your entire life." I didn't know what to say I just sat there as she rocked and nursed Nessy's little girl. They both soon fell asleep but I couldn't sleep. I was so worried about what I had just witnessed I vowed not to think about it nor would I ever mention it to anyone.

Morning arrived and Julie and Nesy's baby were sleeping soundly. I saw Nessy stir and reach for her baby. As she sat up with the still infant in her arms I felt so sorry for her when she let out a cry that woke everyone in the cabin. She held the little lifeless body to her breast and I wanted so much to help her in some way. All I could do was to sit and watch her cry as she rocked the beautiful little dead girl that Julie had brought into the world.

I fell in love with Julie's new "acquired" little girl. She had the biggest brown eyes I had ever seen. She would giggle and run to me with chubby arms held up each morning when a new day would begin. Her dimples in her baby cheeks were so deep one could envision losing an entire pinky finger in one of them. I never knew love until I held this small little girl. Bill had named her Nonu after a great African warrior he had heard legends of. I always had this little girl with me everywhere I went. It was often said that I should have given birth to her instead of Julie.

Julie moved into Bill's small room when Nonu was a year old there was no room for the baby so Julie left her in the room with me and she and I shared the bed. Birdie complained that the baby was keeping her awake at night and it was soon arranged that she have a small room which had been a large walk in closet.

I looked forward to bed each night so I could hold Nonu as she slept. I would look at the beautiful features of her tiny face and know that I would have to protect her from all harm forever. I ran my finger over the little cut she had on her scalp and cursed Julie under my breath. Julie had cut her hair this day and of course Nonu being just over a year old had put of a fight. Julie was not a pleasant person when it came to holding little Nonu down and I often wondered if she had cut her intentionally I held her as I drifted off to sleep and knew in my heart that this was my child.

I was kept busy throughout my days watching Nonu as well as Mrs. Elizabeth's new little girl Miss Selene. Miss Selene had been born soon after Nonu and I was put in charge of caring for her most of the time. I asked Birdie one day when I was especially tired, "What's wrong with these mothers that they don't want to take care of their own children. Why do I have to do it?" Birdie smiled and said. "God knows who his angels are going to, now you be proud that he has so much trust and faith in you." I pursed my lips as I lifted Miss Selene to the ground after trying to feed her with out much success and said," Well, if God knows that then why don't he send someone to help this tired angel" I picked up Miss Selene and Nonu and started for the stairs to get them ready for bed.

As I was coming out of the nursery after putting Miss Selene to bed I saw Master William standing in the hallway. I put my eyes down and he said, Maggie look at me." I looked up to see him smiling and reaching out to touch me. I reached for Nonu's hand and held her close to me. "How old are you now Maggie?" he asked. "I am fifteen MasterWilliam "I replied as I held my head up and looked into his eyes. I thought he was going to pinch me as he always did and I was not going to flinch. He had a habit of pinching my hip and sometimes my breast. "When you complete your chores tonight I want to talk to you. Come to my door and knock." I was glad he didn't pinch me but I was worried about what I might have done that he wanted to talk to me. I was always trying to be good so that Julie wouldn't take her frustrations out on me. Now what could I have done so bad that Master William wanted to speak with me. I was feeling very nervous and Nonu, in her own little way knew this. I took Nonu outside with me to use the Johnny. "Look at all the bright stars Nonu." I said to her. "Do you know how high they are?" She looked at me in her child wisdom that was just two years old and said "Very very high" I picked her up and said, "Well, if you're so smart then how deep is the ocean?" Her reply, "very very deep". I was so impressed that this small little girl knew this. I thought that she was so smart that she was a special angel that God had sent and this just proved it to me. "I am going to teach you how to read like me". I told her." I want so much more for you, more than I can ever have." Maybe you will grow up to be a special someone." I told her. I wasn't so worried about having to talk to Master William after sharing the vast night sky with my little Nonu.

I told Nonu a story that I had made up and put her in bed. I laid down beside her and held her as she soon fell off to sleep. I very quietly got out of bed and walked out of the door. I walked to Master William's door and knocked. "Come in." Master William said softly. I entered to find Master William already in bed. I thought that this was odd, him wanting to talk to me and he was in his nite shirt and in the bed. "Come over here Maggie." he said. I lifted my eyes to see him as he was tapping the edge of the bed. He said, "We must talk quietly because Elizabeth is right next door in the adjoining room." I slowly walked to the edge of his bed and sat down. "Master William," I said, "What have I done"? "Done Maggie? Who said that you have done anything?" He answered. He sat up and put his hands on my shoulders and started to rub them. "Just relax, sweet Maggie, You are about the busiest little gal that I have ever owned. I watch you sometime and I get tired by just watching." With that remark he laughed and I was feeling puzzled. "Am I in here to just relax?" I asked." I thought that you wanted to talk to me." He answered, "Well in a sense I want to talk but without words. I want your body to talk to mine." Well, was I dumb or just stupid, I thought. As I had this thought he reached around and once again pinched my breast. I could not tell him not to do this but I turned my head around to ask him to please not do it now he kissed me on the mouth. "Oh my God, He wants what Tad wants from me I thought. But No, not Master William what about Mrs. Elizabeth she would kill me for sure. I couldn't keep up with my thoughts as he was pinching me and rubbing me all over my body by now. I couldn't believe this from Master William but sure enough it was happening. As he laid beside me after he had had his way with me he asked. "Who else

20

Maggie?" I answered "Tad". "O.k. but from here on out your not to let Tad do anything else with you. You are my girl from now on. You understand?" I understood and he winked. As I was putting my clothes back on I noticed a big black book on the bedside table. "Master William", I said. What is that book about on that table there?" He looked over at the book and said, that was Mrs. Selena's Bible, Maggie why?" "Oh I was just a wondering." I answered. It wasn't to long after my first encounter in Master William's bed that I had in my possession that very same big black book. It was the best reading that I could ever have had not to mention the weekly sessions with Master William.

When Nonu was three she and I was doing laundry in a tub behind the old wood shed. I was doing the laundry and Nonu was playing in the water. This was a chore that I dearly hated. It was my job to wash out the monthly rags and hang them to dry. As I was hanging them on the line to dry I thought. Wonder why I haven't used any of these rags for a long time. I had been so busy I hadn't even noticed that I had not had a monthly for quite some time. I soon forgot this thought and became involved in my many duties.

It was Julie who brought it to my attention. "You are getting so big Maggie when you about ready to drop that baby?" I screamed. "Baby? What baby are you talking about?" "Well looks like you got about at least four months yet to go". Birdie chimed in. I shook my head as I broke up a fight between Miss Selene and Nonu. "Give it to Miss Selene Nonu." I said. The girls were fighting over a walnut that Nonu had brought into the house and Miss Selene wanted it. I knew as well as Nonu did that it was hers but if Miss Selene wanted it she had no choice but to hand it. over. As Miss Selene ran off with the prize I looked again at Julie and Birdie who by this time was grinning ear to ear. "Looks like you are more that just fat girl. Looks like another little one for you to watch is on the way." This news almost made me want to faint. I had never thought that I could be carrying a baby. It just had not dawned on me. I sat down and said "Oh my Lordy, do you know who this baby's daddy is?" Julie and Birdie looked at each other and then with a smirk on there faces looked at me. "Of course we do Miss uppity everyone knows that you are Master's favorite one. We've been expecting this for a long time. Why do you think Mrs. Elizabeth's been so cold with you now more than she ever was? Everyone knows what's going on between you and Master William." I started to cry at this point. I am so sorry I never thought anyone knew I was trying to keep it a secret. Looks like I can't keep it a secret anymore." Julie puts her arm around me and says. "It's alright it's nothing that you could have avoided. You have no say so in such matters, it's Master William's choice not yours." I hated this part of my life. I should be allowed to make my own choices when I wanted to, I didn't want a baby especially not Master William's. I thought of little Susie and how hard her life is because her momma was in the very same position. I knew how everyone shunned her and now my baby would be shunned just like Susie was. I sat with my head in my hands and cried. I felt so hopeless and helpless. I wanted to control my life but it seemed as if my life controlled me.

As I was feeling bad little Nonu climbed on my lap and hugged me with her chubby arms." I love you Maggie" she said. "I love you too Nonu", I told her.

The time for my baby's birth arrived but I had to attend to Mrs. Elizabeth on the day that I was about to deliver. She also was expecting another child but on this day in late spring she miscarried. As I was bringing her tray up to her bed I almost dropped it due to a tremendous birth pain. When I entered her room she was propped up in bed and she looked quite pale. As I placed her tray on her lap she grabbed my wrist. I couldn't pull away as she said," Don't think I don't know what's been going on between you and William, Maggie. I know that you think he cares for you and your about to be born little slave. Remember that's all it will be to him, another little slave, one he can sell, beat or even drown like an unwanted puppy if he wants to ". At this time I had another searing pain but she wasn't about to see me flinch not even a little bit. I looked her in the eyes and said, "You just wait Mrs. Elizabeth one of these days you are going to be sorry you ever spoke to me this way." She let go of my wrist with a start and said. "Oh I've heard of your fortune telling abilities but don't ever think I could ever be worried about the likes of you." She told me to get out of her room and I was glad that she did. I had some business that needed attention right away. I hurried down the stairs and just as I reached the kitchen I collapsed. I was carried to the birthin cabin and soon after much pushing and crying my perfect little boy entered the world. Julie and Nonu had been beside me during the entire birthing process. Nonu instantly became a little mother. She reached to hold the new baby and called him Frankie. Julie and I laughed and Frankie was what his name became. That evening I was resting in my bed having just nursed little Frankie when Master William entered the room. He was smiling at me as he approached my bed side." I heard that you had a boy Maggie. Let's have a look at the little fellow," he said. I uncovered Frankie so that Master William could look at his son. "Well, I'll be damned, he's got my nose!" I looked at Master William's nose and sure enough it was the same as Frankie's. "Do you think he will stay so yellow looking?" he asked. "I hope not ", I answered ".He don't look right to me". Master William shot me a stern look and said "He looks right to me, I kinda like his color. Anyway Maggie here's a silver dollar for being such a sweet girl and making such a fine boy." He tossed me a silver dollar then left the room without even asking me his son's name and I just sat there holding my first silver dollar and my first new born son.

I found myself loving Frankie about as much as I loved Nonu. She helped watch him as much as a little girl could. Master William never payed Frankie any attention and for this I was grateful. The other children did not treat him any different and he was accepted as their peer. A few months after Frankie was born Master William was paying me as much attention as he always had I would sometime be allowed to lie in his bed for a short while until he fell asleep. On many occasions I would try to tell him some important news about his son but he always responded by. Saying,'That's nice Maggie, You're a good momma." He never asked questions about his well being nor showed any interest in his own flesh and blood. I soon understood just what my role in Master William's life was and I could not expect any more. I went through the motions when I had to share Master Williams's bed. I soon learned that he held no interest in his son.

I was caring for three children and learned that yet another one was due in the late fall. Mrs. Elizabeth was once again with child. Nonu, Frankie, and Miss Selene were a handful. Miss Selene was four but acted like she was much older. She and Nonu were the same age but Miss Selene was the boss. I often had to rescue Nonu from the grasp of Miss Selene and dry her little face from blood scratches obtained from Miss Selene's nails. It was after such a fight between them that I had taken Nonu outside to the pump to wash her face when I heard the mournful cry of a mourning dove. I noticed that everyone seemed to freeze in their tracks. The very air stood still and felt eerie. I walked back into the house to find Julie, Birdie and Susanna standing stiff but going through the motions of doing their tasks. Their faces held a still tense expression. The air could be sliced with a corn knife it felt so heavy. "What's wrong?" I asked as I placed Nonu in her position at the small table for the children." Maggie hush "was the response I received from Susanna. "Just be quiet and act like everything is normal". Well to me everything was normal or so I thought. I fed the children as I always did but I couldn't help notice that something was definitely not right.

Mrs. Elizabeth had decided to spend most other pregnancy in bed and on top of everything else I had to do I now had to take her tray upstairs each day. I had completed doing the dishes when I remembered that I had not retrieved Mrs. Elizabeth's tray. I prepared myself for a tongue lashing because of my delay and held my head erect as I knocked on her door. Miss Selene was sitting on the bed by her mother. She was practicing her needlework when I entered the room. She never looked up at me as I gathered the dishes and placed them on the tray. "Maggie," Mrs. Elizabeth said." Tomorrow at noon I have a very dear friend visiting, Mrs. Sims. She has been telling me of a new religious movement that she is involved in. It is called Spiritualism and she tells me of a medium at their meetings that can give readings. Well. I told her that I had a girl in my very own possession that can do just the same." I started to speak my protests but she continued to talk as if I wasn't in the room. "Tomorrow at noon I want you to show her up here to my bedside. She knows the reason that I am bedfast due to my condition so she will expect to visit me in my bedroom. I want you to demonstrate your gift of mediumship to her. I expect you to give her a reading. If it is good and acceptable she has offered to pay me for your services. I expect it to be good and acceptable. If you fail and make me a fool I will take extreme measures to see that the conquences are quite unfavorable. I know that William has quite an eye for you even though he isn't interested in your little brat of a boy he thinks about you often enough. He loves me and can never love you so if I decided to lets say offer you to a friend of mine that needs a maid for their daughter, I think you understand just where I am leading to with this conversation." I picked up the tray and said. "yes Maam I understand." As I walked out the door I heard her say to Miss Selene," I can make some good money off that gal." My face burned when I heard them both giggle.

I was holding back tears when I entered the kitchen. Julie and Birdie were the only ones sitting at the table sipping tea when I entered. There heads were together in a private conversation. They both looked up at me and saw that I was disturbed, "What's wrong child?" Julie asked. "I have to talk to Mrs. Elizabeth's friend Mrs. Sims, when she comes tomorrow at noon." I said. "What about for heavens sake?" Birdie asked. "Oh, I don't know she wants me to give Mrs. Sims a reading. I didn't even know she knew that I could read. The only book I own is a Bible maybe she wants me to read to her out of it. I'll take it with me just in case. By the way where is Nonu and Frankie?" Julie answered. "Bill took them outside to see a new colt that was born this morning, they're just fine.

I said to Julie." What in the world was the problem this morning? It seemed as if the air went cold when the mourning dove cried what was the problem with everyone?" Again I felt the tension as Julie and Birdie answered. "We were just talking about that when you came in the room. I guess it's time to share our secret with you. Your old enough to listen and never speak a word to another soul about what your about to hear. My ears perked up as I sat down with a hot cup of honey sweetened tea. There was always the sweet nectar of honey in the kitchen.

Birdie spoke very quietly. "This morning what you heard was not a mourning dove. It was a bird sound used as a signal." I asked. "What kind of a signal, and what for?" Birdie said. "Lower your voice Maggie, What I am about to tell you will get us killed for sure. The signal of the mourning dove is used when someone is about to escape for the North. What you heard this morning was the signal for all of us to be on the lookout and to pray for someone so bold." I was shocked. I had heard of slaves escaping to go north but I never thought it was right under my nose. "Who escaped?" I gasped. "It was Jim and his woman Mary." Julie answered. "Jim and Mary? Why I just saw them yesterday and they appeared to be just fine. Why would they want to escape?" The thought had never entered my mind that one of us would want to escape. "What is North anyway?" I asked. "Freedom." Birdie answered. "A place where you don't have to answer to no one. A place where you can learn to read and write if you want to, kinda like a promise land. Somewhere where a person can love himself and can feel the love coming from another. I knew about a promise land I had read about it in my cherished Bible. I had never thought that such a place could actually exist." Why don't more people go there?" I asked." Many of us are not so bold honey." Julie said. "Just scared I guess.' "When you call it a morning dove, do you mean like in the morning when you see the sun rise?" I asked. Julie said, "No mourning dove like when someone dies. You don't know what happened to the people you love, sometimes family, you just know that you will miss them and never see them again." I got a funny feeling when I found myself saying." Won't be to long that we will all have to get unscared. Freedom will be right here in our own back yard and we will have to know what to do with it when it comes." Birdie smiled, "If that is another one of your predictions I sure hope your right sweet child. In the meantime let's pray for Jim and Mary's safety."

I was awakened by the smell of bacon and I knew that I had overslept. I hurriedly dressed and noticed that. Nonu was still sleeping. I woke her to get her dressed for the day. As I felt her little body I felt a tremendous heat. I couldn't wake her and I heard a raspy breath as I held my ear down next to her tiny face. I picked her up and hurried down to the kitchen. Birdie noticed my anguish and said, "What's the matter with you two lazy bones this morning?" "I think Nonu is real sick. She is burning up with a fever." I said. Birdie and Julie stopped their morning duties and approached us as I sat down holding my little Nonu. I had tears streaming down my face as Nonu looked up at me and just rolled her eyes upward and closed them again. "Oh Please God". I cried." Don't take my baby." Julie said". Lay her down over by the stove where it is warmer she will be alright by this evening." What do you think is wrong?" I asked. Julie said, "She just got a bad cold with a fever is all. Soon as I put these onions on her feet she will be just fine." Onions?" I asked What for?" I watched as Julie placed raw onions on the soles of Nonu's feet. She tore rags and wrapped them around her feet to hold the onions in place. "Now let her rest there behind the stove while we get this breakfast ready. You will have to hurry this morning with Mrs. Elizabeth's breakfast because of you sleeping late, we are all late." I took Mrs. Elizabeth's breakfast in to her to find her sitting in a chair by the side of her bed. She looked at me and without saying good morning she coldly said," Maggie you're late". I started to tell her of Nonu's illness but she cut me off. "Mrs. Sims is arriving today and I want this room dusted and clean bed clothes put on before she arrives." I nodded and said," yes Maam. "Mrs Elizabeth continued, "I expect you to be show Mrs. Sims to my room and I also expect you to present yourself like someone I can be proud of owning." I again said, "Yes Maam as I lifted the heavy ironstone chamber pot to carry it down the stairs to empty." You may go Maggie but before you do I want you to light the fire under the water tank so as I can bathe." If you wish you may use my water after I am done because I don't want Mrs. Sims to have to smell any offensive odors while she is here." When you have emptied the pot you come back up here to help me with my bath." I went into a little room off of her bedroom and lit a stick from the fire of the lamp. I then lit the flame under the copper water tank that sat above the copper bath tub. The tank held oil that heated the water in the tank. I had filled the water tank a few days ago knowing that Mrs. Elizabeth was due to take her weekly bath. I left the room carrying the heavy ironstone pot carefully so that it would not fall and spill. After emptying the pot I hurriedly went in to check on Nonu. Miss Selene was finishing her breakfast and was kicking Nonu when I arrived back into the kitchen. I grabbed Miss Selene and told her that Nonu couldn't play today because she was sick. She left to go to the nursery with a scowl on her face and said. "Well, she better get up before long I need her to comb my hair." "I will comb your hair today Miss Selene just go to the nursery and be nice." I had noticed the smell of onions when I entered the kitchen but I hadn't noticed that the smell was coming from Nonu's feet. As I approached her she was looking around the room and had a little smile on her face. I was so glad to see her smile at me I held her and cried. I was so worried about her. Julie came over to us with a big smile on her face and said, "Those onions did the trick." "What did they do?" I asked. "Onions on the feet will pull out any fever." she said." Just remember that it comes in very handy." "Where did you learn that?" I asked. I was taught all about remedies long before I knew you." she answered." When I lived with Sug we all had to learn a trade. 'OL Miss Hatttie taught me all about such things." I know how to take the fire out of a burn and can stop bleeding. Well it's all in your Bible, Thats where it came from. Somewhere in Zeke 16 and 6 and Zak 3 and 21 think that was where she said it was I don't know what she was talking about but that's what I remember."" I was really curious now and I wondered where in my Bible I would find this useful information. I wasn't familiar with Zeke and Zak in the Bible but maybe I needed to read it again. Anyway right now I was just grateful that Julie knew just what to do to make our little girl all better.

I headed up the stairs knowing that Nonu was going to be just fine. I entered Mrs. Elizabeth's little side room which was her powder room, and proceeded to fill her bath. As I suspected it was to warm so I had to go back downstairs, find Bill and ask him to please bring up a pail of cold water. Bill said he would get to it right away and I again climbed the stairs. Bill soon arrived with the pail of water and poured it into the bath tub. Mrs. Elizabeth disrobed and I helped her enter her bath. I scrubbed her back and held her hair out of the water as she completed bathing herself. "Did you bring vinegar for my hair rinse?" she asked. I was laying out her clothes when I answered. "I wasn't aware that you was going to wash your hair to". Mrs. Elizabeth shot me a stem look and decided against arguing with me. "Maybe your right." she said. "With Mrs. Sims coming today it would not be dry by the time she arrives." She stood and I helped her step out of her bath and I dried her off. As she dressed she said. "Now Maggie, you may bathe as well." I removed my clothes and immersed myself into her luke warm bath water. I knew that I wasn't going to receive the privilege of having my back scrubbed so I didn't even think about it. I took a fast bath and stepped out to dry myself off on her damp towel. I saw Mrs. Elizabeth looking at me and I tried not to notice her gaze. "I don't see why William is so enamored with you," she said. You're not that pretty of a girl. Just look at your skinny legs and flat feet. Why my feet are so small and dainty compared to yours. I don't understand the needs of men. I am glad that he takes out his needs on you though rather than me." I held my head down so that she couldn't see the tiny tear that had formed in my eye. I just stood there and asked. "Is that all Mrs. Elizabeth?" I put my clothes back on and stepped out into the bedroom in the sunlight. I caught a glimpse of my reflection in the mirror. I didn't think I looked to bad. My best features were my big brown eyes with long lashes. I nodded at my reflection and wiped away my tear. I look just fine I thought. If Master William didn't think so he would have told me so. With that thought I had talked myself into holding my head back up. After All Master William did spend more time with me than he did with her.

Just as soon as I had straightened up Mrs. Elizabeth's room I heard a carriage approaching. "That will be Mrs. Sims Maggie go and fetch her." I went downstairs to the front door. On opening the door I find that Mrs. Sims had brought a friend with her. Mrs. Sims was a small bird like young woman with the blackest hair I had ever seen on a white woman. Her friend was short and plump and smiled at me as they entered the foyer. Mrs. Sims spoke first. :Are you the Maggie I have heard so much about." I looked at her with a quick eye contact and answered that yes I was that Maggie." "Well, dear would you please show us to Elizabeth's room?" I walked to the stairway and both of them followed. They had their heads together and were talking so low that I couldn't hear their conversation. I knocked on Mrs. Elizabeth's door and waited for the response. "Come in." I opened the door and showed the two ladies their seat. "May I be excused?" I asked. Mrs. Elizabeth said. "Yes Maggie dear, please come right back I want you to read for these ladies." She smiled at me so sweetly that I was a little afraid that something wasn't quite right with her.

I went downstairs to check on Nonu and was so glad to see her eating a bowl of soup. Little Miss Selene was standing beside her and seemed to be worried. I thought she is probably worried that Nonu wasn't going to be able to play with her today. I felt Nonu's forehead and found that she was feeling normal once again. "How are you feeling?" I asked her. She turned up her little face and said, "Just fine now". This news made Miss Selene jump with joy and said," Well, if you're so fine now we can go in the nursery and play with my dolls." I look around to find my Frankie and don't see him anywhere. "Where is Frankie?" I asked. Julie answered; He's out in the carriage house with Tad. Tad asked him to help him wash down the carriages" I knew that even in his very young years he was fascinated with anything that had wheels. He would be fine helping Tad. After making sure the children were taken care of I went to my room.

The Bible that I had read clear through was on my little table near my bedside. I would read it to Nonu and Frankie each night and share with them the wonderful stories of Moses leading the people to the promise land. I sat on the edge of my bed and wondered if this would be the right story to read to Mrs. Elizabeth's friends. No I thought better read them the story of Adam and Eve. They might like this one and would understand it a little better. I tucked my Bible under my arm and headed to Mrs. Elizabeth's room.

I was told to enter when I knocked on the door. Mrs. Sims and her plump friend were still sitting in the same chairs that they had first sat down in. The window had been opened and the white lace curtain was blowing inward as a cool breeze filled the room. "Maggie please have a seat". Mrs. Elizabeth had ordered me to sit amongst her friends as though I was no different than they. My heart was racing so fast I felt as if I was about to faint. I was glad to sit because I didn't know if I could have stood up much longer. Mrs. Sims spoke, "Elizabeth has informed us that you are able to read just as good as a medium that we both know." There was that word again I thought, medium. I had no idea what the word meant, but yes I could read. I wasn't aware that anyone knew that Tad had taught me to read but apparently it wasn't a secret. I answered, "Yes I can read, I have been reading for quite a while now." Again I thought, I wonder why these ladies want me to read to them. It was a known fact that all white women could read. Why did they want me to entertain them with reading. I smiled my prettiest smile and they in return smiled back at me. I opened my Bible to the first book and started to read. "In the beginning God created the heavens and the Earth." I heard a gasp from all three ladies and looked up to see that their mouths were all open wide enough to swallow a complete pig. "Is there something wrong with my reading?" I asked. Mrs. Elizabeth opened her mouth to speak and Mrs. Sims spoke first. "Maggie are you reading from that Bible or are you just remembering the story?" I found myself saying, "I am reading Ma'am, this is how I read." Mrs. Elizabeth was speechless but she stuttered," Well- well then- then by all means Maggie proceed." I read the next verse and all at once I felt a strong urge to tell Mrs. Sims about her husband. I heard a voice so strong in my ear of someone talking to me I stopped reading and looked around for the source of the voice. I was listening to someone tell me her name was Grace and that she wanted to tell Mrs. Sims that her husband was going to be alright. This made no sense to me but I couldn't resist the urge to blurt out this bit of information. As I told Mrs. Sims that her Husband was going to be alright she turned a shade of pale pink. I also told her that someone by the name of Grace had told me this information and she swooned. I saw that Mrs. Elizabeth had sat upright in her chair as did her plump little friend. Mrs. Sims found her voice and said. "Maggie, Grace is my beloved dead mother and yes I have been very worried about my husband. He has been gone for about two weeks without a word and I am very worried about him." You certainly are a medium just as good as the one we have seen." I looked at Mrs. Elizabeth and saw her beaming at me. I looked at the floor unsure of the feelings I was experiencing. It was the plump friend that spoke next. "Tell me Maggie what can you read for me?" OK now I was catching on as to what they wanted from me, straight old fortune telling, no problem, they just called it medium. This was a gift that I was sure of. I looked at the round face of this little woman and said, "No he will not marry you." Her face fell and then I said, "there is another in the spring that you will meet. This is the right one." When she heard this her face lit up and she laughed. "Elizabeth, she is as good as you said she was, can I buy her? I must have her she is a gem." My ears burned and my face felt flush. I was relieved when I heard Mrs. Elizabeth tell them that I was not for sale and never would be. "Tell us more Maggie Mrs. Elizabeth said. I told Mrs. Elizabeth that she would have a healthy baby girl and that her name should be Mary. "That is all that I hear to say to you ladies." I said. Mrs. Elizabeth said that I could leave the room and as I left I could hear the women singing my praises.

The two ladies stayed to visit Mrs. Elizabeth a few hours into the sunset. I didn't see them leave but no sooner than they did I was once again summoned to Mrs. Elizabeth's room. A slight tap on her door and I was told to enter. Mrs. Elizabeth was sitting in the same chair that I had previously seen her in. "Maggie," she said, "open my Armoire and retrieve my nightgown. I need you to help me put in on. I am feeling really tired tonight." I opened the huge ten foot tall armoire and found her nightgown. As I was helping her dress she seemed to be quieter than normal. She turned her face up into mine and I knew something was not right with her. She said, "Just when was it, and how was it that you can read?" I became very still and said, "Mrs. Elizabeth, I have been reading for many years now. I thought that you knew because you requested that I read for your friends." Mrs. Elizabeth said. Oh Maggie I never new you could read words in a book. I was referring to reading another persons energies like a medium can. I just assumed that you knew this." How was I supposed to know this Maam. I never heard of a medium before. I didn't know that you wanted me to practice my fortune telling on them. If this is what you wanted I sure wish I had of known it." Mrs. Elizabeth smiled which confused me because she never smiled at me to often. "Maggie, my friends payed me today for your fortune telling abilities. I mean they paid me a nice sum, not little potatoes. I don't care if you can read words or not I just want you to read like you did this morning for others. Mrs. Sims is going to spread the word about your abilities and I am quite sure I can have a tidy sum stashed away by Christmas." I completed helping her dress and I was hanging up her dress. I heard her say, "By the way did Master William teach you to read words?" "No Ma'am it was Tad." I answered. "Well. we will have to do something about that now." she said." Looks as if William isn't the only one who uses you around here. You must be a very handy little girl. Yes a little girl with a lot of big talents. Anyway I expect you to brush up on you medium, or fortune telling talent I know a lot of people that would be very interested in listening to you." I replied, "yes Ma'am" and I left her room.

I was glad to see Julie and Birdie still cleaning the kitchen when I arrived downstairs. Susanna had Nonu and Miss Selene playing in cookie dough and Frankie was sitting on the floor playing with a small wooden box. Tad or someone had nailed little wood wheels to it. He scooted it around the floor as if it was a great wagon. I felt secure with everyone in the kitchen. Bill was bringing in a load of wood for the cooking stove and it felt like a cozy night at home with the family. "What have you been doing most of the day in Mrs. Elizabeth's room?"Birdie asked. I answered. "The oddest thing happened. Remember I told you I was supposed to read for Mrs. Sims today?" Birdie and Julie both nodded yes they remembered. "When I started to read from my Bible they couldn't believe that I could read from a book. They didn't know this." "What did they want?" Julie asked. "They wanted me to be a medium or something. You know Julie when you told me that I had a special gift from God. Knowing when something was going to happen. Well, this is what they wanted to hear. Not reading from a book, buy reading like telling them about their lives and stuff." Julie and Birdie looked at each other and then at Susanna, who by now had left her cookie baking class to the girls and was intently listening, and said in unison 'Oh lordy, it looks like you are in for a lot of talking to Mrs. Elizabeth's friends. Julie asked. "How did it go? Was it what they expected?" I said I thought that they were pleased because they paid Mrs. Elizabeth a good bit of money. "No". Susanna said."! Can't believe it."

"Sure enough, that's what Mrs. Elizabeth told me." I said, feeling like I had just won an award for being the most important person on the whole plantation.

Susanna not wanting to be outdone in her position of importance says, "Humph, I better get busy planning snacks for when she has more friends coming to visit. I sure will be busy when the word gets out about your mediumship trick."

We all laughed and finished our chores. I took the girls and Frankie upstairs to get them ready for bed and decided to read for all three children tonight. As they sat on the bed around me I opened my Bible to the story about Noah's boat, Frankie's favorite story, and started to read. Little Miss Selene opened her eyes wide and said. "Your not supposed to read, your a slave." I looked her straight in the face and said, "Well I can read and if you don't want to hear a story just go to your own room I don't care." She settled down after this statement and wanted to hear the story. She never said another word to me about reading and she learned a lot of Bible stories from our nightly story times.

I had kissed each child goodnight and had just settled into my own little bed when I heard a slight knock on the door. I opened it to find Master William standing in the doorway. He said," Elizabeth told me a lot about you today. Is it true you can read words?" I looked at his tip of his boots and answered, "Yes sir." He said. "I was also told that Tad taught you to read, is that also true?" I again answered /'Yes sir". "I am not going to punish you but I can't have you teaching those kids of yours to read. Your not are you? "I assured him that I was not teaching Nonu and Frankie to read and this pleased him. I couldn't believe that he didn't want his own son to learn to read. Reading would be so important to the children when they were grown. I knew that I was going to teach them both but I knew what he wanted to hear from me right now. I was hoping that he would not want me in his bed tonight. Nonu had the sniffles and I was worried that her fever might come back. Master William said, I have to spend some time talking with Elizabeth so I quess I won't be wanting you tonight. I said in a silent prayer of thank you God. I shut the door after he went into the nursery to check on Miss Selene. As I was climbing into bed a heard a small voice says, "I love you sweet child." I looked at both children and saw that they were fast asleep.

Little Mary arrived when the trees had shed their last leaves. Mrs. Elizabeth had labored for two intense days in order to bring her into the world. She came in all pink and wrinkled. When I saw her for the first time I saw how very pale and thin skinned she was and I wondered just how it was that God had made her just the same as my Frankie, and even the very same daddy at that, and yet she already had more than he would ever have. Some things just kept me puzzled. I thought that just maybe because she looked so weak and pale God needed to give her a little extra boot in order to survive in the mean cruel world. Yep, some things just kept me puzzled.

I took care of Mary with just as much love as I showered on the other children. I fell in love with her big blue eyes and golden curls. But it was Miss Selene's eyes that were the biggest when Master William brought in the biggest Christmas tree that I had ever seen. He had told me during one of our "nightly chats" that the crops had done well and this was going to be a big Christmas. I helped the Children string popcorn and make angels from twigs to hang on the tree. Susanna and Julie were baking cookies and making candy. The entire house smelled of ginger and honey. It was a cold evening when we were gathered in the kitchen preparing to make hard candy. The stone had been placed on the table waiting for just the right moment, when the candy would leave a hard string. It was very dangerous for the children to be near the candy when it was poured on the flat stone to be cooled and cut. With that in mind I had them away from the table preparing the sugar that the candy would be rolled in when it had been cut and cooled. We were so involved in the candy making process that we never heard the first knock on the kitchen door. Nonu heard the second knock and ran to admit whomever it might be. A small brown skinned woman was holding a little girl that appeared to be as old as Frankie. She had on a little thin dress that whipped around her legs in the cold. The only protection from the cold winter evening air was on the child. It was a wool blanket that was thread bare and I couldn't tell how it provided much protection because one could see right through the holes in it. She stepped into the kitchen and sniffed the warm smells. I noticed that Birdie and Susanna had an air about them over her presence. Julie spoke to the girl, "Hi, Berry is there something you want?" The young girl held tight to the little one although she was squirming to get down and play with the children. "Yes Julie, Mable wants me to invite you and Maggie to our cabin for a Christmas supper tomorrow night. She says to tell you she aint got much to cook but she would like you to come anyway." I looked at Julie and wondered how she knew this girl, Julie said,"0k Berry, tell Mable that we will be there." A big grin lit up Berry's face when Julie gave her and the little girl each a ginger cookie. She left into the cold evening air, holding her cookie in one hand and the little girl in the other. "Who was that?" I asked, "And who in the heck is

Mable?"" Mable is my friend and Berry is her daughter. "Julie answered. "Well I never heard you talk about them where did you meet them?" I said." You funny girl", Julie laughed." They live in your own back yard, wake up." I tossed my head and told her, "I am awake but I have never seen you talking to the folks in the back yard. I knew that they lived in the cabins but I had not gotten acquainted with them nor had I made friends with anyone. When did you?" Julie said." Oh I get out often enough. I am not stuck in here watching kids all day and tending to Mrs. Elizabeth and," she smirked" Master William". Susanna and Birdie were listening to the conversation and couldn't help but to say, Maggie, we all know the people live in the cabins we just don't have to much time to associate with them as friends. We live a little different then they do, you understand. I answered, "No I don't understand. Julie I am looking forward to meeting your friend Mable."

Later that night I lay in Master Williams bed listening to him sleep. I look at his closed eyes and hear his soft even breath. I pray as Fannie taught me to and I ask God in the heavens just what his plan was down here on the earth. I didn't love this man sleeping by my side but at the same time I had to give my body to him when he needed me. I had even carried his son. A son that would never receive a part of this land, a son that couldn't even eat with his father at the same supper table. Why God I prayed what is the reason? I heard a still small voice deep within that said. "Maggie read your Bible. Read Romans 8:17." I crept back into my bedroom careful not to wake Nonu and Frankie. I lit the light and read *And if children then heirs; heirs of God. and joint heirs with Christ: if so be that we suffer with him, that we may also be glorified together.* I read this verse twice and knew that I had been given an answer to my prayer. Not an answer that would make anything different but an answer from God that all was not in vain.

The knock came upon my door earlier than I expected it. I looked out to the morning winter sky to see that the morning sun had not shown its face. "Maggie, time to get up." Julie called. I knew why we had to be up so early this morning I had participated in many Christmas Eve activities and this one this year would be no different. Or so I thought. I washed my face in the cold water and shivered as the cold water slid down my neck. I dreaded washing my face in the cold water that had sat all night in the tin pitcher. The washstand had to set by the window because the room was so small and this added to the coldness of the water. I looked over to see if Nonu and Frankie was stirring yet and decided to let them sleep a little longer. I pulled off my nightgown and replaced it with a long wool skirt that had belonged to Mrs.Selena. Master William had given me many of her clothes and I was grateful for the warm skirt. I looked through my wardrobe and found the perfect blouse to wear for such a fun but busy day. It too had belonged to

Mrs. Selena. I ran my fingers over the hand tatted collar and knew that this was indeed a fancy garment to own. I felt almost like the lady of the house when I caught a glimpse of myself in the mirror. I let my thoughts wander to the day that I would have my own house and my own husband to take care of. The second knock on the door snapped me back to reality. "Maggie, what's the hold up? "Julie asked as she poked her head in the door. "We need your help the people are lining up. Come on." "I'm coming." I answered. I took another quick look at the children and followed Julie down the stairs to the kitchen.

Master William was waiting in the kitchen with Susanna and Birdie. The cookies and candy had been sorted into piles along side small jars of honey. My job was to hand Master William and Susanna two cookies. A ginger one and a sugar one. Julie was to hand them ajar of honey and Birdie was to offer candy. These Christmas gifts were offered to each resident of the cabins as they passed through the kitchen. The children were not to receive the honey as it was to be given to the adults.

Master William told Susanna to open the door and for another Christmas I helped to give out gifts. The gifts were soon given to each resident with merry Christmas spoken to each one. I saw a lot of smiles that didn't reach the eyes. Funny, I thought I had never noticed this before. In fact I didn't remember looking at their faces before. This puzzled me and later that day I asked Julie if she thought the people in the cabins were happy. "Happy?" Julie said. "Why I guess so they are as happy as they can be living under the circumstances" "What Circumstances?" I asked. Julie laughed and said "Oh Maggie you are so naive." I didn't respond because I didn't want to be naive so I just went about my duties.

The afternoon was spent preparing a Christmas Eve feast for guests that had been invited to the big house. Mrs. Elizabeth had allowed herself to be carried to the living room to entertain guests. Mary was now three months old but Mrs. Elizabeth was still weak from childbirth, or so she thought. We were so busy that I had forgotten mine and Julie's invitations to Mable's for supper. The guests were soon served desserts of Christmas pudding and had settled into the living room to sing carols around the fireplace.

"Why don't you two head on out to Mable's for a little while?" Birdie said. "We got things pretty much under control here." I called Nonu and Frankie to me, I was grateful to take them both with me as I had been told by Mrs. Elizabeth to keep Frankie out of sight of the many guests. I was having a hard time keeping them from peeking through the door to watch the guest's children playing with new dolls and trucks. Miss Selene was enjoying the many gifts that had been brought and exchanged with visiting children. I felt pain in my heart as I saw Nonu and Frankie admire the new shiny toys at a distance.

Julie and I walked with the children to Mable's cabin. I was hurrying each child along in order to get them to a warm place. The ruts in the lane between the many cabins twisted one's ankle if one wasn't careful. It was such a rut that sent little Nonu tumbling. I picked her up and examined her knee. It was scratched but not too badly. "Be careful Nonu and watch where you're going" I said. She turned her little face up to me, placed her hands on her hips and said." How can I watch where I am going when you don't watch where you're pulling?" Julie and I laughed which made her even more indignant. We arrived at Mable's door and I realized that this was the first time that I had ever been on the porch of one of the many cabins. Mable opened the door and with a big smile told us to come on in. Berry was stirring something over the fire in a big black kettle which smelled delicious. The little girl, I soon learned was named Ethel, sat by the fire holding a large cat. Nonu and Frankie was excited to see her playing with a cat and soon joined her in chasing the poor cat around the room. Mable said, "Sit down you two." I was about to grab two children as they ran passed me but Berry apprehended them first. She gave them each a pork cracklin to suck on and sat them down with a box of pick up sticks.

I looked around the room and was surprised that it was so bare compared to the big house. The floor was hard dirt but had been swept. In the middle of the room sat a wooden table with two rustic chairs. Against the wall was a wooden bed covered with the wool blanket I had seen on the child earlier. Another bed was against the other wall and on it was a blanket that wasn't as thin as the other one. A grapevine wreath covered with pinecones was the only decoration I saw on the walls. By the small hearth where a fire was burning and the kettle was boiling sat a small tree. It was bare compared to the huge tree in the living room that I had watched Miss Selene decorate. This bedraggled little tree had pinecones, dried moss, and paper hanging on it. Under the tree where I was used to seeing many brightly colored boxes sat three cookies and a jar of honey. I gasped, I had no idea. I had never even thought about the folks in the cabins.

Mable said, "Here child, have a cup of tea. It's real good it's made of catnip." I grew it myself back yonder," I took the cup and noticed that Julie had already drunk hers while I was daydreaming. Mable washed out the cup and poured herself a cup of warm tea from the big black iron teakettle. I saw that she only had two cups and that was why she had waited to drink her tea. Berry approached me and said, "Can I look at your collar?" I reached up to my neck as I had forgotten that I had on my favorite tatted lace collar. "Of course you can." I answered as I leaned toward her. She admired the collar and said, "Wait Let me show you what I have," She retrieved a wood box from beneath her bed and brought it over to where I was sitting. She opened the box and lifted out a lace handkerchief. "That's beautiful Berry." I exclaimed. "Where did you get it?" "Mamma gave it to me when I had Ethel", she said. "She said a very fine lady gave it to her a long time ago." Mable joined in and said, "Yes. that was given to me when I had my son a few years before I had Berry," I looked around and said," Where is he, is he grown?" Mable looked sadly at the little lace hankerchief and said, "I sure hope he is." Julie shot me a look that said shut up Maggie and I changed the subject.

"Oh what a beautiful rug you have on your floor". I said. Mable's eyes changed from sad to proud and said "I made that rug." I said, "Really? How?" "From rags." Mable answered. I would have liked to make it bigger but when we came here about ten summers ago I couldn't get any more rags. Berry was about six when we came here, yes about six,that's how old that rug is.

They last forever and ever. Good rugs. I would like to make some more if I could get hold of some rags." I asked," How do you make them?" Mable chuckled," A lot of cutting and braiding. But come winter they are well worth the work. Gives me something to do in the evening too. I really like making those rugs." My wheels were spinning. I found myself saying, "I can get you some rags. Are all the cabins like this one?" Mable and Julie looked at me as if I was out of my mind and Mable said, "Yes, all the cabins are built just alike some older than the others and some not so airtight but all just alike." I said, "Mable if I get you a lot of rags, will you teach others to make their own rugs?" Mable lit up and said, "If I can make me another one first?" "O.k. it's a deal," I said. Julie just looked at me with disbelief in her eyes. "Where do you think you're going to get rags?" she asked. "Never you mind" I said to her. "I will" Mable said," Well that's about the best Christmas present I have ever had." We laughed and enjoyed her Christmas dinner of pork stew and it was about the best stew I had ever eaten."

Julie and I arrived back in the big house just as the guests were leaving in their carriages. Some had decided to stay the night and it was a late shift in the kitchen for us preparing rolls for breakfast. The children had been allowed to stay up late in order to exchange gifts. We had received new headscarves with matching aprons. It wasn't a surprise to Birdie as she had been directed to be the seamstress. Nevertheless she enjoyed hers as much as we did. Bill received a new white shirt while the children had been given new clothes and a rubber ball. Everyone was pleased with their gifts, or so I thought until I saw Nonu sitting on her little chair holding her new dress and ball. I approached her and said. "Whats the matter honey? Don't you like your new ball and dress?" She looked up at me and said. "How come I didn't get a new beautiful doll like Miss Selene did?" I had no answers, I hated it when I had no answers that would make everything right. I just held her little perfect hand and said, "Maybe Miss Selene will let you play with hers.

You think so?" I knew that this wasn't going to happen but I thought that this might make her feel a little better. She looked at me and smiled and for the first time I saw that her beautiful smile did not reach her eyes either, I thought when did this happen. Her smile had always reached her eyes before. I would have to look at mine and see if my eyes smiled. I held her in my arms and felt so helpless but not hopeless. I was determined to make her smile reach her eyes again. I didn't know how I would do it; I couldn't get her a beautiful doll with silk clothes and shiny hair. I couldn't even get her her own clothes but somehow I knew that one day I would be able to. I made her feel a little better by just holding her. When Frankie saw me holding Nonu he joined us and threw his new ball in the air crying "Catch it, Nonu catch it."

Nonu and Frankie engaged in a ball toss and this took her mind off of her troubles for the moment.

Finally I had completed my duties of dishes, and sweeping. I had just read the children their night time story and had kissed them goodnight. I no sooner felt my eyes close when I heard Master William at my door. Good I thought I need to talk with him and after his Christmas cheer he would be in a more receptive mood. I went with him to his room and after he satisfied his need I said." I visited a cabin tonight and I need to talk to you about an idea I have," He was half asleep and I couldn't quite make out his muffled response but I thought he said, "Maggie, you know I am not interested in your ideas." I ignored him and continued to talk. "I think the cabins might need some repair according to Mable, she said that they were not airtight." Master William leaned up on one elbow and looked at me as if I had no idea of what I was talking about. "Repair? what do you know about repairing cabins?" "Oh I'm not the one to repair them", I answered "But you need to look into it and see what needs to be done." Master William threw back his head and laughed at me but he saw that I was very serious. "I also need to get ahold of some rags. Can you get me some?" I asked. "Rags", he laughed "what for to plug up holes in the cabins?" I was getting angry with him and shot him a look that startled him into becoming serious. I said. "Master William I need rags for rugs in the cabins and I would like it if you would have an inspection in order to see what necessary repairs need done to some of the cabins." He opened his eyes in surprise and said. "Woah, now missy just who do you think you are? Who made you boss all of a sudden?" I stood up beside the bed as I was putting my gown on I said "I'm not claiming to be anyone's boss I just want you to get me some rags and to please check into fixing some cabins. I never asked to join you in your bed but I know just how much you need me to be here whenever you want me. I know how Mrs. Elizabeth tells you to leave her alone when you have a natural man desire. I am not asking for much, not nearly as much as you ask of me. I never put up any fuss when you tell me to be in your bed but if I don't get what I want you will have to go to the cabins for your manly desires and its damn cold out there cause the cabins need fixin!!" After saying that I storm out of his room without asking to be excused and enter my room with determination in my heart. I look at my children and seeing their angelic faces sleeping I tenderly kiss each one and say to God. "Will it matter that I was?" I heard a still small voice say, "Yes, Maggie it will,"

It wasn't long after that night that I saw some work being done on the cabins early one spring morning. I smiled to myself and realized that Master William had listened to me. This came as a surprise because I had understood it to be that he was not interested in my feelings at all.

I was busy giving Miss Selene and baby Mary their baths when Bill entered the room. "Mrs. Elizabeth wants to talk to you when you're done washing the children", he said. I shook my head and wondered just what she needed to discuss with me now. Little Mary was the chubbiest baby I had ever seen and it was a chore lifting her in and out of the tub. Miss Selene was trying to help bathe the baby and this made it even worse when Mary screamed with pain as the soap burned her eyes. I rushed to get clear water from the pitcher just as Nonu fell into the tub of soapy water. "Miss Selene pushed me" she cried as she stood there fully clothed and dripping wet. I grabbed for Miss Selene as she ran out the door half dressed. I was not having a good morning. I lifted Mary under one arm and helped Nonu remove her wet clothes and told her to take her bath. I then ran after Miss Selene in order to have her complete her dressing. After I had completed my job of bathing children I settled them all into the nursery, one nursing on the wet nurse, the other two playing. I hurried back into the bathroom in order to jump into the cool soapy water and take a quick bath myself. My bath completed I prepared myself to talk with Mrs. Elizabeth.

I entered the living room where Mrs. Elizabeth was waiting to talk to me. "What took you so long? I had Bill tell you that I needed to talk to you right away." I looked at the floor and said. "I had to bathe the children Ma'am". "Well, how long can that take?" she snorted. Bathing two little girls can't be that hard of a job. Anyway I have several ladies coming this evening. They are expecting you to perform for them as you have done before for others." "Giving readings?" I asked. "Of course, giving readings." she answered. "You are getting well known for your abilities and I have received many requests for your services." I have received a handsome sum in the past and", she chuckled, "people don't mind paying me for your services." I have even turned down offers of purchase for you. Can you imagine? It seems like Spiritualism is going like a woods afire and I have my very own medium. Can you do any other tricks? I hear tell that some people are floating objects in the air while real ghosts walk around the room. Can you do that?" I answered that "No Ma'am I can't but maybe one of these days I might be able to." She perked up her ears and said "You practice those things; people pay more money for séances. You be in here tonight at six o'clock sharp. That's when the ladies are coming. you hear?" I said. "Yes Ma'am I will be here. Is that all?" Mrs. Elizabeth waved her handerchief at me to dismiss me and I turned to leave the room. Just as I stepped through the doorway she said, "Oh by the way William has informed me that you want rags. Whatever for I would have no idea. I have requested that each lady that gets a reading from you has been instructed to bring you a bag of rags". She narrowed her eyes and looked at me as she said," I told him that I thought that this was ridiculous and embarrassing but he insisted that if I was to offer your services to my friends I was to ask for a bag of rags for you. Humph is that all you think your worth?" My heart was leaping right out of my chest with joy but I remained calm. "Yes Ma'am thank you" was all I said as I turned on my heel and left the room. yess!!!

I was thrilled and the remainder of the day went as smooth as silk. The ladies arrived each with a bag of good clean rags, and the readings went well. I now read a Bible verse to each lady before I received anything to tell her. I was soon doing at least two readings a week with even some men, and my pile of rags was building by leaps and bounds. I couldn't wait to give them to Mable.

Julie and I once again went to Mable's cabin. I felt bad that I had not seen her since Christmas and now it was early summer. It was early evening and the folks were coming in from the fields. I saw women carrying their hoes over their shoulders as easily as Mrs. Elizabeth and her friends carry their lace parasols. Each one eyed us suspiciously but smiled and spoke to us as we passed. Children were running in the warm new grass barefooted and I was reminded of myself when I had first arrived here with no shoes. The children seemed to be enjoying themselves while running and laughing. I needed to let Nonu and Frankie out to play with these children I thought. Perhaps they would be as happy as these children appeared to be. It had been a long time since I had seen Nonu laugh like that.

We soon were standing on Mable's porch looking into her open doorway. Everything seemed the same as when we were there Christmas except that the tree was gone. Mable came from the side of the house and I was delighted to see her welcome smile that took up her whole face. "Julie and Maggie", she exclaimed. "What brings the big house people out here without an invite?"Something wrong?" Julie smiled as she reached to hug her and said "No dear nothing wrong. In fact we have good news for you, Maggie? "I hugged her as well and we sat down on the porch stoop. "I have a lot of rags for you are you still interested in teaching rug making?" Mable threw back her head and let out a whoop. "Am I!" she shouted "When can I start?" Julie and I laughed it felt so good to be in the presence of Mable that I found that my laughter brought tears with it. "I have so many rags, girl you won't believe it. Enough that everybody can have a warm floor come winter." Mable slapped her knee and said, "Let's get started". I never thought that rags could make someone so happy but they seemed to brighten our entire evening. I saw a young boy watching us as we laughed. I said. Come over here son I need to ask you a favor," I noticed that he hesitated at first but he came right over to us. "Do you know Tad?" I asked him. He answered. "Yes, he is working right now in the stable." "Would you run and get him for me?" I asked. He ran off to get Tad and others joined him without even knowing what important mission he had been assigned to. Mable had gone into the cabin and had prepared tea for us sweetened with honey. I asked, "Isn't your honey just about to run out by now?" She said. "Oh no don't run out of honey we always have enough." I looked puzzled and asked, "Hows that? You only were given a small jar at Christmas." Mable laughed and said. "Got more honey than we will ever need. Get it back by the woods out of the bee hives." I looked at Julie and she was as surprised as I was. "Back by the woods? I asked." Mable said "Sure look all around you. Clover everywhere. Where there is clover there is bees and where there is bees there is honey. Back by the wood is where all the hives are. Master William makes a lot of money from his bee hives. "Then why

43

did he give you honey for Christmas if you have plenty?" I asked. Mable answered, "What we get for Christmas is strained what we get the other times is full of hive and is darker. Honey that is not good enough to sell." Berry had now joined us having completed her daily chores and was sitting with us on the porch. She said," Make a lot of candles too." "Candles?" I asked." Yeh, we take the bee's wax and melt it over behind the cabins and make candles." I had never realized this I knew that we had always had candles in the house but I didn't know that they were made in my own back yard. I was really getting an education and I was enjoying each minute of it. "Can I see the candles being made?' I asked. "Sure" Berry said "Come tomorrow that's one of the jobs that I do."

I looked up to see Tad coming across the yard with the boys. "What do you need?" He asked when he saw me. "I need you to help Bill carry a lot of rags from my room and bring them here to Mable." I said. Tad grinned at me and said "It's nice to talk to you Maggie. I've seen you a lot but you didn't speak to me. How come?" I stood up and said "Tad, this is not the time nor place to talk about anything right now. I will talk with you soon but right now will you please go and help Bill?" He scuffed his toe in the dirt and turned to go toward the big house. Mable was jumping up and down with delight knowing that now her wished for rags was soon to be a reality. "I would like very much to visit you tomorrow when I can get away from my duties. I want to learn myself how to make the rugs and I want to see how candles are made too. Oh and I want to see the bees." I was talking so fast Julie said, Hold on girl,one thing at a time. "I am just excited. "I said as I saw Tad and Bill bringing the rags." I didn't know this world was out here and I want to know everything about it." Mable drew down her eyes, shook her head and said, "Oh, sweet innocent child I don't think you will want to know some things that your gonna learn."

As soon as I completed my last chore of the day I was ready to visit Berry and Mable. The chore of washing windows was one I never liked and I was glad that job was completed. I sat in the kitchen sipping my well earned cup of tea while Nonu and Frankie danced around the table. I had told them they were going out to play with some new friends and they were both excited. Miss Selene asked if she could join us and Nonu was the first to tell her in no uncertain terms that she was not going outside with her. Miss Selene pouted and was acting very unlady like as she rolled her eyes and made faces. "I will tell Mother that you can't go outside if I can't go with you." She said. This news made Nonu upset and was afraid that her outing would be canceled. I took Miss Selene aside and said, "If you don't settle down and act like a lady I will see to it that Nonu has a bad cold and will have to go to bed for a week. If this happens who will brush your hair and button your shoes? You will have to do these things all by yourself and I know that you don't want that to happen. Now do you? You go to your Mama and ask her to help you with your new stitches now. We are going outside." Miss Selene flipped her shoulder at me and left the kitchen. Julie looked at me with her mouth open and said," A cold? How you gonna give Nonu a cold that will last for a week?" We laughed.

Mable was in her cabin when we arrived. She had started to cut the rags with an old pair of rusted scissors. "Is that the only thing that you have to cut those rags with?" I asked. Mable said, "I used to have a nice shiny pair but I don't remember what ever happened to them. I sure could use some new ones." Again I found myself saying, I will get you a new pair." Julie shook her head and I myself didn't know how or where I could get new scissors but I was going to. Her rug cutting was a difficult task but she had wound several balls.Mable said, "Berry has been waiting for you all day. She is out back making candles and she told me to tell you to join her when you got here." I looked for Frankie and saw that he had ran outside and was playing in the dirt with other small boys -Nonu was standing with me and as I left to go to the back of the cabin she took my hand. "Are you scared about something?" I asked her. Nonu looked up at me and said, "No, I am not scared I am just confused." "About what?" I asked. "I was wondering why Mable and Berry can't live in the big house like we do." How come she has to make rugs for a dirt floor and we have beautiful rugs under our feet on wood floors?" I squeezed her hand and said." Honey you have questions that I have no answers for." I have asked the same ones over and over. I just know that we have to have faith in God and know that he has a divine plan for us all."

Berry smiled and motioned us over to where she was stirring boiling wax in a big black kettle Nonu forgot her confusion when she spotted several young girls standing around with string wicks in their hands. "This looks like fun". I said. Let's learn how to make candles. We learned to dip the long strings repeatedly into the hot wax and cool them after each dip in a bucket of cold water. The heat coming from the fire was almost unbearable but it wasn't long until our candles were as fat as the completed ones hanging over a wooden rack. "May I take ours with us?" I asked. Berry said, "Yes, you sure can". This made Nonu very proud She enjoyed making her candle so much that I thought she might grow to be a professional candle maker.

There was so much to see and it seemed as if people were joining us just to meet us and introduce themselves. We were living on the same plantation but it seemed as if we were living in two separate worlds. We watched as others dipped their wicks into the hot wax. Everyone wanted to make a candle to show us their talents and we felt so much love coming from everyone.

Mable and Julie joined us and Julie made a candle. which came out lopsided and wouldn't hang straight. Julie decided candle making wasn't for her but she kept hers just the same.

"Would you girls like to stay for supper?" Mable asked. Julie and I needed to return to the big house in order to make sure all duties had been completed and children were in their beds. "We can stay just a little while longer." Julie said. "We will help wind some rags for you but we have to go soon. Julie and I followed Mable back into the cabin while Nonu stayed with a group of little girls still gathered around the kettle. "She enjoys being out here". I said to Julie. "This is real good for her to be away from Miss Selene for a while." Julie said. "Don't tell Miss Selene that she is enjoying herself without her she will see to it that she doesn't get to come out here again." I nodded knowing that Julie was right.

Inside Mable had started to prepare supper. On the kitchen table I saw a pile of chicken feet and had no idea what they were for. "Whats the chicken feet laying on the table for?" I asked. Mable looked at me as if I had lost my senses and said, "Why silly girl we are gonna have stew tonight." "With Chicken feet?" I asked. "Of course, with chicken feet don't you make chicken feet stew?" I shook my head and stammered" well, no not with chicken feet I make stew with chickens. Where is the rest of the chicken?" By now Julie had shot me another one of her shut up looks but I refused to let it drop. "Mable, I asked you, where is the rest of the chicken?" Mable looked into my eyes with a look I wasn't sure of and said, "I would expect that the rest of the chicken is in your stew pot in the big house kitchen." I sat down with a thud because it felt as if I had been punched. "In my stew pot?" I asked. Mable answered. "Yes in your stew pot. Out here we get the parts that folks in the big house won't eat. chicken feet, intestines, pig ears and tails. You eat the best part of the pork and chicken. All's we get is the feet and tails." I said," Mable I am so sorry I didn't know this." Never in my life had I felt so guilty because I had just eaten fried chicken last night for supper. Everything became real quiet as I watched her place the chicken feet into the pot along with fresh greens and potatoes. Her hands placed each item into the pot as if it was a treasured gift direct from God.

Julie and I thanked Mable for sharing with us as we left her home. I called Nonu and Frankie to me. Frankie didn't want to leave his new found friends and put up a fight. I picked him up as he kicked and screamed and proceeded to carry him. Nonu took Julie's hand and we walked to the big house. I looked up at the huge house where I had called my home for my life and felt that I didn't want to enter it anymore. I wanted to stay with Mable and eat her chicken feet stew. I for the first time in my life felt as if I did not fit anyplace. I held my squirming little boy to my heart and said a silent prayer. Dear God, show me what I might do to be of service to you. I know that there is so much that needs to be changed in the world. Help me to be a part of that change. Amen.

"It's been a long time since we visited Mable". I said one fall morning to Julie." I wonder how her rugs are coming along. I never did get her her new scissors and I feel bad about that" An entire summer had passed and I had been so caught up in child rearing and household chores that I had not thought too much about Mable and Berry. Perhaps I avoided visiting her because I felt so helpless to help her and guilty that I had more opportunities than she had not to mention better meals on the table.

"Let's visit her this afternoon when we get a break." Julie said. "That sounds like a good idea". I answered as I polished the silverware. It was Sunday and the afternoon meal was complete. Julie and I were finishing up in the kitchen. Birdie came in to join us in our conversation. I had a brilliant idea. "Birdie, you're a seamstress do you have an old pair of scissors you don't need anymore?" Birdie answered," I have two pairs and that is all I have ever had. If I lose a pair it might take a long time to replace it. I take good care of my scissors." My face lit up. "Dear sweet Birdie Do you think I could have a pair?" Birdie drew down her plump chins and shook her head, "No I need my scissors. Can't let them get out of my sight not even for a minute," My brain was searching for a solution. What would it take to persuade Birdie to part with her extra pair of scissors? All at once I had the answer. I ran to my room and opened my little box of treasures. I still had my shiny rock, my little handmade doll and tied in my handerchief a silver dollar. I removed the silver dollar from its knot and turned it over in my hand. I remember the sadness that I felt when Master William had given it to me. This will do I thought. I ran downstairs and said. "Birdie may I please buy your extra pair of scissors?" "With what? You ain't got no money." she said. I opened my hand and offered her the silver dollar. She took it and bit it." "Well it sure is a real one." she said, "I don't know. I ain't sure I can get another pair of sissors with this. The peddler's wagon hasn't been here for a long time. He might have died you know." I stood on one foot and then another until she made up her mind. She once again bit the coin and plunked it in her apron pocket. "I will go get you your new scissors". she said. I jumped up and down with joy. That afternoon Julie and I visited Mable.I knew that I would never forget Mable's loving face as I handed her her new shiny pair of sissors. I understood that my greatest joys in life would come from giving.

Julie and I were about to leave when we noticed that many folks were walking with each other in small groups. "Where is everyone going?" I asked. Mable said, "It's Sunday night. Time to go to church." "Church?" I asked as I looked at Julie. Julie shrugged and said "I don't know anymore than you do." "Are you going to church Mable?" I asked. "Mable said, "I plan to I just thought that you were company and didn't want to go with me." Of course I do". I almost shouted. Julie do you want to go?" "No I can't

Julie" answered. "You go ahead. I will put Miss Selene and Miss Mary to bed for you." Julie left and Mable and I started toward a small cabin that sat far back behind the others. As we walked Mable said." We only have church once a month. This is our Sunday night that the reverend visits us." "I didn't know that there was even a church here". I told her. Mable continued. "The reverend visits other plantations each Sunday and has services here once a month." In the cabin many were sitting on wood benches while others stood in groups laughing and sharing. I immediately felt that God was in this place as I sat down near an elderly lady. She looked at me and smiled. Her clothes were worn and her hands were rough. She looked at me and I saw the brightest flicker in her warm brown eyes. I feel so welcome here I thought. I didn't see many familiar faces but the ones I saw were full of warmth and love. I was Content to sit and watch others as they hugged each other and shared stories of children and health. I didn't see any one who might be the Reverend until I felt someone take my arm from behind. I stood up to see the most beautiful bronze man I had ever seen in my entire life. I looked into his rich black eyes and saw my - future. "Hi". He said "I am Reverend Mason. I have never seen you here before." I could only look into his eyes and couldn't find any words to say." He said "Welcome", with something else which I didn't catch, and walked to the front of the room." I sat back down spell bound and thought to myself, I bet he thinks I am stupid. I couldn't even tell him my name. I had never felt such a current coming from another person. He was the most magnificent person I had ever laid eyes on. I listened to each and every word he spoke. The singing that I heard from the congregation that night sounded as if a thousand angels had gathered. Their singing told me a new way of living was coming and that I needed to prepare myself for God's great changes. It was time for the alter call and I went willingly. As I knelt at the feet of that magnificent man of God I understood that I too was one of God's children and I now understood my mission. I cried tears of joy and tears of sorrow. I gave my entire soul to Jesus lock stock and barrel. I wasn't owned by anyone that night. I was God's pure child and I was free.

I felt different after attending my first church service. I couldn't put my finger on it but deep down inside I knew I was changed. Perhaps I was just growing up and understanding my role as first a person of God and second a person to others, as others saw me. Life went on as usual. Each day I would hear a small voice inside my head that said, "It's almost time." I did not know what it was almost time for and each day I would fight off an anxious feeling.

I went through the motions of doing what others expected from me. I knew that before long all would be changed but I didn't know just how much my life would change in just a few short years ahead.

I expected change and when one morning I couldn't find Frankie I nearly lost it. His small cot had been slept in but it was now cool to my touch. I looked in the nursery, in the pantry and everywhere else I thought a young boy of eight years could be. I knew that he often visited Tad in the stable or carriage house but I had always given him permission each time he ventured outside. Susanna and Julie were in the kitchen when I entered. "Have either one of you seen Frankie? He wasn't in bed early this morning when I woke." "Maybe he is out this early morning with Tad." Julie said. "No, I wouldn't think so. He would have woke me to ask if he could go out. I know him, he knows that I would worry about him." Miss Selene and Nonu came into the kitchen still wearing their night clothes. Nonu was now sleeping in Miss Selene's room and both girls were now about to enter their early teen years. "Whats all the fuss about Miss Selene asked." I asked. "Have you seen Frankie?" Miss Selene and Nonu both said "No, not since last night." I had to start helping preparing breakfast. "Why is everyone all dressed up today"? I asked as I looked at Julie and Susanna wearing their best clothes. "Did you forget about the wedding?"

Susanna said. "Oh of course." I said. "The wedding. No I didn't forget I was so worried about Frankie I just wasn't thinking." "It seems like only yesterday that I was changing John's diapers and now we are expecting his bride Sophia to arrive this day." I said. Julie said, "Yes and your not even dressed many of the company will arrive by noon and we have to get this food prepared. The dusting needs finishing and the children's clothes need laid out." I started to ask again about Frankie but was hurried out of the kitchen with a polishing cloth thrust into my hand." "Hurry with your duties Maggie. Worry about Frankie later." Susanna shouted as I left the kitchen.

As I was putting the final shine on the glass lamp shades Mrs. Elizabeth bustled into the room. "Oh Maggie, Have you noticed that your little brat isn't in the house this morning?" she asked with a sneer to her lip. I looked her in the eye and said, "Yes Mrs. Elizabeth Ma'am have you seen Frankie?" "Humph, No I haven't and I really don't need to." she said. "I don't think anyone needs to see your little green eyed uh - bastard. He was put out in the carriage house with Tad early this morning. His bed was made and he was put in it. I told William that with all these people coming for the entire week he needed to be where he belongs. I can't have people seeing him and knowing that William might be his father. Frankie, as you know, is not big house material." "Not big house material!" I raised my voice. "Be careful little miss. Remember who you're talking to." Mrs. Elizabeth said. She continues, "From now on your kid will live with Tad over the house. He will be taught to repair the carriages and he will do just fine my sight." My hands drew up into fists and I was so angry that I started cry." Mrs. Elizabeth you can't do this". I said. "Master William said that I could keep my children with me." "Well," Mrs. Elizabeth said, "He will be just fine in the carriage house I know what is best for you and your children." "I said through my tears of anger." No, you know what you think is best for you.

You can't face the fact that you can't have a son for your William. I had his son and you can't live with it. Now you don't want anyone else to know that his son came through me. You think that by hiding him and saying to me that he is not big house material that this will make him go away. Well Ma'am he still exists and he will always be there to remind you that Master William makes love to me. Maybe he don't love me but I can sure tell you he sure as hell respects me." Mrs. Elizabeth looks at me as if she wants to kill me on the spot. Her hand flies through the air and lands with a smart sting on my cheek. I turn on my heel and say as I leave the room." Not big house material. Humph, that boy will own a big house someday and he will not let the likes of you even come in the back door."

I stormed out to the carriage house to see if my Frankie was taken care of. He was working alongside Tad washing down a carriage. "Mamma, I get to go with Tad to pick up some people today. Can I go?" I knelt down to hold him to my heart and looked into his beautiful green eyes. "Frankie, do you like to help Tad?" I asked. "Of course I do I really like to help fix the carriages and wash them." He said. "Well, from now on would you like to stay out here in Tad's room and sleep here as well?" Frankie looked at me with a puzzled look and said." No Mamma I want to sleep in my old room with you." I held him tighter and said." Master William says that now that you are a big boy you must stay out here with Tad. I won't be far away. See that window up there? I will look out each night and see that you are O.K.. Do you think that will be alright?" "Where will Nonu sleep?" Frankie asked. "Nonu sleeps in Miss Selene's room. I answered. "Well that's O.K. I just don't want no one sleeping in my bed." He said. Can I come in to eat breakfast and dinner with you every day?" My tears came again. No dear you must eat out here with Tad." But he can't cook good mamma I will be hungry." He by now had started to cry. I said

"No you won't be hungry I will see to it that you will eat what I do. I will bring you your meals whether Mrs. Elizabeth likes it or not." This made Frankie feel better and I as well. "I will be out here to check on you often I am not going to forget that you are my special son." I told him. I stood up and scooted him off to continue washing the carriage. I looked at Tad and said, "If you as much as lay one hand on that child I swear I will hurt you." He just stood there as I left to return to my chores in the big house.

"In the year of our Lord 1853 I now pronounce you man and wife" Rev. Charles spoke and John and Sophia were married. John and Sophia left soon after the service. Some of the guests stayed for an entire week and Julie, Birdie and I were run ragged. I had to help women bathe, dress, wash out personal garments and watch their children. I was so relieved to see the last carriage leave. Now life could return back to normal.

"We need more help around here." I said to Susanna as she sat smoking her pipe on the back doorstep. "Aint gonna do you no good asking". She said between puffs. "I been asking for years for extra help in this here house. Last time any help come was when you and Julie arrived and I had to beg for you two for years." "Well it ain't right". I said." To much work to do around here for such a short staff." Susanna laughed, "You think we are staff?" You been reading to many uppity books gal. We aint staff we are just plain owned folks that have to do all this work for free. If we was staff we would get paid for what we do." "I guess your right." I said. "But I still say it ain't right." Julie entered the conversation. "What do you see ahead Maggie?" "Your always reading for Mrs. Elizabeth's friends and telling them what's going to happen for them. Look and see if you can see anything for me." I sat down near the fireplace and became real still. My gaze shifted to the fire in the hearth. In front of me coming out of the fire I saw a tall white man with a tall black hat. In one hand he held a flaming paper and in his other he held a small black child. As I watched this vision I saw millions of people, old and young, following this tall man. Many were laughing but most were crying. As I watched the vision faded and was replaced by another. This one was blood red as the fire from whence it came. I saw children with hands held high. They were looking at a figure ascending from above. The ascending figure was dressed in purple robes and held two medallions in his hands. On one was inscribed 1963 and on the other 2010. There was a tremendous wind that seemed to blow out the fire and left everything burned to be built up fresh and new. The vision faded and I was confused about it.

"What did you see?" Julie asked. "I am not sure what I saw." I said. "I didn't understand any of it. It was about the future I am sure but it's a mystery to me. When I saw the vision I felt a mixture of feelings. I now feel as if I need to tell you to be prepared the storm is about to hit". Susanna said "Are we gonna have a thunder storm? Is that all the vision you can get? That ain't no vision, anybody can tell if it's gonna storm by looking at the leaves on the trees. If they are upside down its gonna storm if they ain't it ain't gonna storm Don't need no fortune teller for that news." Julie said, "Susanna be quiet. Maggie got more than a thunder storm. Didn't you?" I nodded and said. "Yes I wasn't referring to a thunder storm Susanna. I was talking about winds of change that you and I can't even imagine. We better hold on to our head scarves when this wind hits because if we don't hold on to something or better yet someone, we are all going to be a sorry sight to behold."

Susanna and Julie didn't understand the reading any more than I did but I knew that something big was just around the comer and that we needed to hold together in order to survive the changing winds.

Miss Selene and Nonu came in the kitchen followed by Little Mary. "Mother said that Mary and I could have another cookie." Miss Selene said. "What about Nonu?" I asked "Don't you think she would like a cookie to?" Miss Selene threw back her head and said, "No I am punishing Nonu right now. She can not have a cookie." I looked at Nonu and she stood with her head down and wouldn't look at me. "What are you being punished for Nonu?" I asked. Miss Selene glared at me as if I wasn't even allowed to speak to Nonu. Nonu didn't answer and I repeated my question. "Nonu", I asked what are you being punished for?" Nonu shrugged her shoulders and continued to look at the floor. Mary said, "Nonu was in Selene's closet this morning trying on Selene's dress." I asked, "Why were you in Miss Selene's closet Nonu?" Nonu looked at me with big tears in her brown eyes and said I'm sorry. I just wanted to see how the blue silk one would look on me." I felt so sorry for her pain and I reached out to take her in my arms. This made Miss Selene mad and she stomped her foot. I said to her, "Nonu I understand how you feel right now. Don't cry baby one of these days you can have silk dresses in as many colors as you would like." Miss Selene said, "That's highly unlikely Maggie." The only way she will get a silk dress is when I decide to give her one and I really don't think I will ever do that." I smiled at the girls and said. Miss Selene we will see, we will see." As they started to leave the room I let go of Nonu and when I let go she found concealed under her arm, a big cookie.

John and Sophia moved to another state and it was a long time since we had news from them. It was about two years after the marriage when I received a letter from John. It read:

My Dearest Maggie,

It has been so long since I last saw your smiling face. I have good news and bad news to tell you. Sophia and I had a beautiful little girl last year. We named her Sophia, after her mother. She is so smart and in some ways reminds me of you. I don't know just what it is that reminds me of you perhaps it is her loving gentle smile that greets me each morning. The bad news is that after giving birth Sophia never regained her health. It is with much regrets that I must inform you that last month my dear sweet wife entered the kingdom of heaven. I am engaging the help of a dear woman by the name of Margaret and she and I have decided to marry. I wish you could be here with me to care for my dear daughter but I understand the many things you do for my father and he would never part with you.

All my love

John (your little boy)

I had never received a letter before. It was an honor to receive it and the others wanted me to read it over and over to them. This was to enter into my treasure box along side my cherished doll and rock. I felt bad for John but I knew he could handle his life as he always was a strong person.

I went to show my precious letter to Frankie. When I saw him I was amazed at the amount of dirt on his face and hands. It wasn't just dirt it was grease. "Tad, when was the last time this child had a bath?" I asked. Tad crawled out from under a carriage and he was covered with just about as much grease as Frankie was. "My stars, don't anyone out here bathe?" I asked as I looked at the caked grease in Frankie's hair. Frankie grinned up at me and said, "A man can get awful dirty when a man works hard as I do". I took him to the pump and proceeded to hold his head under the water. "Tad I need some soap over here." I shouted. Frankie was squirming to get away but I managed to get some of the dirt out of his hair.

After our washing frenzy I told Frankie and Tad that I had something to show them. Frankie's eyes lit up when I produced a letter and read it. "I would like to get a letter from someone." Tad said. "I think that is real good when one of us receives a letter. You're the first one I ever heard of. Yes sir makes me real proud Maggie that I taught you to read. I, in a way am responsible for you getting a letter." "Oh Tad you want to be responsible for a lot of things" I said. "You just remember though that it is my child that you are responsible for now and I expect a lot from you." Tad answered "You know Maggie that I can teach someone a lot of things that will be very useful in their life." He winked. I looked away and changed the subject. Have you received one of the rugs that are being made yet?" "No I don't have anyone that will make me one", he laughed. "Well maybe you ought to sweet talk one of the gals that are making them." I said". I have plenty of rags seeing that I am doing readings right and left for Mrs. Elizabeth's friends. Many of them bring more than their share of rags and there are plenty of rugs being made." Tad became real quiet. "What's the matter? You already got a gal in mind and your thinking of her right now?" I laughed. Tad lowered his eyes and said Master William hasn't talked to you yet?" What about?" I asked. Tad hummed and hawed and then he said, "Maggie I have asked Master William if I could have Nonu. She is about fourteen now and I just thought that she would need a man in her life." I felt myself becoming hot and grasped for my throat. "Nonu?" was all I could say. Tad said," Yes I have asked if I could have Nonu. To live out here with me. It would be good for her getting her away from that mean Selene don't you think? I was without words. I fought back the urge to hit him. "You can't have Nonu living out here with you. She is used to living and eating in the big house. What makes you think she would even want you anyway?" Tad answered, "Well she is a full grown gal now and she is awful good looking. Master William says that he will think about it." I was seeing red by now and my fists were in a tight knot. "No MISTER Tad you may not have Nonu." was all I could say through clinched teeth. Tad now sees that I am more than just angry with him and I am close to a dangerous point and he backs up. "Why?" he says. "Do you really love me and want me to wait until Master tires of you and throws you out here to me?" "Tad, you can't have Nonu she is your daughter!" I scream at him. Tad stands with his mouth open and I storm out of the carriage house." I will have a talk with Master William"! I say out loud." I will not allow him to take another one of the children away from me! He has his children in the same house with him. Why can't I have the same privilege." By now tears were stinging my face and my anger had no outlet. I run toward the woods not knowing where I was running to. I throw myself down under a large tree and bury my head in my arms. "Why God?" I cry "Why?" "Why must everything be a fight? How come I can't do what I want to do?" I become still and listen hoping that an answer will come. As I lay quiet I hear the sweet songs of the free birds and see small happy free squirrels running from tree to tree. I look around me and marvel at the beautiful tall trees and the rich black ground under me. I utter a prayer," God? What happened?" I have read your words many times in your great book; have prayed as Fannie taught me to do. How come? I am a person no less that all these animals and trees. Where in your great plan did something go wrong? I am refusing to feel hopeless and helpless. Many are placed in that position but I won't allow it! I don't have any answers to my great questions God but I am asking you when can I hear the mourning dove cry?"

I picked myself up, without answers and headed back to the house. "I guess it's time to help with supper". I said. "If I ain't there you would think Mrs. Elizabeth would starve to death. But I added, I <u>WILL</u> have a talk with her husband!"

"Master William, You can't let Tad have Nonu." I pleaded that night while lying next to him "Maggie, you sure think you got some say so around here". He replied. "Why don't you want Nonu to go to Tad? I think she and he would produce some good stock. He has several children and they are all good looking and strong." I sat up on the side of the bed and put on my gown. "Well, you're right there. Nonu is good looking and I have never seen a stronger gal. Get the picture?" Master William sat upright and said," You mean?" "I sure do. Looks as if you don't have as much control around here as you think you do, 'OL Tad is is a lot of beds and Nonu's ain't gonna be one of them."

I walk out of his bedroom and go to Miss Selene's door. I peek in and see my beautiful Nonu sleeping peacefully on her little cot at the foot of Miss Selene's bed. I walk over quietly and kiss her on her cheek. I whisper to her," I have great plans for you my angel."

"Maggie I think there is going to be a war." Master William and I were having our usual talk that we shared after his love making. "What makes you think that?" I asked. He withdrew his legs from over mine and sat up on the side of the bed. "Looks as if many folks want to stop the business of slavery. That is the main topic that everyone is talking about." Master William often talked to me as if I was equal to him. I often thought that he shared more concerns with me than he did with his own wife. "Well, Master William what is your views on this issue?" I asked. "You're happy, aren't you Maggie?" He asked. "Wow, I thought, he has no idea. "Master William", I started," Why on God's green earth would you think any of us are happy? Oh sure we sing as we work, we love each other God knows that. And we are grateful that you allow us to raise our own children, most of the time." I added as I thought of my Frankie living "out there" with Tad. "But there are so many dreams that we share, so many wants that we want for our children and their children to come. I personally feel, and I think I can answer for a lot of other people, that I hope that this nasty old war will come on and get me out of here. No, Master William I can't say that I am happy. I live each day with hopes and dreams that I know will never be fulfilled unless something like this war makes the winds change. And I feel it in my bones that the winds is a changing."

I noticed that Master William was not talking and that he wore a frown upon his face. He said, "You know that if this war starts I will have to go away for a while. I am worried that I might lose the farm along with you folks. I sure would hate to lose you gal. You are about the best little girl I have ever lo-uhm had." I smiled as I ran my fingers through his soft hair. "I will miss you to I said But God has a great plan just ahead for us all and who are we to allow our emotions to get in the way of a divine order?" He laughed, "Oh dear sweet Maggie, you speak like a preacher. I sometimes feel as if I have an angel in my arms and then again I know that when I look at your beautiful black face I understand that you could never be an angel." "Why couldn't I be an angel?" I asked. "Maggie you know that angels are all white and shiny. Perhaps you could be an angel's shadow". He laughed at his clever joke and I left the room. I crawled into my bed. As I lay and looked out at the stars I cried.

The morning came with a fresh feeling. I thought to myself as looked into the mirror. I could one day become an angel. I'm sure God makes angels in all colors. The words 'Maggie you speak like a preacher" rang in my ears. A preacher, I thought, maybe I could be one. As I had this thought I noticed that in the bottom of my water pitcher was a small stone. I fished it out and held it close to the window to see it better. It was the shape of a heart. I said aloud, "Now I wonder who put that in my water pitcher. Maybe it was Nonu. I will have to ask her." I slipped it in my apron pocket and went down to the kitchen. Nonu was busy preparing Miss Selene's breakfast. She always wanted something different than everyone else. Nonu had spent many mornings preparing a little something different for Miss Selene. This morning it was eggs fried in the center of a piece of toast. "Nonu, did you put a rock in my water pitcher?" I asked her. "A rock?" she said. "Why would I put a rock in your pitcher?" I held it out for her to see and she looked at it and said." Hey its a heart-Maybe it's a gift from your angels." She handed it back with a little laugh. "How did you know I was thinking about angels when I found it?" I asked. She shrugged it off with a giggle and went about her chores. I looked at the rock again and smiled. "Yes I understand God." I said to myself." I need to teach your people." I put the rock back into my pocket and hummed a tune as I started washing the dishes.

The very next day Berry came to the door. She pushed her face up to the screen door and said, "I thought that you would like to know that Reverend Mason is coming this Sunday." I said, "Berry I haven't seen you for so long, come on in here and have a cup of tea with me." Berry shirked back and said "Oh no I couldn't do that." I asked "Why not? Don't be a silly goose come on in here and have tea with me." Berry entered the kitchen feeling very uncomfortable. She stood by the table just looking around. "Sit here", I said as I pulled a chair out for her. Berry sat and took the tea I offered. "Hows Mable and your little one?" I asked. "They are fine." Berry answered. "So Reverend Mason is coming to the church service this Sunday?" I asked. "Yes Ma'am, he is and it's gonna be a special service. We are all going to the creek 'cause me and a lot others are going to be baptized." I asked, "Can any one be baptized if they want to be?" Berry said as she sipped her tea feeling important. "The way I understand it, if you are wanting to be baptized Reverend Mason will do it." I felt so excited and I said," I really want to be. I read about John the Baptist in the Bible and I have often sat and wondered just how it would feel to be baptized." I knew that Berry did not understand about John the Baptist because she looked at me with a blank stare." John who?" she asked. I answered," Berry that is a Bible story I will have to tell you one of these days." She nodded and finished her tea. "I have to go now, thanks. Maybe you can come this Sunday morning at sunrise. It will be a lot of fun." she said as she left. I walked her to the door" You can be sure I will be there." I said." Tell Mable hi for me." I couldn't wait.

I thought the weekend would never come. Julie and I were preparing Sunday breakfast rolls when I asked her" Julie do you think you would like to be baptized?" Julie shrugged and said, "I aint never give it any thought. It might be the right thing to do though. I have heard of some that got baptized and it changed their lives. Then on the other hand I've seen some folks get baptized and you would have never known it." "Why is that do you suppose?" I asked. "Well the way I figure it once a person is born mean can't no baptizing change it." I looked at her as she punched the dough with more punch than needed. "Who you talking about?" I asked. She got a far away look in her eyes and said." No one that you know about honey. It was years before I knew you." I remembered her only love as I last saw him lying on the ground in his own pool of blood. "Was it something to do with Sug?" I asked. I had never heard Julie mention Sug before and I wasn't sure if she wanted to talk about him now. She shot me her usual shut up look and I acted as if I didn't see it. "Who did you see get baptized before?" I asked. She stiffened her back and said, "A long time before I ever saw your pretty little face I had the opportunity to be baptized. It was when I was about thirteen years old. I was down by the river watching others go under the water while the preacher held their hands. Oh it's a beautiful ceremony to witness I can tell you that. Why the singing alone is worth going to hear. Anyway it was when I was about thirteen I guess when I first saw my Sug. He was helping the ladies into the water when I caught a glimpse of his beautiful strong back. He wasn't much older than me I guess, but he looked older. I was going to get baptized myself that day but it never happened." "Why?" I asked. "Just as a group of us girls were about to be led into the water we heard a lot of commotion. We turned to see about four men on huge horses. Everything became real quiet as all four men waded into the river. They started shouting and yelling bad things to our preacher and told him he needed to go with them. He tried to explain to the men that he was doing the work of the Lord and he would be more than willing to baptize any one of them if not all. They started laughing and grabbing at the women. We all ran out of the water and watched as one of the men approached the preacher. "Baptize me preacher. I want to be pure in the eyes of the Lord." He shouted as the other men laughed. I was stunned standing on the river bank along with the rest of the congregation. The preacher showed no fright as he reached for the big mans hand. He immersed the man in the water and as he came up he shouted." You're all a witness to this preacher trying to drown me. As he shouted this the other men grabbed the preacher and held his head under water until he couldn't breath. "Oh my God Julie, What did you do?" I asked. "Wasn't nothing anyone could do. The preacher was a free man like your Rev. Mason and I guess those men didn't like him for some reason. Any way that is the one and only baptizing I ever saw and it wasn't a pretty sight. Only good thing was I saw my Sug there for the first time. I hope your baptizing is a better one than the one I saw." We completed our chores in silence. That night I said my prayers and after reading my nightly Bible story I thought about tomorrow. I wonder if baptizing will change my life I thought? I would like to take Frankie and Nonu with me and have them baptized to. If God be willin it will change our lives. It it don't something will have to I can't go on much longer living this way.

I woke early before the rooster crowed his daily wake up call. I looked through my clothes and decided on the cream colored dress. It wasn't the best one I had but I thought I didn't want to look too proud. I was meeting my Lord and I didn't want him to think I had airs. I had a white scarf that I had made for such an occasion if one should ever come up. I looked in the mirror and saw my eyes looking back at me. "You look just fine". I said to the woman in the mirror "Just fine". I crept quietly into Miss. Selene's room to wake Nonu. She woke without a start and followed me to my room. "Do you want to get baptized this morning?" I asked her. "I guess so if you want me to." she answered. "I would like that." I said." Let's go get Frankie up." I knocked on Tad's door and retrieved my Frankie. "Where we going?" he asked as he rubbed his eyes. "Today we are going to get baptized." I answered him. "And it looks as if it will have a duel purpose for you". I said as I tried to wash some of the grease off his face and hands.

When we arrived at the creek there were already many folks standing around. I looked for Reverand Mason and didn't see him anywhere. "I wonder where Reverand Mason is?" I said to Nonu. Just as I said these words I felt a presence behind me. I turned to see the beautiful face of a man of God. I felt my legs go weak and my heart beat faster. "Good morning Maggie. It's nice to see you again." I just about fainted as he placed his hand on mine. "Hello Reverand" I managed to say. "How are you this fine morning?" "Are you going to let me baptize you in that beautiful dress?" I stammered that. "Yes I was if he would be kind enough to do so." He squeezed my hand and said. "Nothing would please me more dear sister."

"You didn't ask him if he would do me and Frankie," Nonu said. "Oh I am sure he will." I answered her still in a daze.

The singing started and just as Julie said it was the most beautiful singing I had ever heard. I joined in with the others and felt waves of energy shooting up and down my spine. I looked up at the morning sun coming over the hills and I marveled at all the colors in the sky this bright new day. The singing sounded as if the very angels themselves had settled among us and were joining us in song.I closed my eyes and could feel the breeze of their gossamer wings upon my face. I heard above the singing Master Williams voice saying," Maggie you speak like a preacher."

As I opened my eyes I saw the first of the women being led to the water. When she came up out of the water I saw the morning sun shine upon her head looking like a halo. I whispered to Nonu. "God is in this place."

It was our turn to be led to the water. Reverand Mason led Frankie first and I thought I saw him trying to rub some dirt from him as he held him under. I started to giggle as Frankie sputtered and spit and darted up out of the water toward shore. I held Nonu's hand as she was led next. She looked at me and smiled as she came up out of the water dripping wet. I noticed that today her smile had once again reached her big brown eyes. I thought, angels are in all colors. I felt a hand take mine and I was led to the edge of the water. The sun was shining in the water and was giving off a Beautiful golden reflection. I looked at Reverand. Mason smiling at me and I then looked at his feet. I gasped. I had never seen such beautiful feet standing in the golden waters. I took his hand and he led me to the deeper part of the water. I felt his warm hands as he held me tightly so I would not fall. I held my breath and Reverand Mason immersed me completely under the water. It was only short seconds but it felt as if I was under for minutes As I was lifted up I looked into the face of Reverand Mason. I couldn't tell if I had tears or if it was the water clouding my vision. He was smiling at me and for a short second I saw the face of Jesus. I cleared my vision and looked again at Reverand Mason. He appeared normal to my vision now but I swore I saw someone else holding me. I climbed out of the water and sat with the others. I put my arms around Frankie and Nonu and held them tight while others sang about the Promised Land.

That late morning after the baptizing and the church service I had a chance to spend some time with Rev. Mason. "Won't you come to the kitchen with me and have a cup of honey sweetened tea?" I asked him. "I would really enjoy your hospitality Maggie." he answered. He walked with me to the kitchen of the big house and seemed very uncomfortable when he first entered. "Have a seat Rev. Mason I 'll fix us some tea." He sat down with his hat in in hands and looked around the kitchen. "Is this where you spend most of your time Sister?" He asked. "Yes sir I do, when I am not looking after the Mrs. of the house or cleaning these huge rooms." I answered. "Where do you call home?" I asked. He smiled and said, "No place in particular. I travel a lot and I often spend the night in barns when I am not invited to stay where I preach." I looked at him in astonishment. "You have no home?" I asked. He said, "Well in a since the whole of God's kingdom is my home.I just haven't settled down under just one roof." I asked do you like it that way." His face smiled at me and said, "It's a lot better than being owned by any one man who tells me when and where I can go. I carry freedom papers with me." I asked him. "How did you get freedom papers?" My wheels were turning. I didn't know how one went about obtaining such precious papers and I was about to find out. He said," I did a good deed for a man once and he issued me these papers." He produced a tattered piece of paper and I read it. It was indeed papers freeing this man of God. "Oh I would love to have such papers for myself and my children I said. "You must surely be a man of God to have such papers. He said, "From what I hear soon everyone will as free as me when the war starts." There was that war mentioned again. He must have heard the same as Master William had heard. "Tell me more about this war coming". I said. "Looks as if there is a big war pot simmering on the stove. It's about to boil over and when it does it will boil with a big bang." Rev. Mason sipped his tea and smacked his lips with authority. "What will happen to everyone when this war starts?" I asked. Rev. Mason looked over his cup and said," Either death or freedom. That's all I hear. I felt a chill go up my spine. "What do you think will be the outcome", he asked. "I don't know but I fear when I think about it." I answered.

"There isn't anything we can do but pray and pray daily", he said. "But let's don't talk about war now, let's talk about you." "Me?" I asked. "What about me."

"Maggie I hear tells you're a prophet, and I have been told you can read the Bible. Is that true?" "Well I could be a prophet and yes, I have read the Bible" I answered. "I talk to a lot of Mrs. Elizabeth's friends and they seem to tell others about me. When things happen that I tell them what I see. They tell me that these things come about. Maybe I am a prophet." I laughed.Rev. Mason said, "Maggie I would like it if you would do Sunday services each Sunday at the church. I can only come by this way every two months or so. With a war so close I can't even say I can ever come back and I want to make sure that the folks here will have a preacher." I looked at him with my mouth open and said, "A preacher? Me?" Rev. Mason stood and walked over to me and said. "Yes my dear sweet Maggie, you. Would you do this for me and for God and of course for God's people?" I stammered,"Of course I will! I can't believe you think I can do it! I would be delighted to have the chance!"

He continued, "I have spoken too many of the congregation and they all agreed that you would be an excellent preacher. They all seem to hold you in high regard. And I took the liberty to tell them that church would be held next Sunday and that you would conduct the service. So all is in order?" I sat down with a thud and said "Yes sir I can do that."

I said my good-bys to Rev Mason and sent him along his way with a hardy lunch packed. A lunch that would last him for several days. As I saw him ride off on his horse I had the feeling that I would never see him again. I felt a tear sting my cheek as he turned to wave one last wave to me. I thought to myself "There goes one of God's angels and I have been blessed."

Sunday came before I was ready for it to come. I was nervous as Nonu and I walked to the church clutching my precious Bible. Many were seated when I entered and many were still coming. All were glad to see us as we joined the others in our morning greetings. I walked to the front of the little church and opened my Bible. I read the first verse my eyes fell on. 2 Kings verse *And Elisha came again to Gilgal: and there was a derth in the land: and the sons of the prophets were sitting before him: and he said unto his servant. Set on the great pot and seethe pottage for the sons of the prophets.*

I thought to myself "This is what Rev. Mason and I talked about. The derth in the land, could be the upcoming war, the great pot could be the simmering war pot we spoke of. Even the word Prophets was in this scripture. I opened my mouth and the words of God filled it. I spoke of war and having faith. I wasn't even aware of where I was going with this sermon and I was as surprised as everyone else was. I was home and I had my calling. Yes, I guess I could be called God's prophet.

"Maggie, Maggie wake up" Master William was standing next to my bed in the middle of the night. I woke to see him standing fully dressed.

"What do you want sir and why are you dressed?" Master William said "I have to leave for a while and I wanted to say good-by to you before I go." "Where are you going?" I asked. I have to go and serve my country Maggie we are at war now." I sat up with a bolt and said "War!! Who said?" Master William laughed and said, "The president said. and I have to go fight in the war. I want you to take care of Mrs. Elizabeth and the girls while I am gone. I have asked Tad to help around the house as much as possible and he is to take his orders from you. In fact I have even informed Susanna that you are in charge. She didn't like that but I told her that was the way it was to be." I said, "But Master William I don't think I want to be in charge of anything, I will let Susanna and Birdie run things while your away, and of course Mrs. Elizabeth."" Hah Elizabeth doesn't have the sense God gave a goose dear Maggie. You will do just fine." He said. "Give me a kiss for good luck and I will be on my way". I shall not be gone long it should be a short war and I know people in high places." Master William gave me a kiss on the cheek and left my room.

I watched the sun come up. I wondered. War what will it mean? "Oh well." I said. I have a house to run and children to feed. I must get up and face the day ahead. I couldn't help but wonder what changes the war would bring today in this house, if any.

I go to the front parlor to find Mrs. Elizabeth huddled with Miss Selene and Miss Mary. I notice that they are all three crying and I approach them with care. "Don't worry. Master William will be home before you even know it." I said as I placed my hand on Little Mary's soft blonde hair.

Mrs. Elizabeth looked at me and just for a moment I felt sorry for her pale face and pale blue eyes.

"Maggie, what would you know about anything after all?" Mrs. Elizabeth said. "We women are all alone here and Lord knows what can happen to us with William gone." I said, Mrs. Elizabeth nothing is going to happen to you I am sure of that. The war will soon be over and Master William will soon be back. In the meantime you must not think of such things nor should you alarm the girls with such remarks. I am here as well as a large group of folks. If anything was to happen we would be the first to have it happen to, not you and the girls." Mrs. Elizabeth shook her head and mumbled, you don't know what you're talking about Maggie. What enemy soldier would want you when he could have me or these beautiful girls?" I said. Well Mrs. Elizabeth I guess you might be right but remember if they were to come after you or any one of these girls I would have to be the one they have to go through first and that my dear woman is highly unlikely!"

I left them crying in the parlor and went to the kitchen. Everyone in the house seemed worried and quiet. Susanna and Birdie were fixing breakfast as usual and Julie was sipping her morning tea at the table, while talking with Bill.. "Where is Nonu?" I asked. "Nonu is upstairs making beds." Julie answered. Everything seemed to go on as normal except that we have crying gals in the parlor.

Susanna spoke," We need to maintain this house as usual until the war is over. I don't know yet what affect it will have on us but I am sure we will definitely have some uncomfortable times. We all have to stick together and remain calm as much as possible. Master William left early this morning and Tad and Bill will act as men of the house until he returns. The main thing is that we all must work and stick together.

The federal troops entered Nashville. Nonu and I were hanging sheets on the line when I saw men riding high stepping horses coming down the lane. "Oh my God Nonu!"I yelled. "Hurry and get into the house." We dropped our clean white sheets right there on the dirty ground and ran. The soldiers kept coming and without any warning started to take up camp right under our noses. The sea of men and tents stretched as far as I could see.

As I was attending to Mrs. Elizabeth the evening the soldiers arrived a tall man entered the parlor. "Ma'am", he said. "I am to inform you that your husband William has been sent to Fort Makinac as a prisoner. We are to remain here on his ground until further notice. It would be in your favor if we had full co-operation from you and your people during our stay." I reached out just in time to catch Mrs. Elizabeth as she fainted.

Men were everywhere and it was part of my duties to provide meals for them. As I was plucking chickens early one sunny morning I had an eerie feeling that I was being watched. I understood that there were many present around the farm but I had not noticed any one in particular close by this morning. I looked over my shoulder and looked into the face of a young man of about fifteen years old. "Hi" I said in a calm tone "What you want standing there watching me pluck this old hen?" He smiled and said I been watching you and the other little gal ever since I got here. I was wondering what your name is?" He said as he sat on the ground next to my tub of hot water. "My name is Maggie." I answered. "What's yours?" "Jack" He said. "Where is the other gal I always see you with? Whats her name?" "Her name is Nonu and she is inside in the kitchen fixin some food for dinner." I answered. "Well I think that little gal is awful pretty." He said. I eyed Jack suspiciously and said "Yes Nonu is a very pretty girl and very polite to". I saw a glimmer in his eye as Nonu came out to help with the chickens. He rose and reached for her hand. As he did this Nonu put both hands behind her back and asked. "Susanna wants to know how long until you get those chickens ready for the pot?" "Won't be long "I said. "Tell her to come help and things will go a lot faster." I said with a smirk. I knew that plucking chickens was a job beneath Susanna." Jack was still standing and grinning at

Nonu as she ran to give the news to Susanna. I put down my chicken and placed both hands on my hips. "Jack." I said. "If you got any notions to touch that child you will know just what these chickens are feeling." Jack jerked his head in my direction and said "You know as well as I do Maggie them chickens ain't feeling nothing. They are as dead as they can get." I sat back down and picked up a fresh chicken and said. It looks like you and I are understanding each other son. Now go on and mind your own business." As he left I tossed a freshly plucked chicken in a burlap tote and thought, Mable and Berry would like that one for the Sunday church social.

Days seemed like weeks as I watched the ruination of the plantation. The soldiers had eaten many chickens, lambs and cattle and it was just a chore in itself cooking for endless hours. I ran all day providing care for the many men that had made the plantation their home during the war. I was not allowed to shirk my duties of caring for Mrs Elizabeth and her girls on top of everything else that needed attended to.

"Maggie come here this instant." I heard Mrs Elizabeth call. I dropped my dish towel and ran to find her sitting serenely in the dining room. "Yes Ma'am what is it that you want?" I asked. Maggie the girls and I are feeling that you don't care about our welfare anymore. I want you to stop whatever it is that your doing and comb my hair. It's so long and you know I can't braid it as well as you do. I think if I had my hair freshly braided I would feel better." I watched as she took out the pins and let her heavy hair fall to her waist. "Braid your hair?" I said. "How do you think I would have time to braid your hair? Have you noticed that the whole damn war is camped in the yard? I don't have time to braid your hair have Miss Selene do it she isn't doing anything but flirting with men all day." Mrs. Elizabeth jumped to her feet and said. "I hardly think that she is flirting she is very involved with caring for the men when they need a smile from someone that reminds them of a loved one at home. She even said just he other day that she wanted to become a nurse after this war is over. I think she is doing a fine job of keeping morale up. I stood there with my mouth open as she tried to hand me her brush. "Mrs Elizabeth." I said. "I told you I don't have time now to do your hair. I have to complete cooking and after that cleaning up and then cooking again. I understand that your hair is looking poorly lately but braiding it won't help you to feel better. What would help though is if you would stop sitting around crying and help in the kitchen." "Kitchen?" she screamed. "You have to be kidding me!" I stood my ground and said. "Yes in the kitchen we could use an extra pair of hands. This Sunday I am asking several women from the church to help and I am sure your help would be appreciated. And I might add Master William would be proud of you if you would lend a helping hand." She said, "You can't bring yard people in this house to work I won't allow it. You can't trust them they will steal everything I own." I laughed and said, "Steal? What do you think is going on right now with all those men? They are taking whatever they want right out from the very ground you call your own. Your livestock is being used up, they stole Master William's horses, the very best ones at that, and we are running out of chickens and pigs. And you are worrying about folks that need to help? Many of them have even offered their help and you say you will prevent it? I don't think you can do too much about it now. I am going to ask and I sure will be grateful for any help I can get. Now if you want to sit all day and brood about your hair you go right ahead. Me? I am not going to braid it right now, perhaps later, but right now I have a plantation to keep in order and I would hope to think your concern would also be having a plantation for Master to come home to. I ducked as Mrs. Elizabeth threw her hair brush at me as I turned to go back to the kitchen.

Birdie and Julie were peeling potatoes as I entered the kitchen. Susanna was helping Nonu cut noodles as Bill was slicing a huge smoked ham. He said, "We only got three hams left in the smoke house. After tomorrow they will be all gone. It's going to be a long time before we will ever be able to butcher hogs again. The hogs have been all used up and only little ones are left. They aren't ready to butcher and many of them are going to hog roasts. "Birdie added. Chickens just about gone to. I don't know what were going to do when all the livestock is eaten. We will all starve I guess." I joined in with the potato peeling and said as I looked at my knife,".This sure is pretty silver." Birdie said, "Yes it sure is. It comes from a set that we use only on occasions. I don't know how it got out of the silver box." Susanna stopped and said, "Let me see that". She took the knife from me and turned it over in her hand. "Now how did this get in here I wonder? Anybody been in the cabinet where the silver is?" We all shook our heads as Bill left to get the silver box from the cabinet. He carried the box into the kitchen and placed it on the table. Susanna opened it and we all saw that some of it was gone. "Now who do you suppose took some of this silver?" She asked. Bill said," you know what? We ought to hide it so as nobody will get the rest of it. Looks like everything around here is being taken and I want Master William to have something of value when he gets home" We all agreed and I said, "Where could we hide it though? Everything around here has been gotten into where could we hide it so no one would find it?" Bill said with a grin "You let me worry about that Maggie I can hide it." Bill wiped the knife as he placed it along side the remaining pieces of silverware. He picked up the box and started outside with it. Nonu asked," Bill where you going to hide It?" Bill said, 'Don't worry I know a good place that no one will look into." He laughed as he went out the door with the box under his arm.

I woke and almost forgot that today was Sunday. I dressed to go to church and headed out the door. Many men were waiting for breakfast and others had decided to take it upon themselves to cook over a fire in front of their tents. I held my head up high with my Bible under my arm as I walked to the little cabin we used as a church. "Where you going this morning Miss Maggie?" It was that kid Jack again. "I am going to church Jack would you like to join me?" He smiled and asked. "Where is that pretty Nonu this morning?" I answered "Oh I reckon that she will be along later shes a slow starter in the morning." I didn't tell him that she had to fix Miss Selene's and Miss Mary's breakfast before she could come to church. Jack said. "I think I would like to join you if I would be welcome." I turned to Jack and smiled. "Jack everyone is welcome in God's house and I am sure your momma would be proud if you went to church this fine morning." Jack said "Oh I been going to church, Chaplin holds church every Sunday for those who want to go. But I ain't never been to a colored church before and it might be a nice change." I once again smiled and he walked with me to the church.

Many were gathered this morning but I noticed that a few familiar faces were not there. Mabel was alone and many others that usually were there to greet me was gone. I walked toward the front of the church and opened my Bible to read. This morning I had opened to Psalms 31.1 read and when I got to verse 11 reading; *I -was a reproach among all mine enemies but especially among my neighbors, and a fear to mine aqcquaintance: they that did see me without fled from me. K.j.* I noticed that many were stirring in their seats and I read further: to verse 16; *Make thy face to shine upon thy servant: save me for thy mercies sake K.J.* I stopped reading and looked at the people. I saw that they were whispering amongst themselves and feeling very uneasy. I asked, "What is the matter with you all this morning. Can't you have an open heart and welcome Jack into this house of God?" A man named Hank rose from his seat and said, "Reverand Maggie we don't have a problem with Jack being here this morning. What we are all talking about is how come you to read that part of the Bible to us?" I looked at the faces and now I noticed that more than just a few were missing. "I don't decide what to read before I come here Hank. I just open my Bible and am led as to what I am to talk about. What is the problem with the chosen word this morning?" Hank stood on one foot and then another before he answered. "Well Miss Reverand ma'am it is telling us that God will protect those that we are worried about and we were just wondering how did you know?" I asked, "Know What Hank?" Then Mable my dear friend stood up." Reverand Maggie could I talk with you alone?" she asked. "Of course Mable." I said. Mable left her seat and walked to me. She took me aside and said." My Berry left last night and many others went with her. I gasped and said "No Mable say it aint so." Yes she cried, "and we are all so worried about them.

We couldn't say anything because of that man Jack is here and we thought your sermon would give them away." I held her to me and said "Oh dear Mable I didn't know I am just led to talk about what God puts in front of me. I guess the gift can be awful tricky at times and I am sorry I asked Jack to join us. You go back to your seat dear heart and I will change my words this morning." I saw that the congregation had settled down and I said," This morning is such a fine morning lets pray for our loved ones and then enter into song. We sang for the entire service and we all silently prayed with each songs note that our loved ones would be protected from any harm as they went toward their new lives.

Bill retrieved a large key, a candle, and some matches from the small cabinet in the pantry and cautiously walked out the back door. At night the endless sea of dark, quiet army tents looked like a small mountain range. He retrieved the silverware box from under the back step. With quiet steps he walked toward the family crypt. He thought to himself, I hope no one sees me with this box. If they do they are sure to grab it from me to keep this silver for their own. Master William will be awful proud of me when I give him his silver when he comes home he chuckled to himself as he had this thought. As he approached the family crypt he felt fear when he unlocked the iron door that kept the dead in and the living out. He knew of a loose stone that needed fixed and it would be easy to slide open. The crypt smelled of dampness and felt cold as he drew the door shut behind him. He fumbled with the matches and lit the candle. The small flame flickered, he tried not to notice eerie shadows as the flame danced against the stone walls. He backed up and almost decided against hiding the silverware box behind the loose stone. He once again thought of how proud Master William would be of him when he could produce the lost silver. This thought kept him going. As he reached the secret place where he was going to hide the silverware box. He stopped in front of a flat stone and he remembered the small little boy that always was weak and didn't smile very much. He said in a low tone. "Nathaniel, I have a job for you to do for your daddy. I know that you won't mind helping him out. I am going to give you something to hold on to for safe keeping so the soldiers won't steal it from your daddy." Bill placed the box on the ground and reached up with both hands to touch the cold marble stone. He shivered as the cold marble slid to the side. He was wet with perspiration and knew that he had gone to far now to back out. The edge of the small coffin became visible to his eyes. He reached down and picked up the silverware box and placed it alongside of the tiny casket. "No one would be as brave as I am to open this grave to look in here." he said still talking to Nathaniel. "This is a fine box you can watch over for your daddy. When he comes home I will take it back, won't be in your care for very long child. And Oh, I am sorry if I have disturbed your sleep but this is a very important box and I knew that you would keep it safe and not mind watching it." He slid the cold marble back into place and saw that it looked as undisturbed as it had before. He walked back over to the entrance and waited while he watched two men talking in front of one of the tents. The men retreated back into their tents and he very quietly shut the iron door and locked it.

The next morning Susanna asked, 'Bill did you hide that silverware?" Bill looked up from his morning cup of tea and said with a smile, 'Yes ma'am I sure did." "Where did you hide it?" she asked. Bill stood up to his full six foot stature and said, Well Susanna if I told you it wouldn't be hid any longer. You have a mouth on you that has to talk about everything and pretty soon everyone would know where the silver is hidden. Let's just say that no one will enter in to the most secret place I know of, and it is in the care of some very good hands. He wasn't about to tell any living person and he felt important that he knew something that Susanna would love to tell others. "Hands!" Susanna shouted. "Hands? You gave it to someone? If you gave it to someone I want to know now. It isn't safe with someone." Bill laughed, "It is as safe as it can ever be with this person he won't tell a soul, not now or ever. Don't you worry it is safe and I will give it back to Master when he gets home and lets just leave it at that." He left to go outside and Susanna jumped when the screen door slammed. "Humph, don't know why I don't feel good about that." she said. "Oh well, gotta get busy."

Madgelyn Hawk

It seemed like an endless battle just to maintain the house and keep Mrs. Elizabeth's life calm. Men were in and out of the house all hours of the day and night. The war was taking its toll on all of us. Mrs. Elizabeth with Mary stayed in her room for the most part and Miss Selene was always "entertaining". She took it upon herself to sing and play her music for the men in the evening hours. Her complexion was rosier than I had ever seen it.

Jack was trying to catch Nonu's attention on one particular evening as I walked into the parlor. "Aw come on Nonu dance with me. "I heard him say as I entered the room. Nonu had her head down and was shaking it no. He took her by the hands and started to pull her to him. Nonu was protesting as men laughed and urged Jack on. "Nonu I need you in the kitchen now." I said. Several men said at the same time, "Heres another pretty gal to dance with." Before I could protest I was grabbed by a tall dirty smelling man. "Let go of me!" I yelled. "Nonu I need you in the kitchen now!" I saw Ms. Selene leave the room and dart up the stairs. The men were pulling at me and Nonu and I could hear laughter and comments being made that sent chills up my spine. "You take the little one Jack you have been talking about her enough,nows your time to break that filly." I felt hands all over my body as I watched three men holding Nonu down. As I felt my dress tear I heard a thundering noise that rattled the windows.

"Stop right there or I will shoot all of you!" I was so startled to hear Mrs. Elizabeth's voice in such a loud manner. I looked over toward the door of the parlor and was shocked to see Mrs. Elizabeth pointing a rifle at the room full of men. "Maggie, Nonu get out of here right now. I am appalled at the both of you carrying on with these men in such a manner!" Nonu cried "Ma'am I was ~" "Shut up girl and get out of this room before I shoot you!" Mrs. Elizabeth shouted. I knew not to open my mouth as I grabbed Nona's hand and ran out of the room. The men cleared the room as well and Mrs. Elizabeth went back to her bedroom.

I held Nonu's little shaken body as she cried in my arms. I was still in a mild state of shock mainly because I had never thought Mrs. Elizabeth would come to my rescue. "Are you alright honey?" I asked. She dried her eyes and said, 'Maggie when we ever gonna get out of this nasty place?" "Nasty place?" I asked. "This is home I don't know if we ever will get out of here alive." I had a horrible thought at that time and I took Nonu's face in my hands. "Please don't ever try to run away from here. I would be so worried about you I think it would kill me." Nonu just looked at the floor and wouldn't answer me. My blood ran cold. "Nonu promise me you won't run from here I couldn't bear it if I didn't know where you were. I tried to look into her eyes and all I received back was a teary blank stare.

I lay in my bed that night and said a prayer to God. "Please Dear Lord, Please see to it that we can all stay together until the great promise is

70

fulfilled. Please protect me and mine and keep your sheep from straying. Amen.

Mrs. Elizabeth became involved with the running of the plantation. She was even helping with some small chores around the house. She had joined me in the chore of washing windows. "Why Mrs. Elizabeth." I said, "What has changed your attitude? I thought you were going to spend the rest of your living days hiding upstairs in your room." She shot me a short glance and as she rubbed the window with a small effort she said "Gotta make sure this place is still standing when William gets home. Can't have those soldiers destroying my best people along with my home." I smiled at her response and continued with my window washing.

As I stood on a chair looking out over the vast yard covered with brown tents I noticed that many of the men were running and shouting. "Well, what do you suppose?" I said out loud. "Looks as if something is stirring up the whole place like ants running around in the rain." Mrs. Elizabeth stopped what she was doing and I heard her gasp. "Maggie get down off that chair and close the shutters fast!" she yelled. "What's wrong?" I cried. "What's going on out there?" As I leaped off my chair and started to close the shutters I heard a shot that broke the very window that we were just standing in front of. I grabbed Mrs. Elizabeth and threw her to the floor. She cried "Oh My God the damn Yankees has just turned the air blue." We ran to the kitchen to see where the rest of the house folks were. Bill, Birdie, and Susanna were standing in a huddle while Miss Selene and Miss Mary were under the table. Frankie had ran to the kitchen and he and Nonu were huddled in a corner. Julie was entering the kitchen from the back stairs entrance. Susanna yelled, "What in the sam hell is a going on out there? "Mrs. Elizabeth said, The God damn Yankees is out there shooting up everything and everyone." Just as she said this the door crashed open. A tall, bearded man dressed in a blue uniform stood glaring at us. "Who is in charge here? Is there a man of this house?" he bellowed. The man smelled of gun powder and sweat. Mrs. Elizabeth pulled her shoulders back and stuck out her chin. "My husband William is the man of this house and if you have any business with him you can take it up with me. I am in charge while he is gone!" I was standing with my mouth open as I saw him approach Mrs. Elizabeth and smile. "Well little Mrs. William it looks like if I had any business that needed taken care of I would certainly come to you my sweet cream colored belle of the South. It just so happens though that I took care of my business just last night with a pretty little brown wench so I won't be needing your business just right now." Mrs. Elizabeth spit right in the eye of this big burly man. We all thought that he was going to kill her on the spot but he just wiped the spit off his face and said. "We are staying here awhile and I would appreciate it if you would just do your woman things like cooking and cleaning. I will tell you this once though if I see your little smart ass sassing any one of my men I dare to say I will indeed take care of my "business" with you." He turned to leave the kitchen and Mrs. Elizabeth took Mary and Miss Selene upstairs. "Come on Nonu!" Miss Selene shouted. Nonu looked at me and as I nodded for her to join Miss Selene she waved at me. "We will be fine down here just stay away from the windows.!" I called to them as they ran up the stairs.

It was a bloody battle right outside the very walls I called home. We soon all became nurses as we bandaged wounds and held dying men's heads. Some of the men were as young as my Frankie and I couldn't help but wonder what their life would have been. In the evening hours the gunshot was still ringing in my ears. I thought the night would never end and in the early morning hours it became quiet. I dared to look outside. I saw men lying in various positions all over the ground. Many were moaning but most of them were silent and bleeding from wounds. They were wearing gray uniforms as well as blue ones. It seemed to me that most of them were gray. I walked toward the carriage house to check on Tad and Frankie. "Please God let them be alright." I prayed. As I walked through the men I felt someone grab my ankle. I looked down into the face of Jack. "Maggie," he said in a whisper. "Say a prayer for me dear lady of God. This is the day I will go and meet my Lord." I knelt and placed his head in my lap and he smiled at me as he died. I wiped his hair off his bloody forehead as I did this I saw a gold chain coming from his clinched fist. I didn't want to see it because it probably was a locket or something that he held dear. I did not open his hand I just placed it near his heart.

I placed his head back on the ground and stood. I need to hold my Frankie, I thought, I walked toward the carriage house and upon entering I stumbled over Tad.

"Oh God where are you hurt?" I cried. He said" Just my arm, I think." I looked at his arm and saw that a hole was shot clear through it. He wasn't losing much blood and I saw that the wound looked clean. "Lay still." I told him "I will get Bill." I ran back to the house and shouted to Bill. Hurry I need help! Tad has been shot and we need to get him off the ground and into his bed." Julie and Bill ran with me to help. We managed to get Tad upstairs to his bed." Run outside and pull me up some plantain and some burdock leaves." Julie instructed Bill. "Got to make a poultice. Get some poke root too if you can find some." Bill left to get the ingredients while I started a fire in the fireplace to boil water. Julie ordered, "Hurry and get that fire hot enough. We need to get the poultice on as soon as possible. We don't want infection to set in. He could die if we don't act fast. Maggie run to the house and get my sleeping powders and your Bible we will need them. I hurried back after retrieving the powders and my Bible. Bill soon came back with the herbs and placed them in the boiling water. Julie said. "Maggie find the part in the Bible that stops the blood and read it three times over Tad." I thumbed through my Bible and said "Where did you say that verse was?" Julie answered with an air of authority, "You're the preacher gal and I have to tell you where to find something in your own Bible. Its in Zeke 16 and 6. I said, "Zeke, humm oh! Ezekiel chapter 16 verse 6. Of course!" I turned to the book of Ezekiel 16:6 and read aloud. The Bleeding stopped at once and Julie went to work applying the herb soaked rags to Tad's wound.

I looked around and didn't see Frankie. Tad was almost asleep because Julie had given him nerve root and catnip to induce sleep. "Tad where is Frankie?" I loudly said. He fluttered his eyes and pointed towards the door. "Tad! where is Frankie?" I now shouted. This time he didn't answer he was sleeping near to unconsciousness.

Julie and I looked at each other and my heart jumped into my throat. I ran down the stairs calling out Frankie's name.

I looked everywhere for him and couldn't find him. I was crying and ran into the house to see if he had gone in to play with Mary. Miss Mary and Miss Selene were sitting in the center of Miss Selene's bed when I opened the bedroom door. "Girls have you seen Frankie?" I asked. They both said "No" at the same time. "If you see him will you tell him I want him?" I said to them. They both nodded as I closed the door. As I started down the stairs I thought, that's odd those girls acted as if they were scared of me. Poor little girls I am going to have to have a talk with them after while they are in a state of shock. I need to find Frankie first though.

As I went back through the kitchen I ask Susanna if she had seen Frankie. "No Maggie I haven't seen him nor Nonu for that matter. It's been a while since I saw Frankie but Nonu hasn't been down stairs yet this morning. Maybe they are together." I said, I hope so. Nonu can keep him out of trouble."

I went toward the cabins. Sometime Nonu would visit Mable or some other friends that she had made from out back.

Mable was in her house when I arrived. Since Barry had left she didn't leave her house much except to work and to go to church. I knocked and Mable came to the door. "Maggie dear come in", she cried. "How are you dear? Have a seat." she said. As I sat she said "What brings you out here with all this fighting going on in our own front yards?" "I am looking for Frankie and now I guess Nonu is missing to." I said. Mable got real quiet and said "A bunch of folks left last night when the fighting was going on do you suppose they went to?" My face went pale, "Left? My kids? You don't think so, do you?" Then I remembered how Nonu looked at me when she asked me when was she ever going to leave this "nasty place". I also remembered her waving to me when I sent her upstairs last night with the girls.

I couldn't think of anything to say. I just sat numbly in Mable's cabin. I couldn't even cry I didn't know what to do. There were no words to speak and no outlet for my pain. I just couldn't stand the thought of my babies gone, and where did they go, and would they be alright. Mable didn't say anything to me she just let me sit there until the shadows grew on the wall.

I didn't even know how I walked back to the big house. I was standing in the kitchen when I heard Miss Selene yell "Maggie! Maggie I am talking to you! Will you answer me?" I looked into the face of Miss Selene and saw her mouth form the words, "Where is Nonu?" I stared blankly at her and shrugged my shoulders and shook my head. Julie noticed that something was wrong and grabbed me as I fell to the floor.

I must have slept for days. When I awoke the sun was shinning into my open window and the breeze was blowing my thin curtains. I first thought of Nonu and Frankie and wondered how the sun could shine and the breeze could still blow. I could hear the folks talking and children laughing. I was at a loss as to what they could be laughing about. Julie came into my room carrying a cup of tea. "Oh you're awake are you?" she asked. I answered, "Yes I am has there been any word from Nonu and Frankie?" Julie frowned and said, "No honey not a word. Don't you worry now I am sure they are just fine. Been many folks get up North just fine when they leave here" I needed to cry and couldn't. "How do they get there Julie? I hear that the dogs catch them and chew them to bits." Julie sat on the edge of the bed and pulled me close to her. "There are people that take them under their wings. These people take them from one safe place to another. I am sure the kids went with a group of folks that had good connections. Just you wait you will hear from them someday. Now you know Nonu would never forget you or me for that matter." I managed a smile for Julie and I knew that my smile would never reach my heart again. "I can only pray that the people that helped them are led by God." I said. I drank my tea and decided to venture downstairs and try to resume my life. Julie left me alone to get washed off and dressed. I looked at myself in the mirror and saw that I hadn't changed much from the little scared girl that I once was. I was older but deep inside just as scared. I washed my face and put on a clean head scarf and dress. I tried to smile at myself but I couldn't manage it. Oh well I thought God has a plan for me and he knows what is right. His plan for Nonu and Frankie is just as important as mine is. I refuse to hope that they are just fine. Hope is a doubt. I will know that they are fine. After all I have to trust God or I will not be of service to him or his sheep. I smoothed out the wrinkles from my bed and headed down the stairs to the kitchen.

When I went downstairs I heard a commotion in the yard. Folks were shouting and running toward the road. "Whats wrong?" I shouted at Mrs. Elizabeth as she ran through the house. She grabbed me and spun me around shouting, 'William has come home! He has come home!" I ran outside with her to see Master William riding up the lane with folks running and shouting alongside his horse.

I noticed that the dead were no longer on the ground and all the tents were gone. All that remained were remnants of camp fires.

The folks were shouting and patting Master William on the back. Everyone was glad to see him come home. I could feel my heart lighten a little when his eyes caught mine. He jumped off his horse and Mrs. Elizabeth, Miss Selene and Miss Mary each grabbed hold of him and all four walked in the house.

Master William had been home a few days before he and I had an opportunity to talk. I was making beds when he came up from behind and pinched me on the hip. "My dear sweet Maggie." he said. "I have done a head count and I just became aware of the fact that your Frankie and Julie's Nonu are no where to be found. Could you give me some idea where they might be?" I turned to look him in the eyes and answered "No Master I can not. I reckon they left when the Yankees were fighting out in the yard. I was tending to Tad and after that I couldn't find either one of them. I figure they just up and took off. Many folks are doing that you know. Master Lincoln has got the entire world shook up and many folks are running on account of it." Master William sat on the bed I had just made and wrinkled it. I shook my head and said, "Looks like a gal just can't get ahead I had that bed all made and you are making more work for me." I started to cry. He pulled me down beside him and took my hands in his. Maggie I need you to help me get all the folks together in the yard I have something to tell everyone of you." "What is it Master William? Tell me before you tell the others. I said through my tears. He laughed, "No I won't tell you first. This news will have to be told to everyone at the same time. I know you gals. If I tell you something everyone will have a different story to pass on and none of it will be the right story." I laughed at this and felt better just knowing that Master William was home and things would somehow get almost back to normal even without my Nonu and Frankie. He kissed me on the cheek and said," Gal looks at the wrinkles in that bed, you better get busy and do your work well or I will have to spank you." He grinned as he slapped me on the rear end and left the room.

I completed my bed making and went to inform the others that Master William wanted everyone in the yard. "Ring the work bell Bill that will bring them to the yard." The work bell was a bell that was tolled every morning and evening to single time to go to work and time to stop work for the day. If it was rang three times in a row it meant for everyone to gather in the yard for announcements of one sort or another.

Bill rang the bell and the folks started to gather in the yard. Many were murmuring and had a look of wonder on their faces. Susanna said, "Tell them not to worry about anything Bill. Master William just wants to tell them how well we kept the plantation going while he was gone. Nothing to worry about". I looked at her face as she said this and I saw that she was just as worried as many others were.

Master William with Mrs Elizabeth and both Girls were standing on the front steps. He looked almost regal as he stood above us. He cleared his throat and said," The war is now over." The folks cheered and clapped while the children jumped up and down and ran around chasing each other, he continued," I can't tell you how grateful I am and how proud I am of each and every one of you." Susanna looked at me and Julie and nodded because she knew the reason Master William had called us to the yard." When I came home I did not expect this house to be standing. I was so surprised that it is as good as it was before I left. It's got a few bullet holes in it but so does Tad." Everyone laughed at this and looked at Tad. He was healing well except for the fact that he had lost the use of his arm. Master William said /"Now calm down or you will miss the reason I called you all here together." Master William took a deep sigh and said to Mrs. Elizabeth, "Well here goes. Now I want you to listen and to listen to me good people. I don't own you anymore. What I am saying is that no one owns you now. You are as free as I am. President Lincoln signed papers called the Emancipation Proclamation. What these papers say is that each and every one of you are free people. There will be no more slaves and no one can ever be sold again."

The crowd for a brief minute went still and then a quiet murmur started among them. The quiet murmur soon became a shouting like I had never heard before. I couldn't believe my ears.

Free what would that mean? I thought. My mind was racing as I watched folks jumping, laughing and crying with joy. Master William said "Bill ring the bell for the last time." When the bell rang everyone once again settled down. Master William said. "You are free to go or you can stay here." His eyes looked into mine as he spoke. I shifted my gaze and saw the glare in Mrs. Elizabeth's eye. I looked away." Those that wish to stay will be paid wages and be hired hands. I will leave it up to you to decide who wants to stay and who wants to leave. I will give the ones who want to leave their wagons, and a few dollars to help them get settled into their new lives. Please let me know by the end of this week who is staying and who is leaving. I just want you all to know I respect each one of you as a person and I can only wish that God be with you all." I saw that he had tears in his eyes as he and the ladies walked back into the house.

"What are you going to do Maggie?" Julie asked me as we were eating our breakfast after having fed the family. I'm not sure" I answered her." I guess I will stay here with the rest of you folks as hired help. I would like to find Nonu and Frankie but I am afraid to start the search by myself. Even though we are free now to come and go there are a lot of mean people out there stopping a lot of us. I guess I will just stay here." Julie responded, "Yes this is really the only home you can ever remember having." I nodded. "Julie?" I asked. You going to leave to go back to Sug?" Julie winced when I mentioned his name. "No, I don't think I could ever find him." Bill took her hand and squeezed it. "Anyway I want to stay with Bill even if I don't love him he is a good man." Bill laughed and said, "Girl you love me you just don't know it yet." We all laughed together. Birdie said," I am needed here to make Mrs. Elizabeth's and the girl's clothes so I have to stay." We all agreed. It was decided that while others were leaving to establish new lives we were all going to stay with each other.

Sunday came and the church was next to empty. I missed so many faces that I had prayed with and loved. Mable was there in her regular seat. Many of the folks that had decided to remain were up in their years. I greeted them and took my place in front of the church. "The winds have blown change into our lives. The young folks have left and only us remain behind. Many have started out into the unknown in the hopes of finding happiness and enjoying their freedom. We who choose to remain here must continue daily to work for the Lord. Let us pray for our loved ones and ask that God will keep his mighty hand over their heads where ever they are." The meeting ended in prayer.

As I was walking back to the house I heard a weak cry. I thought it was a cat so I didn't pay much attention to it. I heard a small voice in my head say," Maggie, tend to my sheep." I said out loud, "I just did Lord now I have to get home to help with Sunday dinner." I felt a pull as I once again heard the weak cry. I walked toward the cry and discovered that it came from an empty cabin.

I entered the cabin and noticed that it was as neat as a pin. I then saw a girl lying on the dirt floor. I didn't know her name but I had seen her on some occasions. She wasn't one of the regulars at church so I had not become familiar with her. She managed a smile as I approached her. "Oh thank God." she cried." You're Maggie, the preacher woman." I knelt by her side and saw that she giving birth and was losing a lot of blood. I also noticed that she was a young girl of about thirteen years old. I looked to see how far along the birth was and said," Looks like we don't have time to get you help. We will just have to get this baby out and you will be just fine." She grabbed my hand and closed her eyes. I hear bells Maggie, I hear bells. Is the Master ringing the bell for us to be in the yard?" I said. No dear you've got some work here so don't worry about those bells your hearing. What's your name child?" She managed to say, "Sarah" as she slipped into unconsciousness.

The baby slipped out screaming as Sarah slipped silently away. I grabbed the infant and looked around for a knife.I cut the cord and laid the little boy aside. "Sarah, Sarah" I shouted as I slapped her face. She never regained consciousness as I picked up her small bundle and said, 'God is this a sign that my Frankie is dead? Did you just give me a baby boy to replace mine?" I carried the new little boy into the house. Julie and Susanna jumped as I entered holding a cold bloody newborn. "What in the world have you got there!" Julie exclaimed. "I hurried to get a towel to wrap around him and said,'Its a baby and his mamma just died having him." What are you going to do with him they both asked at the same time." "I don't know I have to take him to Master William he will know what to do."

I took him to my room and washed him off. I opened my trunk and retrieved one of Frankie's baby blankets that I had saved. He was alert and seemed to know that I already loved him. "I have to take you to Master William." I said to him. "He will know what to do with you." I carried the tiny little bundle down stairs and found Master William in his study. "Excuse me Master uh Mister William." Mister William looked up from his books and smiled. He looked down at the baby and said 'Oh Lordy girl what have you got there?" His face looked as white as a sheet. I said in a hurry "No, he's not mine. I just helped a girl by the name of Sarah deliver him." He breathed a sigh of relief and said, "I didn't think your belly was any bigger than it always was but I,for a minute thought that Elizabeth was going to skin me alive." He laughed and saw that I was not amused. I said, "Sir, Sarah is lying dead in her cabin. This is her little baby and now I am bringing him to you because his mamma has died. What do I do with him?" William stood up and walked over to take a close look at the baby. He looked at me and said. "Poor little guy. I knew Sarah was in her cabin. It seems that Emma's man Big Tony got little Sarah with child. When everyone left Sarah couldn't go with them on account of her being ready to drop that baby. She told me that Big Tony was going to come back for her after she had the baby. I just assumed that she had arranged help with one of the older women when her time came. I told her that if Big Tony didn't come back, cause I knew he wasn't going to, she could stay here with her child and be hired help. Looks like if Big Tony would come back he wouldn't want this little guy. He will have it hard enough just feeding the family he already has."

I looked down into the face of the sleeping baby and said, "What will become of him?" William answered, "Maggie he will be what ever you hope for him to become. Consider him yours."

I had not even dreamed of raising another child but somehow this felt right. I took him into the kitchen and said Susanna do you remember where you put those baby bottles we had for Miss Mary? "Looks as if we got another little one around this big 'ol house. Master William just gave me this baby." I said with a laugh. I held him up in the air. "This is the first person I know that is born a free man, and he is mine!" Julie, Birdie, Bill and Susanna all became very quiet and looked at this new free born person. Susanna said, "Wonder what he will become? Free born and all. He's got his own life in front of him can you imagine that? His own life." "What you going to call him Maggie?" Bill asked. "I hadn't thought of that ".I said." I don't know ".Bill puffed out his chest and said Well if he was my boy I would call him Freeman, on account of thats what he is. And on account of that's a proud name to have." I looked at the baby's tiny mahogany face and said, "Freeman is a good name but I think it would suit him to have another one to. How about Christianz. That is a good strong name. Yes Christian Freeman will be his name. I will write it down on a piece of paper that will be his very own record of his birth and name." We were all so proud of Christian Freeman and everyday as he grew he grew to love all of us as his own family.

Little Christian was growing like a weed. He was six months old and always a happy baby. I had just put him down for the night when I heard a knock at my door. Upon opening the door I found Master William standing with his head down as if in sadness. "What is it Sir?" I asked "Come on in here and sit down." He sat on the edge of the bed and reached out for me. I sat down beside him and he kissed me on the neck. "Oh Maggie I love you. I really do love you". I allowed him to have his way with me and upon completion I asked "Why are you feeling so sad tonight?" He said, I have bad news for you and bad for me as well." What could it be?" We have been through the worst of times how could it be any worse?" We are rebuilding the plantation. You came through the war practically untouched in your business affairs what could be the problem?" He held me in his arms and said, 'Elizabeth and I have had words." "Oh" I laughed. "That's not new. She always cools after a short while.I just gave a reading for a friend of hers this morning and when she introduced me to her friend, she seemed just fine." He smiled "Are you still doing those readings?" I had forgotten about that. Yes, this will make my news a little better to give you I have been worried that you would not have enough to live on." I sat up "Live on? what are you talking about?" William sat up and said." Maggie, Elizabeth wants you out of the house. Now I don't want you out but she insists that you are not to live here with us any longer. You and Christian will have to go." Go? Go where? I don't have anyplace to go. This is my home!" William said. "I have made arrangements for you and the child, you will be able to continue doing your readings where you are going." "Where am I going?" I asked, "I want to stay here you said we had a choice. Either stay here or go away. I chose to stay here as hired help right along with Julie and the other house staff." "Why?" I asked "Why does she want me out of this house?" William once again tried to hold me in his arms but I drew back. "Tell me why." I said. "She knows how much I love you and she claims that both of us under one roof is an embarrassment to her. At sun up I want you and Christian ready to go I will be out front with a wagon. Now don't you worry I will always take care of you no matter where you are on God's green earth I will promise this until eternity my dear sweet Maggie." He left the room and I sat on my bed and cried.

It was early in the morning hours when I decided to wake Julie. I knocked on her door several times before Bill answered. "Whose there?" "It's me Maggie. Can I come in?"I asked. Julie was up and at the door when I opened it. She saw that I had been crying. "Whats the matter,why are you crying?" she asked. "Julie," I said. "Master William has told me that I can't live here no more.At sun up he is taking me away." She said "Where to and why?" I answered her as I started to cry again, "I don't know, but Mrs Elizabeth doesn't want me to live here under this roof with her William. She said I was an embarrassment to her. I am so scared Julie, will you go with me?" Julie looked at Bill and shook her head,"0h my little baby girl I can't go, you will be alright your a woman of God. God would not put you in a place that was to his unliking you know that. Where is your faith? You have to know that God has a special plan for you and when God moves he moves in mysterious ways. We can't always know what is ahead for us but without faith we will never find out just what his great plan is." I stopped crying and said, "Your right I will be just fine I know I will. Its God, me,and baby Christian. I will be brave and hold my head up as Fanny told me to do." Julie said "That's right we can visit each other I am sure you won't be far away. Not to far that Master William can't visit you often, if you know what I mean." As soon as she said this she looked down. "Oh honey I am sorry I didn't mean anything bad by that statement. I am sorry I said that." I said, "Thats o.k. your right I won't be very far away. I am leaving at sun up will you explain to Susanna why I am not in the kitchen this morning?" Julie hugged me and said "I sure will dear. Now don't you worry God is in control of his children and he will not let them fall. You preach this often enough, it's funny that you need to hear it from me." I left her room feeling better about my new venture. I went downstairs and fixed Christian several bottles of milk and went back upstairs to wait for sun up.

I started to pack my trunk with everything that I had acquired during my entire lifetime. My Bible first of all. My beautiful clothes that were once worn by Master's first wife Mrs. Selene. My little doll and a pretty rock that glistened in the sun, rolled up in the now aged rag that my dear Fanny had handed me many years ago. As I held this small bundle containing my doll and rock I once again felt like that small, scared, big eyed, little girl. I placed the bundle in the trunk and closed the lid. I shut my eyes and prayed to God above that his will be done and not mine.

Christian made his usual morning whimper. A knock came upon the door as I sat down to feed the baby. I opened the door to Bill. "Master sent me here to fetch you Maggie. You got everything ready to go?" I nodded that I had everything packed and he picked up the small trunk and took it downstairs to place it on the wagon. I bundled up Christian and followed Bill downstairs. I passed through the kitchen to find Julie, Birdie, and Susanna waiting to tell me good-by. I could hardly constrain myself from crying out from my fear and from the pain of separation from my one and only family. Each one vowed that they would visit me from time to time and assured me that I was going to be o.k..

I climbed up into the wagon and closed my eyes as Master William called out the order for the horses to pull us away. Where to I had no idea but I was not going to open my eyes and look back.

When I finally did open my eyes I saw that we were pleasantly riding through beautiful country. I had never noticed that the world continued outside the boundaries of the plantation. I thought to myself. Well, of course I knew that this country side existed because when I was five I had to travel through it. I was so sore and tired then that I had not noticed my surroundings. On this trip outside the plantation I was seeing for the first time beautiful country. I looked at Master William and he returned my look with a smile. "You o.k Maggie?" he asked. I nodded my head and held Christian close to me. "We are almost there and I am sure you are going to be very surprised when we get there." I remained silent during the trip. Master William said," You are only going to be about two hours away from the house. I can visit you often, maybe at least once a week. Would you like that dear sweet Maggie?" I looked at him in the eyes and tried to smile as I nodded. My tears started to flow once again but I wiped them away before he noticed.

"Master, uhm Mister William" I began. "If Nonu and Frankie wants to find me, I mean if they come back for me will you tell them where I am?" I noticed that his shoulders slumped and he looked at me and said. "On such a day of liberation for you Maggie I hate to give you any bad news." I looked at him and said, "Bad news? What are you talking about? Bad news? If you know anything about my Nonu and Frankie you best be telling me right now! I need to know if they are alright." Master William handed me a letter. I turned it over in my hands and said, "How come you didn't give me this letter when it came?" He said, "It's not addressed to you Maggie it is a letter to me." I looked at the strange seal on the envelope and proceeded to open it. I read:

> *To General William Hording:*
> *It is the purpose of this letter to inform you that the Mallato young boy named Frankie was killed in battle.*
> *It is our intention to thank you for the service of such a fine young man in the ranks of the Northern Army.*

I couldn't read any further. I looked at Master William and he looked away. I managed to say, "Our son? Killed in battle? What does this mean? I thought he left with Nonu. Have you known this all along and not told me? Our Frankie left with the Union soldiers?" Master William pulled the wagon over to the side of the road and said, "Let's walk over there by that big oak tree."

Christian was sleeping so I laid him down on a blanket on the wagon floorboard. I jumped down from the wagon. My legs felt numb as I started to walk toward the big oak tree standing in the greenest field that I had ever seen. Master William followed me and tried to put his arms around me as we stood under the tree. I pulled away from him. "Maggie, I did not know Frankie had left with the Yankees. I just assumed like you did that he left with Nonu." I could not cry. I couldn't feel anything and this concerned me. I wanted to reach out and hurt someone or something but I couldn't do that either. I thought if I try to slap or hurt Master he will undoubtedly kill me right here on the spot. The anger I felt was enough to get me killed immediately. Master William pulled me down on the ground with him and started to kiss me. I stood back up and said, "What do you think I am? I have feelings just like you do, I hurt and feel pain just as strong as you do and even stronger than you I hurt! It was our own child that died and you act as if you don't even care! What kind of a man are you? You say you love me! What is love to you? A feeling of satisfaction after you have had your way with me? I don't understand you nor do I understand the ways of God! Why would God give us such a beautiful child and then never really let me have him. You can have your children, you can see your children grow up and have children of their own. Why am I not allowed the same privilege?" I was now screaming at Master William and he was just sitting on the ground looking up at me while I continued to scream. "I have always followed the rules of God's plan and I cannot understand why I have to live such a life of pure hell. I want to be able to see my children grow up. I want to see them happy and smart. Reading and writing just as good as any one else on God's green earth. I want to run but by God I have no where to run to!!" I was running in circles, ranting and raving when Master William pulled me to the ground. "Maggie, my dear sweet Maggie let me help you." I shouted at him," The only way you can help me is to kill me! Kill me now! Help me to go to Jesus's arms. I don't want to be here any longer!!" He allowed me to hit him with my fists for a minute and then he grabbed my hands. "Maggie listen to me!" he shouted. "I am so sorry that Frankie is dead. I don't know where he is buried but I will put a marker for him in the slave cemetery. I can at least do that for him and for you. I know that won't bring him back but you now have another little boy to raise. I promise you that I will do all I can to get him educated. I will do that for Frankie's sake. You and he will never want for anything. I will promise you this." I calmed down and allowed Master William to hold me as I thought of Nonu and wondered if she to was dead.

Master William and I walked back to the wagon. He helped me into the wagon and I picked up Christain. I woke him just to see him smile. Master William looked at him and said, '* Well, he certainly is a cute little guy." When Christian heard Master William's voice he broke out in a huge smile that made us both laugh.

After completing our journey in silence Master William said, "Here we are Maggie. Your new home!" I looked up as Master William pulled the wagon into a long lane that led to a small white house. I saw the newly built house for the first time through my free eyes. The small white house had a wood porch that contained a wood rocking chair. Flowers in individual wood boxes blew in the soft breeze as if they were greeting us. Master William pulled the horses to a stop and he jumped out of the wagon. He hurried around to my side to help Christian and I down. "This is where you're going to live!"he exclaimed. "I helped build it myself just for you. Just wait until you see what else I have to show you!" I couldn't believe my eyes. I walked on to the porch and placed my hand on the rocking chair. It rocked as if to welcome me. "Come on Maggie!" Master William shouted. "Come on, see what else!" I followed him inside to find that the house had been furnished with the finest furniture that I had ever seen. It was even better than what was in the big house. The living room had a fireplace and in front of it sat another wood rocking chair. This chair was bigger than the porch one and was made of dark wood that shone in the sunlight streaming through the window. I looked around at the tables and the setee and I was speechless. I couldn't believe that this was to be my new home. The rug on the floor was so plush that it felt as if my feet might become lost in the beautiful swirling pattern of roses and vines.

"Where did all this furniture come from?" I asked. "From here and there." Master William laughed. "I have been getting this house ready for you for several months. It had to be the home of my sweet darling so it is only the best that I could find." I walked to the next room and was presented with the cutest kitchen that I could ever imagine. It was just like the big house kitchen only scaled down to fit this little house. There was even lace curtains hung in the windows. "You did this all by yourself?" I asked. Master William's face shone with pride and he answered. "Of course I did Maggie, and just for you." He pulled me into the other room and I gasped when I saw the dark cherry wood of the biggest bed I had ever seen. I placed Christian down on it and laughed when I almost lost him as he sank into the feather mattress. "Over here Maggie is Christian's room." Master William said as he pointed to a small room adjoining this one. In Christian's room I saw a small bed next to a wooden cradle. On the walls shelves held toys made for a small boy. "Oh Master William I can't believe that you have done all this for us." I started to cry as I placed the baby in the cradle. "Whats the tears for now Maggie? Doesn't all this make you happy?" He asked. I answered. "I will try my best to be happy here Master William. It is a lovely house with beautiful furniture and I am very grateful to you for it. I do wish that Nonu and Julie could be here with me and my Frankie. Then I think I could really be happy." I looked around and saw a small brown bird light on the windowsill and then fly. "Yes Master William I can be happy here.Master William said, "Maggie no more Master. Just call me William now. Call no man master ever again Maggie." I was reminded of my Bible when I had read the words. *Neither be ye called Masters: for one is your Master, even in Christ.*

He once again grabbed my hands pulling me he said," Come on outside I have something else! I have another surprise for you yet. No wait let me blindfold you first." He pulled his handkerchief from his pocket and tied it around my head covering my eyes.

He led me out the door to the back yard and paused. "O.K now remove your blindfold" he instructed. I reached up and when I removed the blindfold I fell to my knees.

I was kneeling in front of the most magnificent little white church I could ever only imagine. William helped me to my feet and laughing said, "It's yours dear Maggie! It's your church. I have put posters up in the colored sections of town to let folks know about it. I have also have instructed Elizabeth to tell her friends that you are doing readings here. I have told many folks to notify their hired help that there will be a church just for them. I am sure you will have many peoples coming here to your church for Sunday services. I was dumbfounded. I opened the door to the beautiful church and saw that it was filled with benches just waiting for the people. I felt the sun shine on me as I walked toward the newly built podium. There was even an alter railing built around the raised platform. I felt a chill run up my spine as I knelt at that alter. William knelt alongside me and reached for my hand. I couldn't return his grasp. It was a silent moment with God that we both shared on that day. A moment that would forever lock us into each others lives for all eternity.

I watched William's wagon until it was out of sight. I was alone with baby Christian and God. I was filled with so many feelings I felt a little confused but at the same time very sure of my self. I was to be about God's business of teaching his flock and he had just provided the means to do it. All things in my world had just been changed, against my will, but changed they had been and I realized that I had a job to do. I went into the bed room and just stood and looked at the beautiful bed that I was almost afraid to touch let alone consider it mine. I smoothed the quilt covering the thick mattress and noticed that the quilt was made of deep purple and blue patches of rich velvet. I withdrew my hand and placed it in my dress pocket. I had never dreamed that anything of such beauty could be mine. I fell to my knees at the side of the bed to give my thanks to God.

I heard wagons approaching. I stood up wondering what William had come back for,and went to the front door. Two men were driving two separate wagons. They both got down off their wagons and approached the front porch. "Are you Maggie?" One asked. "Yes sir, I am." I answered. He continued," We were instructed to deliver this here horse and wagon to you on this afternoon. It's been bought and paid for by a Mister Harding. You know him Gal?" I answered, "Yes I do know him." He looked over my shoulder into the house and said, "Where is Mister Harding? Is he home right now? He lives here, right?" I said, "No sir. Mister Harding does not live here. I do." He looked at his companion while the other man said. "Where is your man? You live here all by yourself in this new fancy house?" I was now sensing that I might not be safe in the presence of these men. I drew back my shoulders and said, "No sir I live with my man in this house. His name is Christian Freeman and right now he is sleeping." This seemed to satisfy them. "I have a paper for someone to sign saying that we delivered the horse and wagon." One of the men said. "I guess if you will just put an X here on this line Max here can witness that you signed it." I took the pencil from him and wrote my name on the line and handed it back to him. They both stood dumbfounded for a minute and I saw a look of disgust overcome their faces. They neither one said another word and each rode off in the other wagon leaving me a lovely brown horse with a wagon.

I walked over to the horse and immediately fell in love with her. As I patted her I said "Where in earth can I keep you sweetie?" I looked at the wagon it was a nice wagon with big wheels trimmed with green paint. I thought to myself I can go anywhere, even to visit Julie if I want to. I was overjoyed with the idea that I could travel anyplace in the whole country maybe to visit Nonu when I found out where she was. I was crying as I felt the smooth wood of the wagon. Thank you God, Thank You." I cried.

I unharnessed Sweetie, as I called her, and tied her to the railing of the porch. "I will have to get some fence for you so you can have room to run around in.Maybe I can have Bill or Tad come over to help me put up a fence for you. Until then I guess you will have to stay in the front yard tied to the porch. I am sure you won't mind that. I will just move you around though where you can eat as much grass as you like. How's that?" Sweetie seemed to understand as she watched me with her big brown eyes.

Christian woke from his nap with a cry. I fed him with milk that I had brought with me. I was hungry myself and I wondered what I was going to eat. I placed a happy,dry,fed baby on a blanket on the floor. He rolled over on his stomach and picked at the roses woven in the rug. I explored the kitchen. I first looked in the wood cabinet and was thrilled to find that there was flour in the flour bin. I discovered potatoes in the bottom drawer. I opened the upper doors to find a can of lard, salt, pepper, and other seasonings. I was excited. I opened the small pantry door to find two huge hams hanging from ceiling hooks. "Oh my God. William has thought of everything." I exclaimed aloud. I sliced off a piece of the ham after I had found that the dishes, pots, pans and silver were also included in this perfect kitchen. I put a few pieces of wood in the stove and looked around for the sulpher stick and the sandpaper. When I found them I placed the match in the folded piece of sandpaper and withdrew a lit stick. I lit the stove and when it was hot enough I prepared myself my first meal. A meal that was just for me that I could eat first. As I prayed before this meal I prayed that Nonu was safe and not hungry. And if it be God's will I will soon know of her where abouts.

Evening came upon me to soon. I wasn't prepared to spend a night alone for the first time in my life. I held Christian long after he fell asleep not wanting to separate from the only living connection to my security. As I held this tiny sleeping child I wondered what would lie ahead for him. I uttered a prayer for his life ahead and asked God for the opportunity for Christian to become an honest and God loving man.

I placed Christian on my bed and drug the heavy cradle into my room. I placed it beside my bed and then very quietly laid him into it. As I looked at him smiling in his sleep the thought entered my head as to what I was to feed him when by tomorrow noon I would be out of milk. I had placed the milk in a cool spot under the porch hoping that it would not spoil. I hadn't noticed a spring house perhaps; I thought I just hadn't looked around enough for one. I thought to myself, first thing early light I will look out behind the church for a spring house. "There has to be one I am sure." I said aloud. My thoughts ran now to an outside visit to the jhonny. I had remembered it as just being out back from the kitchen door. I looked around for a candle and ventured outside.

I stepped out the back door to the most quiet space I had ever been in. It was so still the only sounds I heard was a bullfrog. Ah I thought bull frogs mean water and water means a spring house. I have to explore that in the morning. I thought. The sky was as velvet as the comforter that covered my bed. I looked at this velvet night sky and smiled with open eyed wonder as a shooting star fell. I stood still as I pondered the meaning of the shooting star. I was reminded of a little girl that once stood peering into the faces of men as I listened to the auctioneer's voice say, sold to that man over there. Now this same frightened little girl had been picked up and placed into new beautiful surroundings. The star represented to me that star that had shown the way towards the new babe in the manger and it now appeared to me to show me the way. I had a mission to do and I was ready to take on any task that God ask of me. As I stood looking at the place where the star was my attention was drawn to a strange light in the sky. At first it appeared to be another falling star but as I watched its glow it simply darted around in a circular pattern and then disappeared from view. I became frightened and ran to the jhonny to complete my business and hurried back into the house. I, for the remainder of my life never spoke about this to anyone, nor did I ever forget it. I knew that God had given me his sign.

I slept soundly and when morning broke into my window I awoke with a start. "Oh goodness I have overslept." I said aloud. "Mrs. Elizabeth will be furious with me." When my feet hit the floor it dawned on me that I didn't have to get up unless I wanted to. I could lie in bed until the baby wakes if I choose, I thought. I laid back down into my soft pillow bed and for the first time in my life I was free to do as I wanted to. I felt guilty laying there in that huge soft bed but not guilty enough to want to go back to the big house.

I decided to arise and explore before Christian woke. He was due to sleep at least another hour or so. It was just cracking dawn-I slipped into my mules and walked into my beautiful living room and just stood and admired my new surroundings. I walked into the kitchen and delighted at seeing the sun starting to shine on the glass windows. I put some wood on the stove which still had embers. I looked around for a bucket and found one under the dry sink and started out to find water. I passed the jhonny and looked up at the sky remembering the strange light I had seen last night. I talked to myself, "Maggie pull yourself together. You didn't see anything odd or unusual last night. Silly girl you were just tired" I decided that I had only imagined a strange light in the sky. I walked around to the back of the church and smiled when I found a cute stone spring house. "Thank you God." I said. I entered the cool stone house and found a bubbling natural well of running water. William had built the stone spring house over an artesian well. I also saw small copper box sitting over the stream on little legs. The bottom of the box was immersed in the stream. I opened it and found a crock full or rich white milk. I dropped my bucket I was so amazed. It was if the God's angels were watching my every move and they knew what I needed. I placed my bucket in the running stream of cool natural water. Upon reentering the house and after placing the bucket of water on the dry sink I looked into the cabinet, and sure enough there was tea and a shiny new tea ball. I smiled. I didn't even know William knew that I drank tea I thought. I fixed my tea and walked back into the bedroom with a pitcher of warm water in one hand and a fresh brewed cup of tea in the other. It was refreshing to wash off in the clear, warm water. I decided upon a blue dress with a white apron It was time for Christian to awaken so I retrieved some milk from the spring house. I was so grateful that it was there because his milk under the porch had soured.

Upon entering the house I was a little startled to notice that a clock in the living room chimed seven o'clock. I couldn't remember hearing it yesterday. I wondered why I had not noticed it before now. I walked over to see the clock better and saw a piece of white paper sticking out from under the clock door. It was a note from William:

> *Maggie;*
> *I must leave town for a while. Before leaving I passed by this way to see you. I stopped by quite late only t to find you sleeping soundly. I knew that on your first day in your new home that you would be very tired so I allowed you to sleep. I took the liberty of setting this clock. And if you will*

look in the box in the spring house you will find milk for the baby. I must be out of town for at least two weeks on business so I won't be able to come and check on your welfare. I will send some one to put up a fence for the horse as I see it has been delivered on time. I will bring you a gift upon my return. Until then my dear take care of yourself William.

"Well." I said out loud. "It isn't one of God's angels but thank you God anyway". I found myself to be at leisure. This was almost too unbearable for me as I was so used to having my entire day filled with demands. I was not comfortable with having spare time on my hands. When Christian was taking his afternoon nap I walked around the yard feeling that the entire world had forgotten me. I cried for Julie, I cried for Nonu, I cried for Frankie. I was feeling so sorry for myself that I was even crying for me. I asked God aloud, "God, what am I supposed to do all of my days? I can't believe 1 am to only care for Christian. How can I care for the other people that I love and miss? I am sure Nonu has no idea of my where about. Maybe Julie doesn't know either. Lord I had a purpose when I was living in the big house. I had chores that took up my entire days. Am I to understand that now you want me to spend my time walking around in this yard? What's the meaning of having a beautiful house with beautiful furniture if I can't share it with others? Now Lord I don't mean to sound ungrateful but I need to ask you again the aged old question that I have always asked you, Why? Why have I been taken apart from those I love? Why have I been given such a perfect house and I am sure my Nonu doesn't have anything as nice as this, nor Julie. Julie still has nothing, is that fair?"

As I was walking and crying a wagon approached. I wiped my tears on my apron and watched as the wagon drew closer. I saw a lovely white woman sitting on the wagon seat driving her two horses. "Hi, are you Maggie?" she asked as she pulled the wagon to a stop. I answered, "Yes, ma'am I am Maggie." She had the biggest brown eyes that sparkled as she smiled. My name is Natalee. I live just over that yonder hill there." She said as she pointed "May I speak with you?" she asked. "Of course," I answered. "Would you like to come into the house?" She stepped down from the wagon and said, "Yes, I would like that very much." She followed me into the house. "Oh, you have beautiful things." she exclaimed. I put my head down and said, "Thank you. Would you like a cup of tea Maam?" Natalee took my face in her hands and lifted my head to look into my eyes. "Oh, you've been crying is something wrong? Here you sit and let me fix you a cup of tea." I started to protest but she guided me over to the rocking chair and said, "Honey have a seat. Let me wait on you. Where is your tea?" I couldn't speak I just pointed towards the kitchen. As I sat watching her preparing tea I just shook my head. My world seemed to all at once be upside down and I didn't know how to right it. "Here dear, a fresh brewed cup of tea made just for you. I hope you don't mind but I made one for myself." Natalee said as she handed me a cup of tea. "Mind if I have a seat?" she asked. "Oh of course have a seat I said as I stood up. Natalee laughed, No, of what I have heard about you I am the one who should be standing you sit back down. I can sit over here." A look of puzzlement came over my face. "What have you heard about me? I have been here not yet one day and I don't want anyone to be talking about me. I am not doing anything as to give folks something to talk about. At least I don't think so." Again Natalee's face lit up with a smile. "Oh you are the talk of the social circles dear Maggie. You reputation as a medium is one of the main topics of conversation. The word is out that you are available to give readings now that you are settled in your new home. The reason I came to you is to have you do a reading for me, if you would, and I am prepared to give you a handsome donation towards your ministry." I sat down.

I gave Natalee a reading. I discovered that she had lost her child two years ago and wanted to know if her little three year old girl was happy in heaven. Her baby's name was Rose and since Rose's death she and her husband Matt had been unable to have another.

Natalee was pleased with the reading and handed me one dollar. We were to become bonded which would develop into a friendship.

After Natalee left I looked at the money in my hand. I couldn't believe that what I could tell people was worth money to them. I felt guilty taking her money but she instisted.Natalee had said, "Use it to live on Maggie, or use it to help others who might someday need help." I thought, the people had been paying Mrs Elizabeth for my readings so why now can't I accept their money. I don't need to ask for rags anymore. "Yes." I said aloud. "I will take it without guilt and help someone if need be or use it as God's means for Christian and myself." Once again I thanked God as I walked into the bedroom and picked up a hungry wet baby. "Hey, precious one we are going to be alright you and me." When I said this Christian opened his mouth and laughed. I kissed his sweet smelling baby mouth.

Sunday arrived only three days after I had been in my new house. Sunday morning around eight o'clock I heard wagons approaching. I looked out to see three wagons each carrying at least six to eight people. I answered a knock on the front door. I opened it to have a short brown complexioned man ask. "Are you Maggie?" I said "Why yes I am. What can I do for you folks this morning?" He held his hat in his hand and said. "My wife tells me that this is the place where we are to start coming to church." "Oh!" I exclaimed. "You are all here to come to church? Oh my gosh! yes I am a church, I mean yes this is a church, no not this house but the church is back there I pointed. Go on back the door is unlocked. Please go on back I will join you in a minute" He looked at me as if I was deranged but returned to his wagon and drove it back to the church. The others followed.

I hurried and changed my clothes as well as Christians. I saw two more wagons arrive filled with people. I was so nervous I almost forgot my shoes as I started out the door with Christian under one arm and my Bible under the other. I entered the church to be greeted by many people smiling and greeting one another. Someone took Christian and I approached the pulpit. I looked out over the folks gathered there and saw so many loving faces that my heart went out to all of them. I was doubly surprised to see that several white women including Natalee had joined us. I opened my Bible and placed my hands over the words that I was about to read and said, "Lets pray. "When I had opened my Bible my eyes had fallen on I Kings chapter 8 verse 17 ironically I read about a house being built for the name of the Lord God. I was convinced that God's hand was in the building of this church, his house. After the sermon I was led to demonstrate the gift of prophesy for each person in attendance.

Everyone had gathered in the yard after the service. I was surprised to see that the congregation had brought baskets of lunch with them. Evryone shared in the fellowship over a delicious lunch of fried chicken, ham, salads, baked breads and sweet deserts of cakes and cookies. I met many new folks on that day that were to become faithful members of the church. Natalee and her friends shared lunch with us as if we were all of one accord. I had never before sat next to a white woman and broke bread, let alone several white women.

As I sat on the ground next to Natalee she asked if she could hold Christian. As she picked him up from his soft spot in the green grass he gazed into her face. She laughed and said, "Don't be so serious little one Your going to be a special person in your life. You should smile as God has smiled on you to have such a loving mamma." Christian smiled as if he understood her every word. The other women exclaimed,"0h he is so cute." With all this attention Christian acted as if he was in the limelight and couldn't smile enough. I noticed that his little eyes lit up with each crinkle of his smile. I thought as I watched the ladies pass him around, I hope nothing happens that will stop his smile from staying in his eyes.

Natalie asked, "Maggie where do you get his milk? I notice that he has a bottle next to him, are you not nursing? She then looked down and said," Oh dear,1 hope that that is not to personal." I answered. No, that is not too personal I am not nursing Christian because I did not give birth to him. I was given this child when his mother died. The women remarked, 0h how sweet of you to take an orphan." "Well he is more to me than just an orphan I said, I feel as if he is a gift from God." Everyone agreed.

I said," I am not sure as to where the town is but I must go tomorrow in search of a store to purchase milk and some other things. Perhaps you could direct me to the nearest town." Natalee said, "We have a farm. My husband Matt and I can sell you milk and eggs. You won't have to go far into town for such things. We sell to many folks around here. One more customer would be welcome." I was thrilled to know that God had answered another prayer.

Around two o'clock everyone started on their journey home. Before some left, especially Natalie's friends, they made appointments to visit for readings later on in the week.

That evening as I rocked a sleepy baby I told Christian a little story about a little boy named Frankie and how this same good little boy was now a perfect angel in God's great heaven. I told him that he was always watching and protecting baby Christian as he was now sitting in the same place as he once sat on his momma's lap.

Seasons pass and the congregation has grown triple its size. Many services have been held in the little white church. In the past three years a Sunday school for the children has been established as well as a Wednesday night service. On Friday night special services are held for the teens with different youths conducting the services each week.

Little three year old Christian looks forward to each and every meeting in order to play with all the visiting children. He has a friend. Tommy whom he plays with each time Tommy's parents attends services. Tommy's parents are Becky and Joe. They are always friendly and loving toward Tommy as well as their other four children. Many times after our Sunday pot luck the members give Becky and Joe leftovers to take home with them. It seemed as if everyone had adopted them as their own because of Becky's and Joe's spiritual loving natures. One Sunday afternoon as I was talking to folks gathered in the church I noticed Becky leave to go outside. I was speaking to Patty, a member of the church about a new fabric that I had purchased for a new dress. "Wait here Patty, I will go get it to show you. It is so pretty You will just love it." I walked over to the house and entered the back door. In the living room I found Becky standing as still and quiet as if in prayer. I walked over to her and placed my hand on her shoulder. She seemed embarrassed and said,0h Rev. Maggie. I am so sorry I came in your house without asking permission." I said. "Thats alright Becky you can enter this house without my permission any time you want to. Is something wrong?" Becky lowered her eyes and said, "I was just wondering as of how come I can't have a beautiful home like you have. Tommy works and all but we can't afford a nice house. We are trying to save our money though." I smiled and said "Becky you must have faith. The good Lord knows what you need even before you ask for it. Be patient. He will provide. He will give you what he knows you need." This seemed to perk her up and we joined the others in the church.

I showed Patty my new fabric and joined in with the others as we all enjoyed our Sunday meal. Winter was fast approaching and I was about out of wood. That night William was on my doorstep. "Hi Maggie." he said as he entered the house. "I am sorry I haven't been here for awhile. How have you been?" I answered /'Christian and I are doing just fine." Christian heard him come in and ran to greet him with his hand out. William laughed. "Now what do you want?" He said this as he reached in his pocket and pulled out a piece of candy. Christian took the candy and said," Thank you sir," William said "You are raising a fine boy there with manners and everything." I shot him a pert glance. "What did you expect? I raised several children with manners and everything. Why should this surprise you?" William saw that I was a little short with him and he said. "Maggie this does not surprise me in the least. I have come to know this about you. Why are you on a high horse?" "Oh I guess I am just tired, excuse me." I said. How are the girls and everyone?" William said," Everyone is just fine and they all send their hellos. Julie and Bill want to come visit you but Bill is pretty weak right now. Remember I told you he has been very sick this whole last year. I hope he either dies or gets better he's no help the way he is" "I hope he gets better soon." I say. "Has he ever told you where the silver is hidden?" William looks surprised and asks," Hidden? I thought the soldiers took it?" I look away and say,"Opps. No Bill hid it somewhere and if he is going to die you best ask him where it is." William said. "Yes if I can remember to ask him I will do just that." He sat down on the settee and removed his boots and said," Better put some more wood on that fire ifs supposed to get very cold tonight. According to the catapillers were going to have a cold winter," I said." I need some wood. Do you think you could send Tad or someone over here with some?" "Put that little rascal to bed and we will see just what it takes from you in order to get some cut wood delivered to you doorstep." He reached for me as I left the room to put Christian to bed.

I lingered over reading a story to Christian while William sat and fell asleep in front of the fire. As I rubbed Christian's forehead as he fell asleep I said a prayer. "God I don't know how to tell William I don't want him to bother me. I am a free woman now but I still have no choices. I need what he provides and what he can do for Christian's life. I am sorry to complain dear God perhaps this is your will because I know it's not mine. Amen."

After William had had his way with me for another time in my life he sat up on the side of the bed. As he put his pants on a white envelope fell out of the pocket, he picked it up and said. "Oh I almost forgot. This letter came addressed to you." "Me?" I said." Who from." He said, "I don't know the post mark is Ohio. I didn't even know you knew anyone in Ohio and I am as curious as you are." I turned the letter over in my hands a few times before I opened it. It read:

> *My Dearest Maggie:*
>
> *. I hope this letter gets to you. I am taking, a chance that you are still at the same place where I last saw you as I am sending this letter to this address. I have so much to share with you it •would take more that a single letter to tell you everything. How is Julie and everyone else? I miss everyone so much but I especially miss you. 1 am married now to a fine man named George and we are doing just fine. George is teaching school and I am working as a maid for a prestigious family. I hope so much to vist you some day and once again feel the love from your very breath as you kiss my cheek. I am sending you my address at the bottom of this letter so you Can write me back. I will hold my breath until I see a letter from you. As I am not even sure that you remain at this address or even still alive God forbid. Please forgive me for leaving you, All my devoted love*
>
> *Your Nonu*
> *Box office 202, West Liberty Ohio*

I couldn't believe my eyes. A letter from my Nonu and she was alive and doing fine. I jumped up and down on the bed and hugged the precious letter to my breast. Master William said 'Calm down girl,calm down you will explode if you don't calm down," I laughed and cried all at the same time. I just couldn't believe that I had a letter from Nonu in my very own hands. It was as if she spoke to me from the grave. I was so thrilled that I didn't even see William leave. I read my letter over and over, I even smelled it. To think that she was O.k and had written me a letter was more than I had ever hoped for. I hurried to my desk and took out a piece of paper and opened my ink. Placing my pen in the ink I started to write: *My darling Nonu;*

I had so much to tell her the clock struck three as I completed my letter. I spoke out loud as I folded it and placed it in an envelope."! Have to take this into town first thing to the post master. I wonder how long it will take for this letter to arrive to Nonu. Not to long I hope. Not to long."

The cold winter came as if it appeared over night. I woke in the cold night to put a log in the fireplace and then that didn't seem enough. I checked on Christian to see if he was warm enough and decided to take him into bed with me. When morning arrived the ice had frozen the back door shut which forced Christian and me to use the indoor chamber potty.

I was sure that people would not venture out of their homes to attend church functions so I did not anticipate any one for this weeks services. Just as I had expected not one soul showed up for services the entire week. I could not remember a winter this cold and I was not really prepared for it. We could have used a few extra blankets and some warmer socks. "Momma will have to buy some yarn and have a few heavy over blouses and shirts made for us." I told Christian. "I should have paid more attention to Birdie when she tried to teach me how to knit." In the mean time we will just have to snuggle.

The weather grew a little milder throughout the remainder of the week. It was early on a Tuesday morning when I heard a knock on the door. I opened the door to several men and a couple of their wives. I saw that Peggy was one of the early morning visitors. "Come in, come in, it is so cold. What brings you folks out on such a crisp morning?" I asked. As they entered I noticed that all had sad, grim faces. "Whats the matter?" I asked. Josh, one of the men spoke and said. Rev. Maggie we have out there a wagon with some of our friends in it. We thought it best to bring them to you." I had a puzzled look on my face when I said, What ever for? What do they need? Bring them in by all means." Peggy and the other woman started crying. "What is the matter?" I asked. Peggy said," Rev. Maggie it's Becky and Joe and their kids. They are all dead. Dead out there in that wagon." I gasped," Dead? How did they get dead?" "They froze to death in their wagon one night." One of the men said. "We thought it best to bring them here so as you can perform a proper funeral service for them. "Me and Ike here and the others can bury them if we could bury them alongside the church." I was stunned. I could not imagine Becky Joe and all their children dead. Peggy said, "You know that they was living in that wagon?" I shook my head, "No I did not know that. I knew that they were trying to get a home but I never thought to ask where they were living." Peggy said, "None of us knew. Becky and Joe was so proud. I guess they didn't want anyone to feel sorry for them." Ike asked. What are we going to bury them in Rev. Maggie?" Again I shook my head, "I don't know. has anyone got any wood to make coffins with?" All shook their heads and said, "No, 1 don't know of any wood we could get ahold of." Anyway the ground is froze we can't dig in it until we have a good thaw." Josh said. I said, "Well lets put our heads together," I am sure if we kneel right down here and ask God an answer will come." We all knelt in the living room and bowed our heads. When I stood up I said," We will have to use the wood from the wagon. Save all the nails we take out and maybe we can get at least three boxes. We will have to bundle them up together but as cold as it has been and those babies have been so cold anyway I am sure they would not mind." Everyone agreed. Ike said, "We can do that. We will get as many men on it as soon as we can." Peggy said through her tears, "What will we do with them in the mean time?" I said. We will have to lay them out in the church. Can you guys pull the wagon around to the church right now?" I stood and watched as the men brought all seven bodies into the church. The sight would remain with me throughout the remainder of my life. Becky and Joe held the two youngest. A set of twin boys Nate and Bert not quite a year old. The oldest a boy Casy of seven years. The other two was Sally age five and and Tommy age three, holding each other in order to keep warm.

I stood in silence as I looked at this beautiful little family. I could not cry I felt numb. I looked at Tommy holding on to his sister and pulled his little shirt tighter around him. Everyone was quiet as we knelt next to them. I said. "I was just talking to Becky the other day and I had no idea she had no home. If I had of known I would have let them stay in the church. How could I have been so blind as not to see this?" One of the women, Katy said, "Now Rev. Maggie don't you take any blame. None of us bothered to ask any questions. And even if we had of ask about where they were living I don't reckon Becky would have told us. They were proud folks. Let's let them sleep for now until the men can make some proper coffins for them."

We all left the church and silently shut the door. I looked back to see if perhaps one of them or all of them might have been only near death but I saw no signs of movement.

After everyone drank the hot tea we prepared they started to leave. Ike said, "We will be back with some other men later on in the day to tear the wagon apart to make boxes." Peggy said, we will get the word out that we will have a service this Saturday. We are the only family that they have and it's up to all of us to have a proper service for them." I agree." I said.

That evening men came and in the bitter cold tore the wagon apart. It didn't take to long to have it completely disassembled. The wood was carried into the church and three sturdy coffins were soon constructed. I felt bad that I didn't have extra blankets to cover the family with so as they would not be in full view of the men. I guess they knew that the work had to be done so they worked in the church where the family was laying.

The family was placed in the three boxes in the positions that they had been found in. Each parent holding a baby, and the other three in the third coffin. It seemed as if the entire congregation had received word of Becky's family. Saturday morning the church was full of those that came to the service. I found it difficult to do the service because I had felt close to each one of them. This was my first funeral service and I realized then that I did not like this part of God's work.

The problem was that the ground was frozen and the men could not dig graves. After the service everyone asked what were we to do with them until the ground could be dug. Hank, one of the men said, "Lets place them on top of the ground in the place where they are to be buried and cover them until the time arrives that we can bury them." This was agreed on and each coffin was carried out beside the church and placed on the spot where they would be buried. Straw was a precious commodity but each casket was covered with straw.

That night kneeling beside my bed I prayed. Dear God, I am at a loss. If I have such a gift why didn't I know that Becky had no home? If I am to help others shouldn't I be able to help them when they are in need? I feel bad God that I didn't take the time to ask Becky questions instead of telling her to have faith. She had as much faith as anyone God, Why did this awful thing have to happen to her and her family? I promise to you God that if another person seems to have a problem I will ask questions and try my best to offer help. Amen.

As I stood up to enter my bed I heard a wee small voice in my head say, "Maggie, you can't do it all. Your not God."

The coffins sat covered with snow. I would look at them each morning as I guiltily rose from my warm bed. The morning sun cast tiny sparkles on them as if the angels were sleeping with them covering each box with their gossamer wings. The coffins gave a grim reminder that we had such a long way to go and that not one of us should ever give up.

The southern winter soon gave way to an early spring. We once again gathered around the coffins in prayer and song after Sunday service. Each Coffin was lowered into its respective place. We all knew that Becky's and Joe's family had reached the Promised Land which made each one of us more determined that we would reach ours before we had to leave for the heavenly one.

"Maggie I was just wondering." Natalee said to me one warm spring afternoon. I had just driven over to buy my weekly eggs and milk and we were enjoying girl talk. "I was a school teacher before my baby Rose was born. Since her death I haven't been able find it in myself to do much of anything." I looked over to see what Christian, now four and exploring everything, was doing as I heard him laugh. A calf had knocked him down and was licking his face. "Christian" get up don't let that cow lick your face." I laughed. "Oh he is so funny, I really enjoy him". I said to Natalee.We both laughed as we helped Christian up and held the calf at bay.

"Oh I am sorry Natalee what was you saying?" Natalee continued. "I was just wondering. You know yourself that there are many children coming to church." "Yes" I said" Isn't that great?" Natalee said" Yes I think that is really great, but this might be a touchy subject so I am going to jump right in. You know that these children can't read nor write." I answered, "Yes, I am aware of that." Natalee spoke, "Well I was just thinking what if I offered to have a school session in the church sometime, me being a teacher and all." My mouth fell open," You would be willing to teach the children? The black children?" Natalee dropped her eyes and said "Yes, I would if you would allow me to use the church to do it in." I was dumbstruck. I was so excited that I grabbed Natalee and swung her in circles. Christian saw that we were laughing and ran over and grabbed both of our skirts nearly knocking us over. "Oh Natalee I couldn't ask for anything more! Do you think you are up to it? There are a lot of children that need a school. The word gets out we will have other children that don't even go to the church. I would love that. What will it take to get it started?"

The announcements were made and by the fall of the year we had all ages and sizes of children sitting in our little church. Natalee was so eager to teach them that I couldn't even imagine her not being able to teach after her child had died. She soon had a glow in her cheeks and she was ringing the school bell every morning at 8 o'clock.

Christian wanted to attend the school and I tried to explain to him that he had to wait a couple of more years before he could attend. On several occasions when he would turn up missing from the house I would find him sitting quietly on the front door step to the school/church. Natalee and I decided to let him sit in a couple days a week and he learned as fast as the older children. I was so proud.

"I don't want you teaching at that school." Matt said." Teaching those kids don't look right." Matt and Natalee was sitting in the parlor before preparing for bed. Natalee shot him a sharp glance and said. "Well, even if you don't like it, please don't forbid me to to it. I feel as if I have something now to live for. I would pine away again if I didn't have those bright little faces so eager to learn, looking at me every day. I enjoy teaching them so much." Matt scowled, "If you want to teach then go get a job that will pay you. Get a job at a white school. I am sure you could get a job teaching at a white school. You had one before Rose was born." Natalee said with tears in her eyes. "Matt. I ask you; don't put pressure on me like this. I enjoy teaching at this school. Even if I don't get paid I know that I will someday get my rewards in heaven, so don't ask me to stop." Matt said, "Humph, rewards in heaven. What about the rewards we need now? Anyway I am getting a lot of hassle from my friends with you teaching there and everything." Natalee jumped up, "Friends! You call those men you hang around with friends? You know I don't think they are capable of being a friend to anyone. They have so much ugly in their hearts I don't understand why you even entertain the notion that they are a friend to you." Matt drew a drag from his pipe and watched her as she transformed right before his eyes. He loved to get her angry at him. He needed this type of anger to feed on in order to keep his position in his group of "friends."

He watched as her anger grew toward him and then she stormed out of the room. "I will not quit teaching at Maggie's school. I will continue to help her as much as I possibly can. I think that she is a strong woman and I agree with all she stands for!" Natalee yelled as she stomped up the stairs to the bedroom.

Upstairs she threw herself upon the bed and cried. Matt soon followed her into the room and sat next to her. "Honey, I know that you enjoy teaching. I was concerned that you was not getting over the death of Rose. Now that you have started teaching again I see roses back into your cheeks. I just was trying to make you understand the pressure I am under because you are teaching at that school. You could teach at any other school. You are a damn good teacher. Natalee glared at him through her tears and he saw that he was not going to convince her any other way. He knew when she had this look that her mind was made up. "Let's go to bed." He said." We will talk about this another time."

I walked to the mail box holding Christian's little hand. We often walked and talked over issues that four year olds could have. "Momma why don't Tommy come to play with me anymore?" He asked as we walked down the lane. I looked down at my baby and said, "Honey, Tommy is heaven with the Lord and his angels. He and his family moved up there." This seemed to satisfy him for the moment but I could see that he was thinking. He stopped in his tracks and looked up and said, "Tommy if you want I will be home all day today. Can one of your angels bring you down here to play?" He then looked at me and said," Is that O.k. momma if Tommy comes over to my house today?" I nodded and we once again resumed our walk. I was elated to find a letter from Nonu. We had been corresponding now on a regular basis. I had invited her to visit. I knew in my heart if I could get her to visit she would stay. She and her husband George would find their place in the school and I was sure they would help.

The school had grown just as I thought it would and it was getting to be more than Natalee and I could handle. I was after all still very involved in the running of the church as well as doing readings on regular basis. I found my life to be very busy.

That night after I had kissed Christian and had tucked him in his bed I reread Nonu's letter. As I placed it in my drawer I said to myself Well, Miss Nonu you can't come here just yet, but it won't be long that you will be right here in this very house." With that thought I blew out the lamp and crawled into bed. Just as I settled into bed I heard a soft knock on the door. I sighed and climbed out of bed, padded to the door and upon opening it I said. Oh, hi William, come on in."

Roy, Max, Charles, Carl, Richard and Matt sat around the wooden table. Matt jumped as Roy hit the table with his fist. "I don't care if your wife does teach there that place needs burnt to the ground!" The weekly meeting was being held in Max's barn and some of the members of the club had not yet arrived. Charles said," Maybe we should discuss this when everyone else is here." The others agreed but the issue was to hot to put aside. Matt said, "I don't think that Maggie woman is hurting anything. She is doing a good job of teaching the children around the countryside." Roy threw back his head and one couldn't help but notice how rotten his teeth were. He said. "What in the hell are you talking about Matt. That woman of yours got you saying some dumb things. She must be awful good doing her wifely duties if you know what I mean." Matt jumped to grab Roy but the arrival of three other members caught his attention.

Harly, Earnest and ol' Jack entered the barn. "Hey what's all the commotion about?" Harly asked. "This air in here could be sliced with a knife." Matt said," It ain't nothin. We were just having a talk is all." Roy snorted.

'OL Jack was the oldest of the group so this entitled him to be the leader. He pulled up a chair and said "What's on the agenda this week?" Got any trouble makers that need put back in their place?" he snarled.

Max said, "Is this meeting officially under way?" 01' Jack said, "It is now I am here." Everyone laughed and settled down to the business of the week.

"The floor recognizes Earnest," 01' Jack said. Earnest stood and said," We hear that the widow Smith is entertaining a man that has been hired to care for her farm." 01' Jack spoke, "You mean entertaining him in an entertaining sense?" Earnest answered, "That is the understanding I got sir." "01 Jack said, "Who wants to go and have a talk with the widow Smith?" Harly said, Maybe two or three of us should ride out there tomorrow night. We can try and talk some sense to her and forewarn her before we have to take any action." Charles jumped in, "I will ride along I will volunteer." 01'

Jack continued. "That's a good idea who will ride along with Charles?" Harly, Max, and Carl volunteered and it was settled. "What's next?" 01' Jack asked. Richard said, "Been a lot of uneasy feelings about that Maggie woman. The one who has her own church and now has opened a school for the colored children. "The others nodded, all except Matt. Max said, "She has a fine house." Carl said, "Better than mine I hear." The other men said in agreement, "I have heard that to." Charles said," I hear that she is awful uppity. My wife told me that she saw her just the other day hurrying into the post office and when she passed my wife she never once cast her eyes down." Again the men agreed with each other. 01' Jack added, "She got quite a fortune telling business going on there. I think she makes more money than I do. Also got a lot of white folks listening to her and taking her advice." Carl said, "She is going to get the colored folks around here pretty sure of themselves."

Matt said nothing and 01' Jack noticed this. "Matt," he said, "What do you think about this uppity colored woman?" Matt said, I have met her once or twice. In fact my wife thinks highly of her." The barn became quiet. The owl that was sitting in the rafters stopped preening himself as if he to was listening.

'OL Jack spoke in a quiet voice, "Matt am I hearing you right? Are you saying that you think this Maggie woman is no problem?" Matt said, "I have seen no problems from her. She is a God fearing woman and I hear from my wife that she is a strong willed little woman." 'OL Jack reared back in his chair and looked at Matt. "Matt, you will want to be selling some grain this year won't you?" Matt said," You know I have to sell the grain It's what I live on. If I don't sell my grain I can't keep my farm going." 01' Jack looked at the others, they all grinned, an evil grin. 'OL Jack said," Boys, you remember Bob that was with us last year?" Thy all nodded and kept grinning. 01" Jack continued, "You all remember how he decided that we didn't know how to keep order and how he decided not to agree with us?" Again they all nodded. "Why don't you tell Matt here just what happened to Bob. Harly?" Harly showed pride that OF Jack had called on him to tell the story. He said, "Bob went down. You can't get no money from burnt crops." Everyone laughed. Matt saw that he was trapped and decided to go along with his fellow club members.

Roy said. "You know we have to be awful careful. That William Harding is a tough man to have to contend with. I know that this Maggie is his woman." 'OL Jack said as he rose from his chair. "All the more reason to make the fire look real natural.

What's the job on the schedule tonight Carl?" Carl answered, "Got a man that claims a boy stole his pigs last night. Not to far from around the other side of the Briggs house." All the men rose from their seats and looked like an eerie, somber sight as they each one looked out of the eye holes of their white sheets.

I was sitting on the front porch after the children had gone home thinking about the weekend's service when I saw a wagon approaching. Christian was playing on the front yard and as the wagon got closer he stopped playing to watch it as it turned into the lane. "Christian, looks as if somebody is coming to get a reading. You play real quiet and momma won't be long." He was used to the people coming for readings. He at times looked forward to them because folks often brought their children with them and he had playmates.

As the wagon got closer I saw someone laughing and waving a hat. "Oh my gosh it's Julie! Its Julie!" I exclaimed." As she pulled her wagon to a halt I was off the porch as fast as I could jump and run. "Julie, Julie I am so glad to see you! How have you been and how come you took so long to visit me?" Julie climbed down from the wagon with tears in her eyes. "Maggie, you look great girl!" she said as we hugged each other. Christian stood silent as he watched us both exchange hugs and a tearful greeting. "Oh my stars is this Christian Freeman?" Julie asked. Christian on hearing his name ran over and smiled up at Julie. "Hi, Ma'am. Yes my name is Christian Freeman." he said. "Julie held his little face in her hands and said, "My, my what a handsome and such a polite young man..." I said," Come on in,come on in. Let me make you some tea. Would you like something to eat? "Julie and I held hands as we entered the house.

Her eyes opened wide as she gazed around the room. "Wow, girl you must have some good poon tang. To have Mister William keep you as good as this." I half heartily laughed and said," Julie stop it, I am not proud of this place." She saw that I didn't take to lightly this kind of kidding and she said, "Oh honey I didn't mean anything bad I was only jabbin at you." I said, "I know, but let me show you something I am proud of!" I walked her to the church and talked all the way. "We have a school established. We have thirty children enrolled right now and at least fifteen starting next year. Can you believe that?" Julie said, "Maggie, I am proud of you. We all heard about the good work you are doing here. Oh, Birdie and Susanna send their love."

We walked back to the house and sat down on the front porch. "What brings you to visit me after all these years?" I asked. Julie said, "Well, have you heard the Bill died last month?" My mouth fell open. "No, William said nothing about that to me." I said. Julie said. "Yes, 01' man was to sick to long. He was too weak to heal I guess. Anyway he died last month." I said," I am so sorry, Julie are you alright?" She smiled and said. "Yes I am just fine. I am an old woman now and I need to do something before I go to be with the Lord." I said," You don't appear to be old. How old are you anyway? I have lost track of the time." Julie leaned back her head and closed her eyes. "Let me think for a minute." I waited. She opened her eyes and asks. "What year is this anyway?" I answered," 1869." "Oh yeh that's right, let me see. I guess I am about 51 years old now." She said. "That's not old." I said. Julie said, "No maybe not, but it sure feels as if I have lived a hundred years." I took her hand and said," Well, for a hundred year old woman you are sure held up good together." We both laughed. Julie said, "If I am 51 that makes you around 40 or some whereabouts." I said, I am 39. I am looking at 40 in the winter. My bill of sale says that I was born in 1830. William gave it to me so that is how I know my birth date. January 3, 1830. Anyway what brings you to my house after all these years?"

Julie answered. "I am on a quest. After Bill died I ask to be let go from my duties. I have saved some money and I am going to find someone." "Sug?" I asked. Julie looked at me with a start and said, "Now what makes you think that? Sug might be dead or long gone by now." "Well." I asked then who would you be looking for?" Julie looked at me with a smile and said,"Oh your right I am going home. Well, not home so to speak but the place where I was once happy. With my Sug. Yes, with my Sug. I have to find out if he is alive or not. I have felt his breath on my face many times in the night. This has kept me going for all these years. I knew that one day I would set out to find him." I felt a chill when she added, "Dead or alive I will find him."

We sat silent for a while Just sitting there holding hands.

Julie stayed the night and at early sunup I watched her wagon until it was out of sight. I said a prayer for her, Dear God, I ask if it be your will that Julie will be able find her Sug. Please see to it that her journey is a safe one dear Lord. Amen.

After she left I said aloud, 'Oh dam! I forgot to ask her if Bill told where he hid that damn silver. Oh well I will ask William." Then I said "No I won't, I don't care!!"

"What's the matter with you all of a sudden?" Natalee asked Matt as he sat in the library on a Saturday morning. "You act as if you are sick or that something is terribly wrong." He looked up from his book and said, "Natalee, can't you see that I am reading?" Natalee walked over and took the book from his hands. Sitting on the floor at his feet she looked up at her handsome dark eyed, husband. "What is the matter? I know that something is bothering you now why won't you share it with me?" Matt stroked her dark curls. "Yes dear I am very concerned." he said. "Seems as if your friend Maggie has created a stir," Natalee said," What do you mean? Whatever are you talking about? Is it your friends? Are they concerning themselves with Maggie?" Matt stood up. "Yes, you said that she was a strong woman. Now some are concerned that she may be a little to strong." Natalee jumped to her feet. "Too strong! I don't understand what you are saying Matt. What are you saying? Please tell me!"

Matt drew in a deep sigh. "Looks as if she is in danger and her school to." he said. "No!! I won't hear of this! I won't! You stop this talk right now. I am telling you right Now Matt if something happens to Maggie or her school and church I will kill you. I am not kidding! I will just kill you!! I will not have you talking like this in this house!! Matt reached for her as she was standing with both fists on her hips looking as if she might be serious about killing him.

"Aw Natalee your not serious. Stop these kinds of threats right now." He said. She moved out of his grasp. "Matt, if anything happens to my dear sweet friend you will find out how serious I am. I cannot leave you but By God you will make me a widow!"

Natalee stomped out of the house and hurried to hitch up a wagon. "Where you going?" Matt yelled. "You better not be going to tell Maggie anything!! You better not!!"

As Natalee rode away in the fast paced wagon Matt sat down on the porch step and watched her go with a smile on his face.

"Maggie, Maggie!" Natalee screamed as she pulled her wagon to a halt. I came out to greet her wondering what all the excitement was about. Natalee grabbed me as she tumbled out other wagon. "Maggie, you're in danger! You're in great danger!!" I took her by the shoulders and asked," Danger? What kind of danger? What are you talking about?"

She yelled, "Mart's friends ride around in the night with white sheets over their faces! He just told me that they would be coming after you soon!" I felt faint, "Me? What ever for?" I asked. "He says that folks think you are to strong or something I don't know! I do know that you are in grave danger and I am here to warn you!" I said "O.k. lets calm down," Who are Matt's friends?" Natalee answered. "I don't know! But you have to do something before they have a chance to do something to you." I said, "Let me think. I know I am expecting William in a little while. He is bringing me some honey that I am out of. I will ask him what to do about this. In the mean time let's calm down and have a cup of tea."

Natalee was still at the house when William arrived. "William." I said, "This is a dear friend of mine. Natalee." Natalee curtsied as William took her hand. William said, "It's so nice to meet you Natalee. Who is your husband?" "Matt Thompson sir" she replied. "Matt Thompson I think I have heard that name. Doesn't he have the farm next to this land?" Natalee answered. "Yes, he and I live just over that yonder hill."

As we sat in the living room we all three sat very silent and awkward. I said, "William, Natalee has brought me grim news. It seems that I am in some kind of danger." William lifted his eyebrows and asked, "Danger? How so?" I turned to Natalee and said. "Natalee?" Natalee started to cry. William rose to take her hand and said "My dear what are these tears for? If anything is wrong or if anything has put my Maggie in danger please I need to know about it." Natalee withdrew the daintiest pink hanky from her sleeve and dried her eyes. "Sir, I am ashamed to reveal that my husband Matt entertains the evilest of friends. It is through talking with my husband that I learned that Maggie is in the gravest of danger. I came here to inform her of this danger and she advised me to share this information with you." William let go of her hand and said. "Am I to assume that your husband is in the Klan my good woman?" Natalee lowered her eyes and started to cry again. She said in a low tone," Yes sir he is." I grabbed my throat and gasped. "Natalee!" I exclaimed ", why didn't you tell me this?" Natalee was really crying now and she looked at me with tears streaking her face. "If I had told you Maggie you would not let me be your friend. You would not let me teach in your school." She cried, "Oh, I have made a mess of things I am so sorry."

William took her in his arms and held her to him. "Natalee, you have not made a mess of anything. You have been a brave woman to have crossed this line. I am most grateful to you to have you share this information with me. I will take care of it right away." He smoothed her hair. Natalee just stood there held in his arms for a while. She withdrew and said. "Thank you William. I am glad to have made this acquaintance."

William did not stay long. He assured us that I was in no immediate danger, and told us not to worry. "He is a very handsome man, Maggie" Natalee said, you should be proud that he loves you so." I answered, "Yes I suppose I should be."

That night when the moon was the only light a lantern was shinning through the boards of Max's barn. "O.k. Matt, you have your instructions." Ol' Jack said. "The church goes first and then house. Make it look like the church fire sparked the house. Roy you go with him." Roy sneered at Matt as he nodded his head in acceptance. He said, Looks as if this will piss your ol' lady off pretty bad. You might find yourself sleeping in a barn just like this one." Everyone joined in jeering Matt. "You'd, better get ready to visit the town whore cause your woman is going to put you out." Ol' Jack shouted 'Stop this! We have serious work to to here and we have to get on with it!"

Matt and Roy rode quietly through the woods. The white sheets blew behind them as they rode. Max looked at Roy riding in front of him. He thought. Looks as if ol Roy is a ghost He blinked as he thought he saw the white sheet glow and float up to hover above Roy's body. He shook his head and the sheet appeared normal again.

"Hold it right there!" a loud voice caused them to stop their horses. "Matt Thompson! Get off that horse right now and you too fellow! If you don't dismount we will shoot." Matt and Roy looked at each other. They dismounted and stood by their horses. "Drop those reins and get over here!" Matt looked and saw that there were at least six men. On a closer look he saw that they were all pointing rifles at them. "Take off those ridiculous sheets and reveal your faces. You're going to die and we want to see the glory in your face as we kill you. Roy shouted "Glory? What Glory?" One of the men answered. "Glory to die away from such an evil life!" The others mumbled their agreements.

Just then another figure arrived on a horse. "I will take it from here men. Good job." He pointed out three of the men and said go check on Max's barn. See to it that the fire took hold." You other men wait over there in case I need back up. I want to handle this alone."

William got down off his horse. Matt Thompson? Wife of Natalee?" Matt nodded his head and said 'Yes sir, what can I do for you?" William pursed his mouth and looked at Roy. "Whats your name?" "Roy sir. We were just out taking a ride on our horses' sir. I am sure that you are fully aware of our duties. Someone has to keep those colored folks under control. Why you being a man of honor Sir I am certain you can understand just how wicked and mean those colored folks can be. It is our God given right to make sure things stay in tight control So many of them now free we have to keep things in order. Why I was just saying the other day to a friend of mine. That our next job was going to be one I was looking forward to. Seems as if we got a little wench running a fortune telling house along side a church." He laughed a nervous laugh." She even got the nerve to start a school to educate the young ones coming up. Now you can see how that will cause problems in the future. Why don't you come along with us? I plan to have my way with this uppity wench; if she is still alive after I finish with her I am sure you could enjoy her yourself."

Matt rolled his eyes. He knew that by the expression on this tall man's face that Roy had said to Much. William was so mad that he was finding it hard not to shoot Roy between the eyes. He bellowed. "Shut up!! You shut Up, You bastard!! "Matt come here by me!" Matt moved over to William's side. William asked," This is your friend?" Matt looked at Roy standing in front of him and said. "No Sir. He is no friend of mine." William said in a firm rough tone. "Roy get down on your Knees!" Roy started to protest and William said, as he pointed his rifle closer to Roy's head. "On your knees now!" Roy fell to his knees. William handed Matt the rifle. "Shoot him! Shoot him to kill him!" Matt said with a shaky voice."! Can't sir, I can't kill another person." William threw back his head and laughed. "You can't kill

106

another person! Hah! What about all those you have killed while wearing your white hood? Just because your face is covered does that make it the right thing to do? Well your face is in full view right now Matt Thompson and if you don't kill this man I will have to kill you with him. I know that you have a pretty little wife with the name of Natalee. Who do you think will take care of her if I have to shoot you?" Matt trembled. Roy said, Stupid! You have the gun shoot him!! Shoot him. What the hell is wrong with you?" Matt looked around to see where the other men were. He saw them standing not far and knew that if he shot this tall man standing at his side that he would have no chance. He would be shot for sure.

William said in a long drawl," You gonna make us stand out here all night Matt?" Shoot him and get it over with. If you do I assure you you will not die yourself. My woman Maggie has told me all about her friendship with your wife. I in no way intend for any harm to come to you. Not now or ever. Matt took this opportunity to bargin. "If I shoot him the others will burn my crops. I need my crops Sir I can't afford to have my farm burned. William said, Ah I see now. I didn't think that you were a true Klan member. I have many connections. So many that you would never understand how things work on such a grand scale. I can not kill this man. But if you don't I can't keep your farm safe nor your wife."

Roy looked up at Matt and William and took one more chance. "If you let me live I will go away I will drop out of the Klan and move far away. No one will know where I went. I promise this. William ignored his plea. "Well Matt, What's is going to be. Looks as if your at the turning point in your life right now. Either shoot this bastard or get shot yourself." Roy shouted. You son of a bitch Matt. If you kill me I swear I will somehow get even with you! Someday and somehow you can bet on that!!"

The shot rang out. Roy fell and Matt slumped to the ground. William shouted to the waiting men. "Check to see if he is dead." The others walked over and examined the body of Roy. "Dead!" One man called out. William said "Well done Matt! Good shot!"

The men started to mount their horses. William said to Matt as he stood over the crying man. "I will keep to my word. No harm will come to you. We have already left a calling card at Max's barn and there will be further contact with your fellow Klan members. I advise you to lay low for a while. Matt stood and watched the men mount and ride away. He stood and looked at the dead body on the ground. He picked up a twig sturdy enough to dig with and started to dig a hole. When he completed digging a small opening in the floor of the woods he stood and removed his white robe. Looking around for the hood he picked it up and threw the garment into the hole. and covered it over.

107

After making sure that no one would detect his digging place he mounted his horse and started for home.

The school was growing as well as the congregation. Christian was learning so fast. He was now seven years old and was reading as well as I could. I was surprised when Natalee's husband started to attend church with her. She was doing more than her share with the running of the school. As we were cleaning up after the children had gone home I said, I have told you about Nonu?" Natalee laughed and said. "Yes, Maggie I feel as if I know her. You have told me so much about her." I said, "She and her husband George might be coming to visit me soon. I told you her husband was a school teacher didn't I?" Natalee smiles and nods." I said, "If I can get her here to visit I am sure she and George will see how much we need them they will probably stay." Natalee said," Yes, we sure could use some help around here. I fear the children are suffering because I can't give them all the attention that they need." I said," Honey don't worry; I am trying my best to get help. In the meantime we will just have to make do."

That afternoon as I was tending to the garden I felt a cramp in my lower back. Christian was pulling weeds. I said," Christian come help Momma into the house. I don't feel so good." Christian stopped his weeding and helped me to the front porch. "What's the matter Momma?" he asked as he looked up at me with concern in his beautiful brown eyes. "Oh, just tired I guess. I will sit here awhile and rest. You go finish weeding the peas and don't worry about me. I will be just fine."

I rested little through the night. I knew what my problem was and now the entire community will have to know about my condition. I have tried to keep it a secret and now I can't hold this secret any longer I thought. I lay in my bed and swore under my breath." I don't know how this has happened. I am so busy Lord how could you ever expect for me to watch and raise another child. Damn that William." I tossed and turned the biggest part of the night. Between patches of sleep I would feel a burning pain. I said aloud, "I wish Julie was here. She would know what weeds I should brew for a soothing tea." I will have to ask William when he comes around if he could get a Dr. to visit me. I don't feel to well and Lord I am so tired."

Morning came and it was Christian waking me. "Momma, Momma. I am leaving for school now. Are you feeling better?" He leaned over and kissed me on the cheek. "You sure are feeling hot this morning Momma. Want me to open your window?" I said, "No dear, I am fine. Would you tell Natalee I can't help her today? I think I will just rest for a little while longer. You go on to school now and learn a whole lot. O.K.?" Christian patted my hand and went out to school.

I needed to go to the jhonny. I stood up and felt as if I would faint. "Oh Lordy." I said as I steadied myself on the bed post. I couldn't remember ever feeling this sick in my life. I started for the door but only got a few feet away from the bed. As I lay there I spotted the winter chamber pot under the bed. I crawled over to retrieve the pot. I sat down and as I tried to let down my water I let out a loud cry. I felt as if I was on fire. I managed to pull myself back into the bed and laid there until I heard the front door open.

"Maggie? are you alright?" Natalee walked into the bedroom. "Her face went stone white when she saw me. "Maggie! What in the world is the matter with you? You look so sick." I said, "I am not sick I am just about to have a baby." Natalee's mouth fell open, "A baby!! she shrieked. "How in the world did you keep this hidden? I didn't even guess that you were carrying a baby. How?" I said," I have been making my clothes bigger and wearing fuller aprons. I have tried to keep it well hidden. I am not proud of the fact that William visits me and now that I am about to have another one of his children." Natalee asks." Does William know?" I answered, "Yes, I told him." Natalee asks," What did he do, or say?" I rolled my eyes, "He said that he was sorry." Natalee scowls, "Is that all? Is that all he says about it?" I try to smile and say, "Natalee you must understand that a child of his would be an embarrassment to him. He doesn't want to face the fact that he is going to have another child with me. He hasn't been here for about three months now. He has his own way of dealing with things."

I could see that Natalee was angry. "Well, if he wants to hear a fiddle he will have to pay the fiddler!! She spouted. I managed to laugh. Fiddler? I said," Girl, if it was only fiddlin he wanted to hear I sure would have loved to learn to play a fiddle instead." We both laughed and Natalee's mood was lightened.

Christian came into the room. "You feeling better Momma?" he asked. I took his hand into mine and said, "Honey I am feeling better just because you and Natalee are so concerned about me. Don't you two worry now I will be just fine. I need a little sleep right now though." Natalee said," Maggie I will see to it that Christian has something to eat before I go. Do you want anything to eat?" I said, "No not right now. I just need to rest. I won't be down to long. I would appreciate it if you would fix Christian something before you go."

Natalee and Christian left the room and as I drifted off to sleep I could hear them laughing in the kitchen. I smiled.

I woke with another sharp pain. It was dark outside so I realized that I must have slept the remainder of the day. I needed to use the potty again. I stood up only to have pain knock me back down. "Christian! Christian come help Momma!" I shouted. Christian ran into my room and helped me lay back down in the bed. I was wet with sweat and was in constant pain. "What is the matter Momma? Christian cried. I said through my pain. "Don't worry Just get in the wagon and get Natalee." He cried. No, I can't leave you!" I said in a firmer tone," Christian! I need Natalee! Please go get her!" Christian started to protest once again and as I cried out in a pain he ran outside. I breathed a sigh of releif when I heard him leave in the wagon.

I was alone. Completely alone for the first time in my entire life. I felt so close to God in this quiet. I was enduring more pain with this child than I experienced giving birth to Frankie. I said aloud, "Hurry Christian! I need Natalee."

I thought that I was going to pass out. I needed to push. Each time that I pushed I could feel something gushing from me. I thought, Must be a lot of water with this baby. I tried to sit up and when I did I saw a pool of blood running all over my beautiful velvet spread. I laid back and just as I did I felt a whoosh. I sat up and grabbed a perfect little girl. I looked at her crinkled little face and ran my finger into her mouth. She let out a cry that sounded like a weak kitten. I reached over and retrieved my scissors from the drawer of my bedside table. Everything seemed to be moving so fast all of a sudden. I cut the cord and tied it in a little knot.

The little girl reminded me of Frankie and I felt as if I was looking at him. I was feeling so confused. "Frankie?" I said. "No, this isn't Frankie. This is a little girl with beautiful golden red curls." I said as I wiped her face with the sheet. I was still feeling the water coming from me. "That's odd," I said. "That water should have stopped by now. Oh well. Maybe it's because I haven't been able to pee for so long." I said aloud." I placed my hand between my legs and felt the water still gushing. I felt so weak and strange. I didn't notice that my hand was covered in blood until I wiped it on the sheet. "Oh My I don't think this is right." I said as I held the now sleeping little girl. I said "Oh Dear God I am so tired and I now need to sleep. I pray that Natalee gets here pretty soon this baby needs her help."

"Maggie! Maggie! Were here! Hold on I am coming! Natalee shouted as she ran up the porch steps. Matt had come along with them because it was in the middle of the night. "Christian, you wait right here I will see to her." She said. Christian cried," Momma are you alright?" as he started for the bedroom. "Matt, keep Christian with you please this is woman's business." Matt held Christian back and said, "She is going to be fine son. Now don't you worry. Natalee will tell us when you can go in the room." Christian calmed down and sat down in the living room with Matt to wait. Matt said, "Everything must be alright I don't hear anything." Natalee entered the bedroom and saw the pool of blood on the floor. She hurried to Maggie's side. She placed her hand over her mouth to keep from crying out. She looked at her dear sweet friend holding her new born little girl. She saw the tiny curls wrapped around Maggie's fingers. "Oh dear God, Please just let her be sleeping." she said. "Maggie. Maggie" Wake up dear I am here now." she felt Maggie's wrist. "Oh dear God." she cried" Oh dear God!"

She lifted the sleeping baby and kissed her on the brow. The baby opened her eyes and looked at Natalee and started to cry. "Oh no, dear sweet little one don't cry. Don't cry. I will take care of you. Yes I will take care of you. No one will ever know that you not mine. My very own little Emily Rose."

The entire congregation was gathered in Maggie's church. Many white folks had come to pay their last respects. Natalee and Matt stood holding Christian's little hand. He kept looking up at the new baby and patting her as Natalee held her. The baby was wrapped in beautiful pink blankets trimmed in pink satin ribbon. Natalee was thrilled and alive once more because William had given her little Emily Rose.

There was no preacher to offer the service. It was decided on that Maggie's students deliver the eulogy. Birdie, Susanna and Tad had arrived with William. They all stood together as they looked at Maggie. Birdie was crying as she placed a white flower in Maggie's hand. William looked as if the whole world was resting on his shoulders.

The men carried the casket to the waiting grave with William following the crowd. He stood and looked around in order to not focus on the wooden casket. He saw the garden growing without weeds, the flower boxes filled with bright colored flowers. He looked at the beautiful little white house and remembered how scared she was when he had to leave her alone. She had tried not to show her pain and fear but he knew it was there. He couldn't remember her laughing.Perhaps I just wasn't paying attention; he thought I am sure she laughed sometime. His gaze fell on the white church. Oh how she loved that church, he thought. And how thrilled she was to provide a school for the children. He felt a tear slide down his cheek. He looked at the people most of them openly crying and some just shaking their heads.

As the little wooden casket was lowered into the grave it became real quiet. The only sound that could be heard was the cry of the mourning dove.

Many folks left after the service. Some lingered to talk a little longer but they soon left as well. Natalee and Matt stood holding Maggie and William's daughter. Natalee noticed how William would not look at the infant. He had seemed pleased when Natalee and Matt had asked him for the little girl. "I will watch Christian." Natalee said. William said. "I would appreciate that very much. I know how much Maggie wanted the school to continue and I was wondering if you and Matt would be interested in keeping it going?" Natalee said as she picked a piece of lint off Emily's blanket. "I will do my best to keep the school going. I will be so busy with this child I can only hope that Nonu will arrive and decide to stay." William said "Nonu? Has she been notified of Maggie's death? Natalee answered. No, I have not written her yet. I plan to do so in the next couple of days." William said. I will give the house and church to you for the care of Christian. I promised Maggie that I would provide for him until he is grown. As for the infant I will provide for her if you and Matt need anything for her welfare. I can not take her home with me nor can I ever allow my wife and children to know about her." He looked at the ground and a tear fell. He wiped it away hoping that Natalee had not noticed. Natalee had noticed the tear and reached out to place her hand on his. "William, I loved Maggie and I would be more than pleased to care for Christian. I will continue to keep the school doors open to the children as long as I can. I can't thank you enough to have the honor of raising this dear sweet little girl". Natalee reached up and placed a kiss on William's cheek. He reached up and felt the place where Natalee's kiss had been and walked away never to look back.

"A wagon is coming A wagon is coming!!" Natalee was sitting in the yard holding Emily as the children enjoyed recess. "Miss Natalee, little Ruth said," A lady and a man is coming here in a Wagon." Natalee stood up as the wagon pulled to a halt. "Are you Natalee?" A pretty young, black woman ask as a handsome man helped her down from the wagon. Natalee answered,'Yes, I am. What can I do for you?" She reached out her hand to Natalee and said, "I am Nonu and this is my husband George. Natalee stood with her mouth open without taking Nonu's hand. "Oh goodness I didn't know you were coming." She said,"0h where are my manners please come in the school and have a seat." she took Nonu's hand. "I have heard so much about you and I am so glad to see you!!" Nonu laughed and said 'Well I really want to see Maggie first is she in the house?" Natalee's face fell. Nonu asked "What is it she's alright isn't she? I got a letter from her last month. I knew that she was going to have a baby and needed my help. George and I decided to surprise her with our visit. It seemed like we were never going to get here, It was such a long trip." Natalee dropped her eyes and said," I am so sorry. Maggie passed away last week.." Nonu grabbed George, "Passed away? Died? Oh my God! Maggie died? I can't believe it. No say it isn't true.!" Natalee said," I am sorry to say that it is true. I am so sorry." Nonu asked, "What about the baby she was carrying?" Natalee held Emily tighter and said, "She lost the baby. We placed it alongside her in her casket." Nonu was now crying and said, "Is that your baby?" Natalee looked at the ground and said "Yes Ma'am it is. This is Emily Rose my new little girl." Natalee turned the blanket down and Nonu gasped as she looked into the face of Frankie. She vowed to herself never to say a word.

Nonu and George stayed on to keep the school open. Many a child passed through the doors of Maggie's school never to know and love the woman that was so concerned for their education and for their spiritual lives.

Heaven 1- Part 2

*I knew a man in Christ above fourteen years ago, (whether in the body, I cannot tell; or *whether out of the body, I cannot tell: God kno'weth :) such a one caught up to the third heaven K.J.*

Maggie, Maggie dear time to wake now. I slowly opened my eyes. I was not in my bed. I was not holding my newborn little girl. I looked around me and saw a white room. Nothing in this room was familiar to me. I sat up. I was still feeling confused. I looked around for the person that was calling my name. No one was there. There were no windows but a breeze was blowing over my face. I looked at myself. My hands were still my hands; my feet were not swollen as they were just a few minutes ago. Where is my baby I thought and where am I? A door opened and I was so alarmed to see a man clothed in white robes enter. He had the prettiest smile and the smoothest darkest skin that I had ever seen on a person. "Hi Maggie we have been waiting for you to awaken. My name is Whitman and I am your guide." I looked at him as he held out his hand to me. "My guide? Guide to where? Who are you? Where am I and where is my baby girl I just had?" He held up his hand and laughed, it reminded me of Julie's laugh. Maggie slow down. I am here to explain everything to you. You are just fine,and so is your baby girl."

"I want to see her right now! I want to know that she is fine." I was starting to feel a little irritated. He stood next to me and took both my hands in his. His touch felt so warm and soothing that my irritation left as fast as it had come upon me. "Maggie, *I* must tell you that you are no longer living on the Earth plane that you are so familiar with. This will be your new home until it is time to leave us." I did not understand and I said. "I am so confused. I was feeling confused when I was giving birth. This is the strangest dream that I have ever had." He smiled as he still held my hands. "Maggie. This is not a dream. You are fully awake. More awake than you can ever be. In fact you've have just awakened from a dream." I started to cry. I asked, "Am I dead? Did I die having the baby?" He nodded. I sat and held his hands and cried. Whitman stood and held me to him until I felt better. I was permitted to cry.

I wiped my tears as the sadness left me. It felt as if the tears washed away everything that I held within. I felt like a child again all full of wonder and questions. Can I leave this room?" I asked." Is this Heaven? Where is Jesus? I want to see My Frankie" I felt so excited. I had read so much about this place and now I was here." Is this the waiting room?" Whitman said. "Yes, you will be leaving this room. Look around you now you can see all the others that slumber. I looked around the room I had not seen any one earlier when I woke now the room was full of activity. Beds stretched as far as I could see. Many were being attended to by men as well as women dressed in white robes, and other beds were still as the occupants slept. "You will soon be leaving here to join others and all will be explained to you."

I could not believe how good I felt. I thought of Christian, Nonu and William. I wondered how they were reacting to me dying. Some how I understood that this was the right place to be and I felt no sorrow. I knew that my loved ones would carry on without me.

"How long have I been here Whitman?" Witman smiled and said "Three days of your time." On the third day all are awakened when they come here. It takes us three days to prepare for the waking." I did not understand so I just nodded.

"Time to go." Whitman said. Will I meet Jesus now?" I asked. Whitman smiled as he took my hand and pulled me to my feet. I followed him. Many were leaving with their guides. We walked down a long hallway until I noticed that we were standing in a large room. I didn't see the hall end into the room it just became a large room. The room was so bright. I looked at the ceiling it was a crystal clear glass dome. Above was a beautiful blue sky with clouds that looked like they glittered. The room was quiet although it contained hundreds of people. All sizes, shapes and colors. All in this room had a robed person standing with them. I heard someone speak. "Good Morning. I am glad to see each and every one of you. You have now been made aware of your condition." I looked for the person speaking but saw no one. We were just hearing his voice. Many of you will understand that you are now fully awake while others will come to this understanding soon. Don't feel overwhelmed and confused. We are here to answer any and all questions as well as provide the best opportunities for your growth and development. Your guide will be with you throughout your stay here. By the time you leave us you will be fully aware of your special abilities and of your truly special self."

The guides were taking many of the people out of the room. Whitman turned to me and said "Let's go."" Go where?" I asked. Whitman said, "We have many things to share with you and if you will follow me I will start you on your journey."

I followed Witman outside. The grass was greener than I had ever seen grass. The sun was warm but not to bright. I looked around and saw others reclining, and talking with each other. Many were in groups sitting on the ground listening to a white robed guide. Is this a park?" I asked. Whitman said," Yes, it can be likened to a park. Many are here to rest and contemplate while as others are here to learn. "What do you wish to do Maggie?" I looked at the resting people and then looked at the groups. "I would like to learn I guess. I have so many questions."

Whitman guided me to a group sitting under a green shade tree. I sat down and thought I saw Becky in another group. She looked at me and waved. Yes! It is Becky! I thought. I waved back at her and smiled. Whitman joined the guide that was talking. I watched as he placed his hand on the man's shoulder and then there was just Whitman standing there. I shook my head as if to clear it. I looked around and others were as surprised as I while most of the group listened and watched as if this was a normal thing to witness. Whitman spoke,

"This is the Third Heaven. Many of you have been here now for quite a while and some of you have just arrived. This is the time for leisure. To do as you choose. From here you will be guided through the lives you have just led. You will understand the needed pains and trials that you each one endured and have passed many tests. Tests of faith. The knowledge that you achieve here in the schools will be of great service when you return to your place of birth. To your native planet. If you want to know of the where abouts of loved ones you are permitted to meet them and share with them provided they are still residents in the mansion rooms. You will learn about God and his ultimate plan on Earth as well as other inhabited spheres in existence. and some not yet occupied" As I sat and listened to him I started remembering that I had heard this talk before. Everything was starting to look familiar to me. I had been here before.

Heaven 2

I sat for several hours. The many things I heard were all so confusing but vaguely familiar. I was not feeling tired when Whitman was replaced with another robed figure, this time a woman with the brightest blue eyes I had ever seen. Whitman came over to me and said. Let's go to the halls of reflection.

In the place called the halls of reflection my memory was refreshed with all the past lives that I had led up until now. I was so surprised to see how each one of them was a reflection of the one just lived. I looked at Whitman and ask. "Why are so many of the lives similar in many respects?" Whitman answered, "You have encountered many lessons. You have repeated things not learned. When one fails to learn from one's actions one is sure to repeat the action." I said. "I feel as if I have made many mistakes." Whitman placed his hand on my shoulder and said in a soft tone," Maggie, no one makes mistakes, everything that we have done in our lives have been lessons to learn. Remember, no mistakes." I felt real good about this. I was afraid that I would be reprimanded highly for the mistakes or lessons that I had set into motion. I looked at all I had been through as Maggie as well as other lives and said, "What about judgment? Am I to be judged?" Whitman said, "One of the hardest lessons one has to learn is that man is his own judge. We as a counsel can help you to understand reasons behind each action. It is up to the individual to judge self, not another."

I felt as if I had been through a trying life but I now understood the reason. I had set in motion this life's plan when I was here before. It was explained to me the before I was born as Maggie I had sat with a group or counsel and agreed upon each factor of my life. Everything I did was based on the decisions I had made in the previous life. Often many things were set into motion in lives that could date back far back. The most surprising thing I learned, or rerememebred was that many of my lives were played out on other planets in other galaxies. I asked." You mean that everything I did I agreed to do?" Whitman answered with a smile, "Yes. I'm afraid so. As you sat with your counsel members your life soon to be lived was as a road map. You agreed to certain conditions and to certain circumstances. The many things you have done, some were new and others were to settle issues." I asked, you mean that all is predestined?" Whitman answered, "No, many things are predestined but each one has free will." I asked, "How can that be?" Whitman said, "As long as one will allow God to be the first most in ones life, if one will have or allow God's will to act through them then all will be in divine order in one's life. If one decides to take one's life into his

117

or her hands, take it away from God so to speak, then that is where free will enters in. Often one will get into many troubles and when frustrations set in or anger then one will create more trouble. A person such as this is creating his or her own hardships. One is always fast to blame another for these problems without seeking a higher spiritual plan for oneself." I sat and listened with awe. "Then it's like a viscous circle?" Whitman said." Yes. It turns into a viscous circle. It says in scripture in Matthew 5:18 that one jot or one tittle shall in no way pass until the law is fulfilled. This clearly says that one will get back just what one sends forth. I said. "Wouldn't is be nice if each child was taught the law of cause and effect right along with the laws of gravity and other known laws." Whitman said. Ah, yes that would be grand. Perhaps the planet Earth would not be such a war planet."

"Time for another lesson Maggie. You up to it?" Whitman asked. I said, "You said earlier that I could visit loved ones. I saw Becky in the group. What about my Frankie? May I see him?" Whitman said." Maggie you can sit in here and review some more or you may go back to the park". I have to check some records to see where Frankie is. If you like I could look of another for you. Are there any others?" I answered. "No, I don't think so. Oh yes, Nathanel. I would like to see him again. I will sit here and review some more. Thank you." I looked down at my records and I didn't notice Whitman leave the room. He was just gone. I shook my head and said out loud, "I have to learn that trick."

I was engrossed in my records when I noticed movement in the room. I watched as a filmy substance formed by my side. The shape of a woman appeared solid. I sat and watched as she smiled and beckoned for me to join her. I followed her to another room. "Have a seat Maggie." I heard although I wasn't aware of her mouth moving. I looked around me and saw a plain white chair and I sat down. "My name is Krymel. I am your oversold or midwayer. I asked. "My oversoul? Midwayer?" Krymel was the most beautiful figure that I had ever seen. Her hair was a glistening light. Her eyes were blue as the summer sky. Her feet were not on the ground. It was if she was floating. Krymel spoke and it felt like a wave of music tumbled in a soft warm breeze. "Maggie I have been through your many lifetimes with you. Hidden but never the less very close by your side. I am the accumulations of all that you have learned spiritually and intellectually while you are in the body and while in classes of these mansion schools. Throughout many of your lifetimes you have been given the gift of prophesy. I am that still small voice that you have heard on many occasions. I have the ability to provide information to you because you have developed your spiritual self and have always looked to God for answers. I asked." Does everyone have a midwayer or oversoul?" Krymel answered, "Yes, but many are not equipped to hear or have the opportunity to develop the self spiritually to understand. Often when one is in danger the oversoul will intercede and help in the form of an angel. I asked. "Are you an angel?"

Krymel said,No. I am not an angel. The angels are of a different order. But we are all a part of God's plan for his children and we each one are derived from God. Many of my functions will be more apparent in your life yet to be. The way is being prepared for your birth in the year of 1948, your time. You will have developed your abilities while you attend your classes at this school." My mouth fell open and I asked," I have to endure more?" Krymel smiled and said 'If you agree, yes. you will function as a prophet in a trying time. Many will be born with the gift similar to your own at this time. Many problems will arise with the people of this time. It will appear as though many have the gift of prophesy but it will be false truths. The teachings of the Master Jesus will not be a part of their so called gifts. Many God given talents will be falsely used. You will encounter many who have claimed the gift but will use it for their own aggrandizements and for their own profit. It will be a changing world with many ills.

Through it all you will have opportunities to teach many people. You are to be commended for your teaching as Maggie and for your help to many. In the life to come you will encounter many that you have just left on the Earth plane. They will once again interact with your life. The life as Madgelyn will be one that will be a religious life as well as a life to learn valuable lessons. In order for you to succeed as a teacher to others you will have to experience many things. If your faith does not falter you will reach great heights. You will be able to make the decision to enter into higher realms of service to God and to many people coming through the veils. I had so many questions. I have another life being prepared?" I asked. Krymel said, "Yes. and as I said I will be able to be nearer to you as you have passed many tests of spirituality as Maggie. You have earned the ability to commune with me as well as others in different realms. I must leave you for now and I will be with you as you enter into your next phase and then on beyond. I am always near by Just ask me of what you need and I will help if it is God's will.

Heaven 3

Krymel left in the same vapor that she had appeared in. I was sitting in the chair and decided to go to the "park" to think about all that I had just learned. As I had this thought I looked around me and I was in the" park". "Wow. I said aloud this is great." I sat down on the softest grass and felt the sun on my face. I thought "What's next? I want to see Jesus soon I have other questions that I need answered.

I looked over to see Whitman returning. I stood to greet him and he said. "Please, Lets sit for awhile." I sat back down and asked, "Did you find my Frankie?" He said. "Yes I did Maggie. You were aware of him when he came back to you. Remember when Christian Freeman was born and you asked if this was a sign about Frankie?" I thought and said, "Yes, I remember that. Christian is Frankie?" Whitman nodded. "Yes, he had to reenter because the timing was right for his mission." His mission? What is his mission?" Whitman said, "I am only permitted to tell you that he is a great teacher of History. A teacher that will help many to achieve knowledge. You would be very proud of him." I beamed, "Yes, I knew he would be someone special." What about Nathanel? Did you find him?" Whitman said, "Yes, he to has reentered. He is serving a life that will afford him many lessons. He will rejoin you in your next reentry. That is all I am permitted to tell you about him."

"I have so many questions Whitman. I am sure I have learned them before but I can't remember. Why?" I asked. Whitman said, "You have not forgotten. This is a new experience for you. You have only been permitted glimpses of the third mansion rooms as a vistor. This time you are a resident. I shook my head. "Third mansion rooms? I asked," I don't understand. You said earlier that this was the third heaven. Could you explain this?"

Whitman said, "After you have rested and enjoyed the company of others we will once again resume your lessons. When you have experienced the time of rest that you are accustomed to you will be accommodated in class rooms with others. There you will receive answers to your many questions. Now I leave you to your time of rest. I will be aware of your needs even when we are absent from one another. You are my charge and I will always be close at hand though I may not be visible I am there."

Whitman left as I was looking at the water. The water was crystal clear. Many were enjoying themselves in the water while some were in water crafts of various sizes. I sat and watched the people enjoying themselves and sharing with each other. I was alone and loving it. I had never had the pleasure of being alone completely as Maggie and I needed this. I thought, I wish I had a great book to read. I have always wanted a book to read that would be a great story. As I looked down I was so thrilled to find a black bound book with pages trimmed in gold. It had one word etched in Gold across the front. It read Madgelyn. I picked it up and started to read. The words held me spell bound as I read about my life to come.

I was enthralled. I was eager to live the life before me. I learned that I would once again share a life with my Nonu and Julie. William would be there and I was glad that we could be permitted to love each other in the life to come. I looked forward to once again having Natalee and John to love. I understood that the names would be different but the same dear souls that I love will be one and the same.

I found that it was tuning dusk and I was getting sleepy. Where will I sleep I thought. Whitman was at my side. "Did you enjoy your book Maggie/Madgelyn?" I looked up at him," Yes I did." He said "Now you would like to know where you will sleep?" I answered." Yes

I feel a little sleepy." Whitman said, "When you have adjusted to this place you won't feel the need of the time passing into night. It is placed in your reality so as not to disturb your natural Earth rhythm. You have been on the planet where day turns to night. It will be such here until you have no need for this structure. Until then where would you like to sleep?" I looked at him puzzled. I, I would feel comfortable in my own bed but I don't see how that is possible now.

Whitman smiled. "Maggie look over there." he said as he pointed. I looked and as I watched a house appeared before my very eyes. It looked so familiar to me. I gasped." That's my house. My home. How is that possible?" Whitman said. "Just because you are here it doesn't mean that you can't go home. You are permitted to go there as long as you feel the need to. It won't be long that this need will also pass. Until then enjoy yourself I will see you in the morning Sleep well dear child."

I walked into my house. It appeared the same. I saw two people sleeping in my very own bed. I thought to myself. Now, who in the world could that be? I got closer and was thrilled to look into the sleeping face of Nonu. When did she get here I wondered. I decided to not try and wake her. I heard a sound that sounded like a whisper. I walked into Christians room and there sleeping in Christian's bed was a man. The sound that I heard was his gentle snoring. I knelt to see who it might be. I drew back with a start when I recognized a man in the place where I had left a little boy." Christian I whispered. My baby Christian." How could he have grown in just one day I wondered? I will have to ask Whitman tomorrow upon my return. I leaned over and placed a kiss on this beautiful sleeping man of about eighteen years old. He smiled. "I love you son" I said. He smiled in his sleep as if he heard me. I silently sat down in my favorite rocking chair and drifted off to sleep.

Heaven 4

I was awakened by Whitman standing at my side. I looked at him and smiled. "I am ready." I said. He nodded and smiled.

The class room was full of every type of person. All were friendly and smiling. I saw Becky and she sat next to me. We soon became friends once again. Sitting on the other side of me I noticed a blue eyed man looking at me. "Hi, my name is Daniel. Mind if I join you ladies after class?" I said," I am Maggie; I would love to share some time and thoughts with you." It was agreed upon that we three would meet and enjoy the company of each other later in the course of the day.

The white haired man stood in the front of the class and spoke. "We are here to discuss the third heaven. You each one have earned the status of being residents of the third heaven. I will explain."

"As you are familiar with your record on the Earth you have read in the book of John 14:2. Jesus's words speak of many mansions in his father's house. Well children, you are in one of those mansions. In the mansion rooms you will have opportunities to learn and progress your souls. Many of you in this room have just arrived from the planet Earth. To be able to go directly to the third level of heaven is a great honor. You have not had to be detained on levels one nor two. It is on this level that you are fully awake to your purpose and to your missions. If not it will soon be reveled to you in a quickening.

You are permitted to visit other levels of the mansion rooms. Many mansion rooms are training areas. Those that are born with special skills are taught here. On this third heaven level of the mansion rooms you have made great personal and social achievements. You have not indulged in the habits of entertaining the physical. Entertainment such as sexual deviations. You have been on a sexual reproduction world it is so easy to mistake love for sexual activities. Smoking, alcohol and drugs are other issues that you have avoided. When you have obtained the privilege to be taught in the third heaven you are certainty choice spiritual beings" I was feeling real good about being here.

When you were released from the flesh you had earned a great deal by passing through the many trials of your lives. You have chosen God and your faith has endured. On this sphere positive education can now progress. You will now understand the meaning of your life as well as why you went through many trials. You have made the choice to continue. Continue through the seven heaven mansion levels to enter into the next phase of advanced learning in the schools of spirit training. On this level you will learn the new insights into spiritual development. You will learn the cosmic meaning of universe interrelationships.

The last time any of you were in the mansions rooms you were in the first two heavens. The training you received there was mainly of a deficiency nature or a negative experience. You had to learn to release fears, hates Jealousies, feelings of revenge, and so much more. In the first rooms one resumes the life they have just lived. You will resume your training at the place you left off when you were reassigned to another physical body. Most teaching time on the first level is devoted to helping the individual to control the habits that one experienced while in the flesh. If one is a smoker it is doubly hard to quit in the mansion rooms. The same is said for other habits.

If one seeks revenge in one way or another this to is an issue that must be addressed and corrected before the person can progress. Judgments of others will be addressed in these first two levels. Correction and cures are the main focus on the first two heavens.

In the first and second heaven many have not reached the mature ability to make personal judgments. It is the decision of the counsels to decide when the person reenters the physical body and what lessons need to be learned. It is ones choice when one enters the third heaven to reenter the physical body or to remain and progress through the mansion rooms.

If you have no further need of the first or second level you will, after ten days on each level progress on to the next level until you have reached your level of assignment. Many of you here today have been able to skip over this rule of thumb. After several times of serving the ten days on levels one and two it no longer becomes a necessity

As you progress your memory will remain intact. You will retain everything that you have learned and all that is worthwhile. You will eat food through out your mansion experience. Although it is not food as you are familiar with it is an order of food that is a living energy. There is no residual waste from this energy. You will still think and act as human because you are of the human order of species. As you progress through the mansion rooms you will become less material and more spiritual. On the second level much time was spent helping the individual to correct mental disharmonies such as intellectual conflicts within one's self.

On this, the third level you are permitted to learn about and to visit the spheres of other orders. You will learn about the angelic orders and will learn of the ability to ascend to higher realms as one who has made the choice to be of service to God. The third level is one that affords the student access to all past as well as future as it pertains to the individual self. On this level one has made the choice to become a survivor and is able to progress on to Paradise.

In mansion rooms number four one has progressed a long way. No longer does that individual need to return to the war planet Earth in the physical body. A desire to reincarnate is of the individual's choice. One will receive one's true name on this level. On the fourth level one is able to know and understand the mysteries of the Kingdom. The expanding mind can now understand various phases of local universe culture as well as cultures of other universes. One develops mutual appreciation, unselfish love and service and the understanding of one's supreme destiny. One on this sphere becomes God knowing. God understanding. God seeking and God finding.

The fifth mansion area is the place where one learns of the various groups of divine beings. One learns of their progress in developing and bringing about changes on the inhabited spheres. One can participate in the guiding of those who are in the physical. On mansion five one becomes universe minded. The knowledge unfolds that some grand and divine destiny awaits all who progress through the mansion rooms. Now one is anxiously and voluntary studying. One is naturally unselfish and worship is spontaneous.

The sixth mansion is one where one learns about the celestial beings of a high order. The understanding of universe administration is begun on the sixth level. The lessons that will encompass the whole universe are now imparted. The archangels will be introduced as much of their functions will be made known to the individual. The mortal nature grows less and less as one ascends to the higher levels. One becomes refined as one leaves behind the traces of animal origin. One can now be assigned to certain mortals as guides. One has reached the level of understanding that will afford another ascending pilgrim much needed assistance.

The seventh mansion world is the crowning achievement. One will receive a forty day spiritual rest. During these forty days one may visit other galaxies, visit loved ones, listen to great orators and fully understand the hidden teachings of God.

Here you will be cleansed of all remnants of unwholesome environments, heredity marks of the human experience, all things mortal will fall away. One will be able to study in the great temples of knowledge on ones own.

One will begin a more devoted worship of the unseen Father. Having ascended as an individual you now will join groups. One may wait for another to catch up before joining the groups. You and other ascending individuals will now begin your journey as spiritual beings. You have experienced being a spiritual being having a human experience. Now will fully understand that one is a spiritual being having a divine experience."

The class was over. So much information I wondered if I could remember all that I had heard. As I was leaving to go to the familiar park I heard Daniel and Becky say, "Hey Wait up." I stood and waited as they caught up with me. "Wow, did you understand all that?" Daniel asked. I nodded and said". *I* understood it now can I remember it. He said we would eat and I am feeling a little hungry. Where do we eat?" As I said this we were immediately standing in front of a building. The building had carvings of angels and flowers. The trim was of the richest wood that I had ever seen. A faint music was in my ears. We entered the building to be escorted to a table.

As I sat I looked around. The walls were crystal as well as the ceiling. Daniel said, "This must be heaven I have never seen anything as beautiful." Becky added, "Nor have I heard such glorious music." The food that was on the table appeared to be fruit. I tasted a piece and felt the sweet nectar as it permeated throughout my entire system. I said," This is tremendous. I think I will love this place."

After we had enjoyed our meals we were approached by our guides. Whitman and two others stood by our sides. Whitman said. "Maggie would you like to rest in your home?" I shook my head and said, "No, I am not tired." He said, "Well in that case you may do as you please. You think of places you would like to spend time in and you will be there" I was enthralled. "Where?" I asked. Daniel's guide said. "My name is Mitchell. May I suggest a place you might be interested in? Daniel has visited there many times," Daniel nodded and smiled. He said "Yes Germany the country is beautiful. Have you been there?" I said, "No, but how can we go there?" Whitman said, "There are worlds unseen to the mortal man. That world is as real as the material one. It is there that we can move and experience things as if we were still clothed in the flesh." I said. "Yes, 1 would love to visit Germany, but I would very much like to visit the holy lands and see where my Lord lived and walked." Whitman smiled, "That to can be arranged. What period of time would you like to visit?" I raised my eyebrows and asked. "Period of time?" Whitman said, "Yes all time is now. You can visit any time you wish." I asked, "I can go to the time when Christ was alive? I can talk with my Lord and savior." Whitman smiled. "No, that particular time is off limits. I am sorry I should have told you that. When the supreme being in incarnate in the flesh that time is sealed off from visitors. You may visit either before or after his death but not during his lifetime. He is in his holy temple at this time. His residence will be made available after you have progressed through the third heaven." I can't wait." I said, "O.K I will visit Germany, Lets go."

Heaven 5

I experienced travel as I never imagined possible. I was slowly remembering being here before I had incarnated as Maggie. I was elated to hear Whitman say, "Maggie, you have been here ten days. The counsel feels as if you are ready to go to mansion four." I was excited.

I arrived and was taken to meadow that seemed to be made of glass. It gave off sparks like lightening. "Is this glass?" I asked Whitman. "No Maggie this is a receiving area. The glass you see is a large crystal. The electromagnetic energies appearing as lightening are utilized here for the ebb and tide of things unseen." I shook my head. I didn't yet understand. I heard beautiful music as I saw glorious angels playing harps.

Whitman said. "If you remember reading in your Bible St. John the Divine wrote about this place when he wrote. *And I saw as it were a sea of glass mingled with fire.and them that had gotten the victory over the beast,and over his image and over his mark, and over the number of his name stand on the sea of glass, having the harps of God. K.J.* I remembered reading this in Scripture. I was so thrilled to discover the meaning of this passage. Whitman said. "My dear soul of God, it is here that you may learn of many things. You have the privilege to commune with the angels and learn of your divine mission in detail. From here you will make the decision to go further or to learn more on your planet of choice. You will learn of many things hidden to your mortal companions. These things will be revealed to you as you mature spiritually whether in the flesh or in the spirit." I must leave you for a short time as I have other charges to attend to. I will soon return until then dear child learn all that you can. You will have many opportunities to share your knowledge to many seeking souls." I found myself alone. I looked around and saw many others and did not feel the need to be a part of them. I knew that I was a part of them. I no longer felt separate from my peers nor from God. I understood that a divine spark of God dwelled within and we were all one.

An angelic being approached. I heard without hearing words." You have requested a meeting with our Lord?" I nodded. "Follow me."

I followed the being to the temple of the most highs. I entered and fell to my knees before the throne. I saw a brilliant golden light and was amazed that it did not hurt to look upon it. I was still and felt the energy as it warmed my deep inner recesses. I heard a voice that was ethereal and soothing. "My dear and faithful soul. Well done my lamb. you have served me well. Do you have questions that you might ask of me? I started to speak and realized that I needed only to think my question. "Why? Why was my life so difficult and why are we to suffer so?" I heard." My child. I have chosen a divine path for the planet from whence you came. This plan in order to be carried out must have a strong body of pilgrims. It is of the ones you speak of that need to be strong to carry out my plan on Earth. If you place steel into a fire it only strengthens it. Your brothers and sisters are strong and in them I will depend. Through them are all colors of a nation

And to them I place trust, responsibilities and expectations.

I left the temple with no more questions I had a song in my soul. It will matter that I was I thought. It will matter that I am.

I was once again joined by Whitman. I sat in classes daily and learned more than I could ever thought possible. So much to forget when I continued on to my next journey in the flesh.

Whitman was standing with other members of the counsel. "Whitman said. It is nearing the time for you to decide. If you want to live the life of Madgelyn or stay and continue your journey here. The stage has been set and it is nearing the time for you to make the final decision." I asked, "If I decide not to go what will happen to the path that has been set in motion for my soul to enter the physical body of Madgelyn?" Whitman smiled. "The path is known to us we are waiting for your acceptance." I smiled and said. "Oh I see. I must have already chosen and forgot right?" Whitman said, Yes that is the way with many. So much to experience that much of it falls back into the depths of the mental body."

He continued, "On your journey in the flesh you will not remember this experience until you have passed many tests. You have a special mission ahead of you and I will be with you all the way. In fact you have earned five guides in your inner band." Five?" I asked He said," Your inner band is the immediate area surrounding you. Within this area are five guides each with a separate function. You have of course your Master. one who has earned the status of a high order which communes directly with the counsel of God. You have a protector, one who is always protecting you from harm in the physical as well as in the ethereal planes. You have one that is referred to as a joy guide. This guide works with the rhythms of the physical body. You have earned a guide that is referred to as a chemist. The chemist's function is to provide the physical with things needed to maintain a healthy physical and mental body". "Such as?" I asked. Whitman said, "When one is craving certain things one needs the added ingredent in the system For example is one is craving tomatoes perhaps that brain has received the signal to provide potassium or some other needed ingredient that the tomato can offer. This balance is maintained and the signal is sent from the chemist" I said, "Oh I see. "Whitman said, "And of course you have me. My title is Dr. Whitman. I am a philosopher. What ever spiritual denomination you will explore I will provide the insight into it."' I asked. What about Krymel

My oversoul or midwayer? I met her earlier." Dr. Whitman said." Krymel is in your outer band as are many others. Hidden from you but not from us. These are divine members of your counsel." I nodded.

"Dr. Whitman I have questions about the physical plane." I said. "I also have a question about the vision I saw in the fire once while in the body. Am I permitted to see the true meaning of this vision?" Dr. Whitman said," Yes. All can be revealed from the fourth level."

Dr Whitman said," While you were gazing into the fire, who you saw was the man in charge of the nation. The one in the tall black hat. This was the president of that period. Lincoln. The one who made significant changes through his mission on Earth. He held a small child representing the race he was about to emancipate. The second figure you saw was a counsel member of the high orders. The medallions held with the dates inscribed of 1963 is when this man called Lincoln will once again make significant changes in the history of the nation on Earth. In the year of your time on Earth 2010 this same man will once again make his appearance as a strong leader clothed in dark flesh. "I understand", I said.

I asked" We all have several opportunities to live?" Dr. Whitman said, "Yes, that is in the order of things divine. Many have this privilege in order to make amends with self as well as others." I asked 'Where can I find this written while in the physical?" Dr. Whitman smiled and said," The scriptures of the Holy Book called the Bible give an excellent account of this record referred to as reincarnation." I have never read such a record in scripture". I said. Dr. Whitman smiled and said, "It is for those who have ears to hear and eyes to see dear child. It is hidden as one of the mysteries. When one develops one's self to a full spiritual understanding one is able to understand the hidden mysteries. Many have and will read the scriptures with an understanding through a literal mind. When one reads the record with such an understanding much confusion arises with many questions. When one advances through the levels of spiritual understanding all things are revealed. When the Bible was translated by wise men the words were written so as all levels of understanding could follow God's plan. As one progress one develops knowledge to understand all words and is fully aware of the allegory. The code was developed in order that each one could understand and be able to meet the needs of each level of spiritual understanding.

I was feeling a little confused as I asked, "Then where does it tell me of reincarnation?" Dr. Whitman said, Think of your favorite Bible story." I thought of the transfiguration on the mount at once." "That's right." Dr. Whitman said. "If this had not been one soul's progress the voice would have said these are, not this is, my beloved son in whom I am well pleased."

I was enthralled to understand this in a new light. Dr. Whitman said, as you progress through your levels of understanding you will have many new insights into the scripture. Never forget the Son of God that was incarnate in the flesh. Before he could make such a sacrifice as the Divine son called Jesus he to traveled many paths throughout the universe. He came to show us and to live as we are as humans in order to teach us salvation and sacrifice. He completed his mission as we all must do in order to progress in understanding. Jesus as God in the flesh wanted to become close to and understand each one of us. In order to do this he needed to experience your realm several times.

I asked," You spoke of Lincoln and the ones to come. Have there been others? Dr. Whitman laughed and said,"0 h, each and every one. In order to help you understand more I will cite you another example. In the year of your time, 1846 a man led a party west. This man's name was George Donner. He was caught in the elements and as a result of this misfortune he resorted to cannibalism. As you have learned in your classes many of the names are repeated throughout one's lives. The spelling is often times not the same but the vibration of the name carries through.' As your name Maggie to Madgelyn. The period of time that you will live will have many others from the same time vibration as well. George Donner will incarnate to act out deeds that he carries much guilt over. His guilt will be in that he condemned with contempt those who acted in the same manner as he did. He became self-righteous and never once forgave himself deep inside while at the same time hating others that he consumed as well as those that acted alongside him. This extreme hate will surface and once again his actions will be repeated.

In your time his name will be Jeffrey Dalmer. "Many will be appalled when his acts of cannibalism are carried out. If one would understand and look at the whole picture one would not be so fast to condemn and judge another." I said, then all things are for a purpose to learn and to help us grow spiritually?" Dr. Whitman nodded. I ask, "What will become of him?" I am not permitted to say I am only permitted to use him as an example to teach.

"Its time for you to rest now." Dr. Whitman said. I didn't want my learning to stop I was **so** amazed at all the understandings that I had received so far and I wanted to hear more.

Heaven 6

The class room was full of excitement on this beautiful day. I along with others was soon to return to our planet of nativity. Earth. I looked around me and was thrilled to see Daniel and Becky. We had learned that we were going to be close in our life to come. We soon were to be prepared for our life ahead individually. This would be our last class together.

Before the counsel member started talking we had a few minutes to share with each other. I said, "Well this looks as if this is the last time we will see each other here." Daniel and Becky held hands. "Yes, but we will all meet again when we are in the flesh? Becky asked. Daniel nodded and smiled at Becky. I noticed a look between them that I understood. "Have you two met before in another life? I asked. They both nodded and Daniel placed his arm around Becky. Daniel said, "I wish you well. You know we three love each other very much. A love that will go beyond our physical minds when we will meet again." I said, "Yes I know. I only hope that we will know each other when we meet." Daniel said, "We will." We took our seats. I was feeling much love and warmth. I was concerned that throughout my next life I was in danger of losing this love that I was experiencing while in the mansion schools.

A counsel member spoke," Children of love and light. It is my pleasure to give you as a group your final class. This meeting will be utilized to discuss the physical realm. The realm that each one of you will soon encounter in the flesh. The journey will at times become as a rough sea. I ask you each one to hold on to your faith. The faith that has gotten you to this fourth mansion room. The history of the planet Earth has been known to you but in this class I will tell you of a plan. A plan for the progress of the planet.

The period of time you are going to will be a trying time. A new era will be dawning and much confusion about one's faith and deep inner convictions will prevail on the earth. Children will be killing children. New diseases will run rampant. Mind altering chemicals will be induced into the physical bodies. I looked at Becky. Did I want to be a part of this? I wondered. I thought that I had just been through a rough period now I am hearing that it has worsened. The counsel member continued. On the planet Earth there on the other hand will be many of you. This group and others will be concerned with the care and well being of the people as well as the planet. Keep the utmost thought in your mind that all is in divine order. There will be multiple births as well as younger women having children. This is due to the fact that we have many souls that need the experiences of this planet. The roles of the female will be greatly changed and the desire for many children will not be expressed. The right to abort will be an available choice. Due to this fact we as counsel members must provide other means in order to have enough physical bodies for the many souls that need a physical expression. Our chemists will help provide the necessary information to the mental bodies of those in the medical field. The information that will produce multiple births.

Technology will be at a level that was once used during one period of the Earths history. In fact it will progress beyond any previous level after each one of you has rejoined in the mansion rooms. The great pyramids located in the Egyptian area were a major turning point in man's technology. Electromagnetic energy was utilized and then lost. The mighty stones were put in place with the knowledge of magnetic energy. This to is soon to be rediscovered on the planet Earth.

So much will happen in the course of your lifetimes. You will produce bodies for advanced souls. You are the means to get higher knowledge to the planet. Most of it will be spiritual knowledge.

Note the procession of the centuries. Nero served as Emperor of Rome and the century closes with Tarjan wearing the crown. The next century one finds Marcus Aurelius on the banks of the Danube: next Diocletian is Emperor. The next is ushered in by Constantine the Great and closes with the Empire divided. Another century and Attila invades Italy, and Rome is plundered by the Vandals and is recaptured by Belisarius in the next. The next century one sees Mohammed's glory and death and another that closes with Charlemagne preparing to rule as Emperor of the west. The next century brings Alfred the Great the robes of Britain and the next finds the house of Capet on the throne of France. A thousand years pass. Harold is now King of England, the battle of Hastings is fought and William the conqueror has arrived on the stage. Another century and Ireland is subdued and King John rules England. Another century and the Ottoman Empire appears. Another opens with Bruce crowned King of Scotland, Bannockbum is fought and Bruce has died. The next century sees Henry the fourth as King of England and the next century the battle of Agincourt is fought. Joan of Arc dies at the stake: Martin Luther is born; America is discovered and modem history is begun. The light of universal intelligence is breaking. We as counsel members can now communicate easier with mankind. The centuries lose their distinctness and we begin to measure time by eras of progress and epochs of thought. The century begins referred to as the nineteenth century and we find that in the midst of its glory and culture, in the midst of its plans, wars, and purposes we find that through all the blood and tears many have prevailed to carry out the divine plan on Earth the plan that was handed down to man through the one called Jesus. The plan of love and Universal brotherhood of Man.

You in this room have been those that have endured and pressed on with this plan imprinted in your deep souls. You have maintained your mission to bring about this plan on the planet earth. As you look around you notice how you see the light that shines from each one. There are thousands in this one room alone and many in other rooms are also holding the light. I release you my dear souls to re-enter and maintain your faith in the name of God.

The stage for your lives has been set and the players are in their positions. It's time for your entrance. God bless and good journeys to you all."

Julia/ Julie -Part 3

1942 is that the year or is that the address that I need to find. Thoughts like this ran through Julia's mind as she ran along the dark alley clutching her new born infant girl close to her breast. As she ran she would keep looking over her shoulder to see if she was being followed. Little Dovie, as she had named her, whimpered. Oh God, it's time to feed her and I don't have a warm place to rest with her, Julia thought. It's a cold December night in Indianapolis and she had only her warm breast milk to offer the infant. Julia found a dark doorway and huddled down and began to nurse her child and as the tiny girl suckled Julia's thoughts ran over in her mind. If they catch me I don't know what I will do and as she had this thought she heard footsteps approaching. "There she is," she heard one of the men yell out to his companions. "Catch her". Julia jumped to her feet and was able to escape into an open door. Someone, she thanked God for, had left it unlocked. Inside the old abandoned building Julia sat on the floor nursing her baby and cried. "I need to get you in a safe place", she told Dovie as she completed feeding her. The place she needed to get to was a few blocks over. Julia looked out the door to see if anyone had been waiting outside for her. Much to her relief her pursuers had gone. She took this opportunity to run in the opposite direction. "If I can get you to your Grandma's house I can leave you there for a few days until I can think of a solution", she told Dovie. Julia walked the streets in the brisk cold of the evening to Mrs. Emory's house. This was the baby's paternal grandmother and Julia just knew that she would offer the needed help. It was her father and his friends that were chasing her, and even though they were against Mrs. Emory she would feel safe with her. As she approached the house she felt a little apprehensive but thought this was her last resort. Mrs. Emory answered the door with a smile that lit up her large brown eyes, and said,

"Oh Julia, I have been so worried about you, please come in dear and get warm." This eased Julia's fears just a little and she was so glad to be in a warm house with someone who showed concern. "Have a seat child and let me have the baby I'll go change her and lay her down". Julia went into the kitchen and made herself a cup of hot tea and waited for her to come back downstairs. Mrs. Emory came in the room and patted Julia on the head and said," why don't you go lay down yourself and we will talk in the morning, O.K.?" "Mrs. Emory," Julia began, "Do you think I could leave the baby with you for a few days? I know you understand and you are the only person I can trust to help." "Oh dear. Now don't you worry things will work out if we trust in the Lord. Just give it over to him and all things will be taken care of. This made Julia feel somewhat better although she thought she felt a bit of nervous tension coming from Mrs. Emory. She finished her tea and went upstairs to sleep in a warm bed. As she passed by Mrs. Emory's room she noticed that she had put little Dovie in a dresser drawer. Julia went in and looked at her sleeping daughter and noticed how much she looked like her father. This was the prettiest child in the world, she thought, and she kissed her on the tiny cheek. Dovie smiled in her infant dream and Julia cried. She whispered a silent prayer to God then went into another room to sleep. As she lay her thoughts would not allow her to sleep. Her mind played out memories of the past and up to the present.

When only an infant herself her mother, Jess and father, Clive were divorced. The year was 1924 and she was not quite a year old when she was abducted from her blanket in the front yard. The kidnapper was her father and throughout many of her early childhood years the battle over her ensued. Julia remembered that during one abduction she witnessed a beheading of a man during a car wreck that she had escaped from unharmed. After a while her mother gave up the fight and she lived with her father. Her father had remarried and his wife did not like Julia. When she was four years old she wet her bed, as she often did, but this particular time her step-mother decided that this pattern needed to be broken. She washed Julia's face in the wet sheets and told her that she had to sit on a trunk in the hallway until her father came home. As if this was not enough, she was told to stick out her tongue and her step-mother put hot pepper on it. Little Julia sat for the entire day in pain and unable to drink water to rinse out the pepper. As she grew into maturity she often had to ward off her father's sexual advances. She often feared these unwelcome encounters especially after hearing him come home after one of his nights out with his fellow club members. He would try to kiss her in an unfatherly type fashion and on many occasions she would feel sick due to the strong alcohol odor on his breath. Julia was a very intelligent young woman but throughout her early childhood her main thoughts were of survival. The war and the depression were the main concerns on everyone's mind during her childhood. She helped in her father's grocery store that was in Indianapolis Indiana. It was called Drake's grocery and was very successful even during war time. Her father, Clive Drake was a prominent figure in the community even though he and his brothers were not on the good side of the law. Julia's uncles, Clive's brothers, were serving time, having been caught during the prohibition period. Clive had escaped the wrath of the law as he had many officials as his friends. He also was a prominent figure that held office in the organization known as the Ku Klux Klan.

Julia was assisting a customer when Robert came into the store. At once she noticed his large brown eyes as they seemed to look directly into her soul. "May I help you", she asked. She was not prepared for his voice when he answered her. As he spoke Julia felt as though she had heard this velvet voice somewhere but knew she had never met him before today. "I am here to deliver some goods that are on the truck ma'am, can you tell me where you want them?" Her heart lunged when she looked into his rich, dark brown face. Oh my God, she thought; this is just about the handsomest man that I've ever seen. Julia was seventeen and from this moment on she would regret ever meeting this handsome black man. Many times after this first meeting Robert would bring deliveries to the store. Julia looked forward to his arrivals and tried not to show her excitement when she heard his voice or saw his face. They both knew that underneath there was chemistry between them but each other was forbidden fruit. If they would ever allow their feelings to be known it would be very dangerous for them since her father entertained Klan member's right there in the very same store where they had met. One day, after Robert made a delivery, he handed her a wadded piece of paper as he left. Julia slipped it in her pocket afraid to look at it until she was safe and alone. All day she kept her hand in her pocket and felt the heated energy coming from the small piece of paper. Her excitement grew and many times throughout the day she felt as though she would faint from just the feeling. Finally alone in her room she unfolded the note and read in scrawled print, *meet me*. Where and how, she thought. If I am caught even showing an interest in him we're both dead. Julia slipped to her knees and prayed. A week went by and Robert did not come to the store. Julia wondered what had happened to him but was afraid to ask the substitute driver for fear someone might pick up on her interest. The following week Robert came back and Julia, with her heart beating so fast that it might explode, wrote him her address on a piece of paper and handed it to him with his receipt. Late that night as Julia was preparing for bed she heard a low whistle and looked out into the yard. Just under the tree she could make out an image of a man and knew at once that it was Robert. She got out of the house as a mouse would if the mouse knew that only a few feet away lay a sleeping cat. As she approached him she knew that she loved him just by the way the moon light lit his strong, bronze, determined features. "Hi", he spoke first. "Man are you brave." Julia said, "I can't imagine someone so brave as to come all the way over to my house after dark." "I wanted to get to know you and I haven't been known to be afraid of anything," Robert said. Julia felt a flutter in her stomach and felt a slight tinge of fear for him as well as herself. She couldn't place the reason for her deep sense of fear that had made her blood run cold. "Hey, I don't even know your last name," she remarked. "My full name is Robert Emory, but I go by the nickname of

Sugar. I would like it if you would call me Sug," he added as he winked. Sug laughed as Julia blushed but deep under her rose colored flush she felt as though someone or something had punched her in the heart. She would not know until much later in her golden years of life that this was her beloved Sug that she had loved so dearly nearly one hundred years ago.

"I want to get to know you better but I know that we have to be careful or we will both be in extreme danger." Sug said. Julia answered, "I want to get to know you also even though I feel as though I have known you forever." "When and where can we meet where we can just sit and talk?' Julia asked. "Meet me Saturday night outside a house located at 1943 Washington Street. This is where my mother lives but she will be gone Saturday night". Sug told her. "1 have to go inside now before I am found out, but I will be there." Julia answered. As she turned to go Sug held her face in his large gentle hands and kissed her softly on the cheek, and whispered, "I love you Julia, and I don't know why. As she looked into his deep brown eyes she was reminded again of that deep feeling of fear that seemed to penetrate her entire soul. Julia ran because all at once she felt that she might never see him again. This feeling confused her because she had every plan to see him Saturday night.

It seemed as if the weekend would never arrive. Julia had a close cousin named Dovie Byrd. They were so close that they often felt like sisters. This closeness stemmed throughout their entire lifetime and between them there were no secrets. In fact when Dovie was born Julia, then six months old, was lying on the very same bed next to Dovie's mother Aunt Esther. This was the year that they were both seventeen years old and like all girls at this age, they were telling secrets. As Dovie straightened her hair before the mirror, Julia sat on the edge of the bed. "My God if Uncle Clive finds out Sug will be killed and maybe even you as well". This remark was uttered under Dovie's breath just barely audible. The girls were sharing secrets and it seems as if Dovie had no secret that could compare with Julia's. "When are you supposed to see him again, Dovie asked." Well, were to meet this Saturday night at his house, he said his mother won't be home" Oh don't go I am afraid for you. You know uncle Clive is in the Klu Klux Klan and he would be thrown out of the club if this was ever discovered." Dovie pleaded. Dovie looked at Julia and noticed a tear was escaping from her big cornflower blue eyes. "Oh, don't cry I know you have deep feelings for him but just play it safe, I am afraid for you as well as for him". "I am so confused". Julia cried, but I have to see him, 1 don't understand the attraction I feel for him. "Well lets not think about it for right now, maybe something will come up and you won't be able to go after all on Saturday night. Get your skates. We'll miss the bus if we don't hurry." Julia picked up her roller skates and dried her eyes and tried not to think about Sug. Perhaps

Roller skating will take my mind off him for a while, she thought. As she and Dovie walked to the bus stop Julia said." I wish that the roller skating rink would allow Sug in. I would love to skate with him." Dovie laughed. Oh, I am sure they would let him in, just as much as they would let us in at the colored rink." Julia felt that this was a sad state of affairs, but not as sad as her state of affairs right at this moment. There were so many things she couldn't understand and her feelings about Sug were so confusing. She did not realize that these feelings would change her entire life.

Saturday finally arrived and it was all Julia could do to keep a steady hand when she waited on customers coming in and out of the store all day. It felt as if her father was watching her a little bit closer but she thought she was imagining this because she felt guilty. The day finally turned into evening and Julia raced home to jump into a hot refreshing tub of water. She put her finest bubble bath in the water and watched as the light transparent bubbles rose to the surface. I am like one of these bubbles, she thought. So translucent to many but so many swirling colors inside. I just hope that one of these days all my colors will be visible to others. Julia slipped into the hot steaming bubble bath and just as she relaxed she heard a man's voice call her name." Whose there?" she asked. Just as she spoke these words she realized that the voice was in her head but just as audible as if the man was in the very same room with her. "Don't go". Julia was sure she heard correctly. The voice clearly said, "Don't go." She sat up with a start and felt a presence in the room that was expanding not only in her head but it seemed to fill the entire room. "Who is there, and what do you want?' she asked. "I am here to tell you not to go to the man's house tonight. The consequences will change your life as well as his and it will be a disaster to you as well as him." As these words were spoken the presence faded and Julia once again was alone in her warm bath. She stepped out of the bath and felt again very confused even now more that ever before. What was that she wondered, she had read about spirit guides and had even attended a spiritualist meeting but had never taken it very seriously. She thought, maybe that was my guide or could it have been the voice of God? Now what am I to do, she wondered. I really want to see Sug tonight but maybe it wouldn't be right. Again she felt tears well up in her eyes as she dressed to see Sug. I will only see him this one time and I will tell him we can't see each other again. Aloud she said, "O.K. spirit guide or whoever you are I will bargain with you, I will see him this one time and never again." She took one last glance of the girl in the mirror and never realized she would never see the innocence of this blue eyed, seventeen year old girl again.

It was a warm spring evening and the world seemed different some how. There was a distinct spring smell in the air but also just under the surface Julia detected a smell of fear. Julia realized that Sug was someone she could never have for her very own right now, but perhaps if others saw how much they loved each other they would be accepted. Maybe she could do a great thing for the world and show people that the heart sees no color. Yes, this is the reason we love each other, she thought to send a message to the world. Julia approached the bus stop and climbed aboard to find her seat. She noticed others looking at her and she smiled back. I wonder if they know where I am going? She wondered. No, I am sure they don't she thought and settled into her seat. The bus stopped only a few blocks from her destination but it seemed like miles to Sug's house. As she approached the house she saw her handsome man standing on the porch looking like a person she had known for years just waiting for her to come home. He came to the gate to meet her and whispered in her ear with a voice that sounded like it came from the very bowels of the earth. So deep and smooth yet so very familiar. He held her face in his strong hands and said," I never thought you would come." They embraced for a long while and Sug said. "Let's go inside, my mother won't be back for at least two hours and I want to hold you for the entire two hours." As they entered the house Julia felt a tug in her very soul knowing that she would have to tell him that this would be the last time they could see each other. "Let me have your sweater," Sug said as he helped her remove it. As he removed her sweater she felt him slide the zipper down on the back of her dress. "Oh God, she thought, I can't tell him no, 1 want him as much as he wants me. Julia had never known a man before and these feelings made her feel frightened as well as sure. Her head swam as he led her into his bedroom and as he held her she looked at the contrast of their skin. I have never seen anything so beautiful, she thought, and at the same time she also thought, so forbidden. That night their daughter Dovie was conceived in love.

A jolt woke Julia from her sleep as Mrs. Emory bolted into the room. "You better leave now child, I'll keep the baby here for you, but you better go now". Julia wiped the sleep from her eyes, "What's the matter Mrs. Emory?" she asked. "Never you mind right now, you just gotta go. The baby will be O.K." "I am not leaving her here if you are this upset about something. Tell me what's wrong!" Julia pleaded. Mrs. Emory grabbed Julia's arm and pulled her down the stairs and to the front room. The room had a strange orange glow that Julia couldn't understand. "Look out there!" Mrs. Emory shouted. "Look what they done!" As they approached the window she felt the heat and saw a large flame in the front yard. "What is that? What is on fire?" She shouted. As she looked closer she saw the outline of a cross. "Oh my God in heaven!" Mrs. Emory cried. "You better get going she screamed, 1 will take the baby to my sister's house but you can't stay here". "Julia ran to the room where she had last seen her sleeping infant grabbed her daughter and said," They found me, 1 will not leave her here. She is going with me!" Little Dovie started to cry at all the commotion as Julia wrapped her in her blankets. Mrs. Emory stood by and watched tears streaming from her brown eyes and wringing her hands. "I am so afraid", she cried. "Why did you have to go and love my son? I am so afraid". Julia didn't have time to console Mrs. Emory as she ran into the dark night clutching her child. She had no place to run to so she started walking the streets of Indianapolis. Dovie had settled down and was sleeping. Julia once again heard footsteps coming from behind. "There she is, grab her!" Just as she tried to turn into an alley she felt hands on her holding her back. The worst hands she felt were the ones grabbing the baby. She looked into her father's eyes and saw hate and disgust. Standing next to her father was a prominent figure in the community. Dr Smith, a dear friend of the family and a strong member of the Klan. The Dr. took the baby and said, "You are a disgrace to the Drake family I have prepared papers to have you committed to an insane asylum if you don't leave the state of Indiana. The child will be adopted out and we will deal with Robert as we see fit." Julia looked to her father for some sort of help but he only turned his head and would not meet her gaze. "Let me take the baby with me," she pleaded. Julia fell to her knees and raised her hands to her father. "Please dad can I keep the baby?" He did not respond but merely handed her bus fare to leave town. The last time she saw little Dovie's face she was looking at her from out of her big pink blanket. Julia reached for her child and the baby's face crinkled into a wail. The Dr. turned away from her, as she was still on her knees on the cold hard sidewalk, and said, 'leave town and say good-by to your baby". She never knew there could be so much pain in one's heart. There weren't even words that could describe this pain. She sat on the cement and thought she could still hear her baby cry even though they had gotten into a car that had stopped for them. I'll find her, she thought I'll look for her; she has a birth mark at the base of her spine that looks like an upside down eagle. She will be easy to identify when I find her, she thought. Julia rose from the ground and realized her legs felt weak, so weak that she could hardly walk, but walk she did and ended up at the greyhound bus station. "Where will this money take me, she asked the station master. "Where do you want to go?" was the reply. She had seen a customer in front other buy a ticket to Ohio and that was where she bought a ticket to. Portsmuth Ohio. It seemed like the bus ride would never end. Julia even hoped it would wreak and kill her but just as soon as she had this thought she thought it best not to think things like this because her baby would need her when she found her. All through the bus ride she could hear her little girl cry. By the time she arrived in Ohio she felt as if she lost her very soul. Julia did not know that she had experienced Karma when she lost her baby girl. Karma is a principle that makes every man or woman the cause of their present conditions due to an action that was set into motion in past lives, making the pattern for this life and for future lives. It is a law of action stating that for every action there is a reaction. In Julia's life in the 1800's she stole another woman's child and raised it as her own. Due to this fact, she in turn must lose a child. Even though this law was unapparent to her she had to experience the loss of her dear little girl and feel the pain that she had inflicted upon another many years ago.

Julia had been given enough money to rent a room and had found a factory job to sustain herself. She found it hard to sleep at night because she was worried about her baby and was just as worried about Sug. She did not want to think that he had been killed but this thought would not allow her to sleep most nights. Eight months had passed and Julia felt like a zombie. It was war time and she was grateful for her job in the factory. Her job kept her mind off things that she didn't want to think about. There was a man at work that had tried to catch her eye but she was not interested in meeting another man. One day he approached her and said. "You know today is my birthday." He was feeling the loss of his wife Winonna who had died of cancer the year before, and was seeking a kind word from someone. It was not only the loss of his wife that he was grieving for but for his brother John as well. John and he had suffered a fight over a woman George was interested in. It turned out that John was seeing this same woman. George was the victor and told John that if he ever saw his face again he would kill him. John was scared to the point of joining the Navy. The last time George received information concerning his brother was through a letter stating that the ship John was on, The Jarvess, had been hit and sunk with no survivors.

Julia involved in her pain of life was not interested in George or his problems. She tossed him a dime and said, 'Happy birthday. Have coffee on me". The next day as he approached her she asked, "Did you enjoy your coffee?" He answered that he had and asked her name. "Julia", she answered. "What's yours?" "Bill" was all he said and walked away. A few days later Julia was to find out his name was not Bill but was George. They struck up a friendship and two weeks later they were married. Julia became Mrs. George Thompson. George never would know the entire secret Julia bottled up inside herself as they settled into married life.

Julia and George were married two years before their first daughter arrived. They had met two dear friends named Elna and Lou Holding. Julia named her beautiful blue eyed daughter Elna Lou. Elna was a perfect baby, but holding her made her pain surface. Julia remembered holding her first daughter and looking into her big brown eyes and once again felt all the fears and pains. I won't think about Dovie today I have to trust in God that she is being loved and cared for. This thought will keep me sane, she reminded herself. At this time little Elna opened her mouth and screwed up her pink face and whimpered a cry like a kitten. Julia's attention was once again returned to her new infant daughter and as she looked into Elna's eyes she decided to love her more that any mother had ever loved a child. As Elna blinked at her she said', I will love you for all your life and nothing can ever take you away from me." Elna was a good baby but Julia felt disconnected from the tiny little girl. She provided all her needs, or so she thought but when it became time to hold her and to snuggle her as a loving mom Julia had a problem with this area of motherhood. Her marriage was far from being a fairy tale because George had a problem with too much drinking and he himself was very cold to her and the child. He loved Elna, and the little girl just worshipped her daddy but underneath George was filled with pain himself and returning physical love was something he could never do. When Elna was two and a half years old Julia once again became pregnant with her second daughter. George became irate over the news of another child. We can't afford the one we have let alone another one," he yelled at Julia. "What are you thinking woman?" Julia had just returned from picking Elna up from Elna Holding's house. Julia had taken full time job as a waitress out of necessity and Elna had offered to watch her baby while Julia worked. "I didn't plan to get pregnant it just happened," Julia cried. George grabbed his hat and stormed out the door. Julia wondered if her life would ever be happy and as this thought ran through her head Elna toddled over and put her chubby hand on Julia's and said I love you mommy. Julia did not answer but lit up a cigarette, sipped her coffee and said to her small child, "Go play.

Julia was give a due date of December 25 for her and George's second child. Christmas day ran through her head as she shopped for a new doll with a wicker carriage for Elna. She will love this doll and carriage for Christmas, she thought, she is such a little mother to her dolls. Her unborn baby kicked and she felt her stomach. Not much longer, she whispered, just a couple more days and I will see my new baby's face. She walked home with her presents only to find George sleeping on the couch while little Elna played in front of the small Christmas tree. She had found a bargain when she bought that tree, it was only a $ 1.00 and it fit just right on a table so Elna could not topple it over. She thanked God Elna was a good child otherwise when she had to leave her with George she would worry because she knew he would fall asleep while she was gone. As she walked up to the bedroom she felt her water break. She felt scared but she had asked George's sister Katy to watch Elna while she went to the hospital so this she knew was taken care of. George would have to help get Elna to Katy's and then take her to the hospital. I will change my clothes before I go, she thought. As she started to remove her clothes she noticed that the water she thought had broken was a bright red. Julia screamed for George as she saw a pool of blood form at her feet. When she arrived at the hospital her hips were elevated in order to stop the hemorrhaging, and she was told that the placenta was presenting first, and the infant was not going to survive. Doctor Houston told George, "I have lost hope for the infant as I have no heart beat but we will do our best to save Julia". On January 3, 1948 at 5:58 a.m. her third new little girl finally emerged covered in blood and hidden from view from Julia. "Is she all right?" Julia frantically pleaded. The baby gave no sign of life and was placed on a table while the Doctor and nurses tended to Julia. A whimper was heard and the nurse wiped the blood from the new, tiny little girl and said," lets hear those cries little one you're just fine." The first time this new daughter was placed in her arms she once again was reminded of a baby she had once conceived in love. Julia thought, another girl, and I was hoping for a boy so I could name him Robert. Her first visitor at the hospital was a friend that Julia had met at work. Her name was Madge Gilmartin. "I was just at the nursery and saw that beautiful little girl, she exclaimed, she has the biggest blue eyes. You have another perfect little girl, how do you feel?' Julia answered with a smile and told Madge she felt fine but really tired. "I brought her a pink sweater with booties. Aren't these cute? Madge held up the little sweater with matching booties and Julia answered that yes they were real sweet and thanked her for the gift. "Madge what is your middle name." Julia asked. "My middle name is Lyn", Madge answered. Julia said," I would like to name the baby Madgelyn if it is alright with you. George wants me to name her Kathleen but I can use that for a middle name." How does it sound to you? Madgelyn Kathleen Thompson". "Oh I am flattered," Madge gushed," I think that name sounds like a handle but I am sure she can handle it." So Madgelyn it was. Madgelyn was also a quiet baby and her big sister adored her. Elna would tip toe quietly to the side of the crib, push her cherub face into the rails and stare for long times at her sleeping new sister. Madgelyn was less than a year old when once again Julia was pregnant with Frances her third daughter, and yet within another year her son George was conceived. Each time she became pregnant George would drink and become angry. He never hit her but he was always mentally abusive. She was afraid to tell him each time she realized she was carrying another child because his wrath was frightening. When her son was placed in her arms she gasped as she examined his small fragile pink body. Directly at his base of his spine she saw a birth mark in the shape of an upside down eagle. The tears welled up in her eyes as she remembered this same shaped birth mark on little Dovie's spine. She wondered if this was a sign from God that they had killed her precious infant." I guess I will never find her now", she cried, as she held her small bundle wrapped in blue.

The world of Elna and Madgelyn became was a magical world as these two little girls bonded. When Madgelyn started to talk she looked at Elna and said', "Hi Nonu". They knew from the start that they were bound at the heart with a bind that went back in time many years ago. This was not an apparent thought but a subconscious's one that would surface well into their adult years. When they were two and five they stood one night out under the stars, holding hands and Elna said, "How high is the sky?" Madgelyn would answer in her two year old wisdom, "very, very high". Then Elna would ask," How deep is the ocean?" The reply was." Very, very deep." Then they would stand with arms around each other and marvel at all the stars in the vast night sky.

As the years progressed Elna and Madgelyn went about the task of caring for the younger siblings while Julia worked. Their summers were taken by cleaning and babysitting. George, their father became like a non-entity in the house. When he wasn't working he was sleeping so his interaction with the family was close to non-existence. He had given up drinking and for this Julia was grateful. The children became a close knit group and would care for each other when the parents were away. Saturdays was always a treat because they all knew that this was store day. When Julia and George came home there would be candy for each of them. They all worked together to have the house clean before Julia arrived. If the house was not clean they would hear about it in the most unpleasant scolding. This was more so for Elna and Madgelyn because she expected more from them as they were the eldest. In 1956 when Madgelyn was eight Elna was eleven Julia gave birth to her second son Mark Raymond then two years later another daughter. Crystal Dawn. The two eldest girls were busier than ever going to school and watching siblings in the evening. Both parents worked from three to eleven so these two girls pretty much "became little adults.

Julia always had a deep spiritual faith in God. On one occasion there was neither money nor food to feed her family. She fell to her knees and prayed. No sooner had she uttered her prayer there came a knock on the door. It was a neighbor with fresh meat. "We just butchered and you came to mind", he said." Would you like to have some of our beef? I just thought that you and your family could use it." Julia thanked him as she graciously took his gift but most of all she thanked God.

It was a pattern for Julia and George to move frequently. Their children were always entering a new school with new surroundings. This played havoc on the children as they could not make friends that lasted. Each child retreated into a world that was filled with ghosts, haunted houses and spirit communication as a norm.

Madgelyn /**Maggie**

I was a petite little girl with extremely bowed legs. One day Julia noticed me at the age of three eating plaster. I had taken a spoon and created a hole in the wall. Julia took me to the doctor and he told her that children were like animals when their system needed a certain mineral they would seek it out. Julia allowed me to eat the plaster on doctor's orders. He assured her that when my body had its fill then I would stop. I ate plaster until I was four and one day I guess" I got my fill" and just quit. I was the type of child that had to explore everything and daily I got my back side as well as my front side beat. One of my earliest memories was that George was watching me and my siblings and once again I was in line for my daily whipping. Julia used to say that she had to beat me for just getting out of bed in the morning. I didn't think I was ever in need of my daily beatings but she was mom so it must be true, I was bad little girl. Oh, I had good reasons for my actions but I was not allowed to talk about reasons. Julia's word was law and it was never to be questioned. Anyway back to my beating on hand. George took a switch from the tree and switched my legs until they were streaked. I thought, as he was switching, that I would never walk again. After he had satisfactorily completed his task I refused to stand on my feet for the rest of the day. I saw that he was scared and kept trying to soothe me as he tried to help me walk. When Julia arrived home from work he said, "I am afraid that I have damaged Madgelyn's legs. I have tried to stand her up and she falls ". We should see if we can get her to a doctor as her legs are so bowed anyway perhaps I have damaged them". I was glad to see mom and it felt good that she was concerned about me. I held up my arms to her and she asked if I would like some candy that she had in the kitchen. Candy through the week was a treat so I jumped off the couch forgetting my injury's and it became apparent that I was not hurt. Needless to say this brought on another whipping and no candy. Yes, I figured that I was a bad little girl in need of my daily beatings. It was at this house when I was four I saw my first apparition. Frances and I were playing in our bedroom upstairs when we both noticed a movement on the wall. As we watched we saw the shadow of an old woman sitting in a rocking chair. It was a side view of a woman with her hair piled on top of her head in a bun. We watched it for a while and it just faded away. I later learned that my great grandmother wore her hair in a bun When my family moved we always moved, it seemed, to a house that was worse than the previous one. We had no indoor plumbing, no heat other than an old black coal stove in the living room and a big black cook stove that choked on wood we children had to gather. It was in the early fifties but we lived like it was the eighteen hundreds. The first move I remember was to an unpainted shabby house in the country. It was small but we were children and it seemed quite adequate. In the front yard was a large rock and many a day I skinned my knee climbing that huge rock. I have since visited this rock as an adult and it is as high as my knees. I am always surprised each time I see it and notice that it is so small. The main feature of this house other than the huge rock was a climbing tree in the back yard, Julia loved the purple roses in front but my love was the climbing tree. In the spring you could get lost in the many apple blossoms that covered this tree and I would sit for long lengths of time just being me. I needed to get away at times from baby sitting and chores. So in the summer I would climb the 'ol apple tree or sit on the rock and just think.

It was the summer I was five when I learned that I had something that would get me change for my piggy bank. Dad had a friend named Monroe that liked me a lot. When I say a lot I mean in the manner that men shouldn't like little girls. I was given nickels and dimes after he touched me in places that were not to be touched by anyone other than myself. I would endure this without crying out because he would offer money for my favors. I always had money in my piggy bank that Julia and George never questioned. Monroe said," If your mom knows she would really know that you are bad and she would be very upset with you". I never told her about this until I was well into my adult years. I could tell by the look in her eyes that even then after many years had passed, she would kill him if she could. I knew this deep inside as a child of what she could be capable of and this alone made me keep the secret to myself.

One Sunday afternoon a knock sounded upon the door. Mom answered and standing there was a man with his hat in his hand. He said, "Maam I am collecting money for my sick child could you help?". I listened and followed as he walked us over to see the handicapped little girl in his big blue station wagon. I didn't feel right as I gazed upon this small handicapped child. She was sleeping in the back on a blanket. I didn't want to give this man my money even though I saw that the child was very ill. Julia said, "All I have is some change I will ask the children if they would like to give some from their piggy banks." Mom asked me, "Madgelyn do you have any money in your piggy bank that you could share with this man?" I answered, "No" and I put up quite a protest against helping him. Mom said, "Well, 1 didn't realize that you were such a selfish child. If you feel right about not helping this man with this poor dear sick child then you just keep your money." I felt guilty but for some reason I knew this was not the right thing to do. The next evening as we sat down to supper dad said," Wasn't there a man with a sick child that that stopped here yesterday?" We all answered "yes" Mom shot me a mean look and I felt guilty all over again. Dad said, "It seems that this man was written about in the paper. It read that he was using his sick child to collect money for to further his drinking habit. He was picked up by the authorities and arrested". I felt really good about my feelings that something was not right and that I had held out on giving my money to this crook. This was my first knowledge that I had an unusual knack of knowing things sometimes even before they happened. I often wondered why Mom had never questioned the reason I had money in my piggy bank I guess she just didn't notice.

We moved the summer I was six to a house in Cable Ohio. We were not in this house long because of the strange happenings. The odd thing about this house was that there was a window visible from the outside that went into a room. When you were inside the house there was no access to this room Dad climbed a ladder and entered this window he found himself in an unfinished room that was completely sealed off from the rest of the house. One night the family was awakened by two blood curdling screams. It was coming from the stairway and those screams made the hairs stand up on the back of our necks. This happened twice and soon after we moved back into the same country house we had just moved from. The old unpainted house was familiar but uncomfortable in the cold winter months. The water Pump was down a hill in the back and water had to be carried in buckets. It was often mine and Elna's job to carry water in two galvanized heavy buckets. The buckets sat in the kitchen with a dipper in it and this was our drinking water. In the winter it froze so the ice would have to be broken off the top before you could get a drink. We had no heat other than a big black stove in the living room. If one of the other kids stood in front of you, you were blocked from the heat. Blankets covered the doors as well as some windows. The kitchen was warm when there was cooking going on due to the big black iron stove we cooked on. The wood had to be gathered to fuel the cook stove as well as the living room stove. We would bundle up in many layers of clothes and go to the woods to bring back firewood. I have memories of snow forming little pyramids in the floor after a freezing cold night. The snow would come in the bottom of the window and form little mounds on the floor. The out house was a brave venture in itself just to wade through the drifts and find the door drifted shut.

In the summer though the house was a comfortable place to be when the apple blossoms and roses bloomed.

About a mile up the road was a little Friends church. Every Sunday Elna and I would walk to church. I loved church and I would look forward to Sunday's services. Each time there was an alter call I would get out of my seat and feeling really bad about my self I would fall to my knees to be saved. I would cry and honestly feel better after these cleansings. It was at the age of seven that I dedicated my life to God.

I was told so often as to how bad I was I thought I needed to go to the altar each time the service was offered. I felt that it helped and then Monroe would visit and I was bad all over again. It seemed like I would never tire of going to church. We attended weekend camp outings and Bible school. I loved it most of all. I would sit and listen to Pastor Turner and just marvel at his knowledge of the scriptures. I would go home and look at the pictures in our big Bible and try to read the stories. It was while we were living in this house was when I had a very personal phenomena.

One moonlit night as I was in my bed I heard a sound of blowing wind and had a vision of sand. As I held up my hands I noticed that they were falling into holes right before my very eyes. "Mom, Mom," I screamed. When she came in the room my hands were normal. "My hands are falling into holes." I cried. "Your hands are fine, now just go to sleep." was her reply. This happened several nights and each time when Mom entered the room my hands were once again normal. I was confused but never frightened enough that it had made an impact on me. The moon was shinning particularly bright one night when I was awakened by an unusual sound. It was in the early morning hours and I climbed out of my bed to look out the window. We were in the country with fields surrounding us. To the side of the house was a large field and out in the field I saw a large plate shaped object hovering above the ground. I looked with amazement and wondered how the little spindly legs could support that big of an object. The legs were red and no wider than hairs holding it up. Later I was to learn that these were laser lights, but at this time in my life I had never heard of flying crafts or laser lights. As I watched it, it just disappeared and I never experienced it again. After this my hands wouldn't fall into holes even if I tried to recreate it. I often tried to tell Mom of my night time vision but I was quickly ignored and was told to take baby Mark outside and to watch him.

One early morning in the warm summer I was sitting in the swaying branches of the apple tree holding a small kitten. I was listening to the breeze as it blew through the green leaves. I heard a mournful sound that frightened me. I climbed down from the tree and ran into the house to see if everyone was alright. I felt silly checking on everyone and I didn't understand why the cry of this bird frightened me. Later I learned that this was the cry of a mourning dove. Many times since I have heard this mournful cry and each time I feel fear and want to freeze in my place.

I started school and soon discovered that the other children did not understand me when I spoke of my experiences and thoughts. I still have a second grade card where Mrs. Klamfoth wrote, "Madgelyn has a very vivid imagination and if she uses it she will go far." I gave up trying to talk to my teachers and class mates about my unusual experiences.

When I was ten we moved again to a big nine room farm house outside of Mingo Ohio. This was our first big dealings with a bona fide haunted house. The house was eerie as it sat on an embankment back a long drive. Once again, it had no modern facilities. We still had to go to the out house, gather wood from the woods across the road, and try to stay warm during winter months. In the summer the front yard was beautiful with trees and underbrush that hid the house from the road. Even though the house was lovely it held spirits that were active with the knowledge that their world still exited. Many of the encounters were of restless spirits of children.

One night as Julia was preparing for bed she heard small feet hit the upstairs floor, run across the room and then she heard a giggle. "Get back into bed." she called up the stairs. Just as she climbed into bed once again she heard the small feet and heard the same laughter from a child. I will bet that Madgelyn is up, she thought. She looked at the clock, and saw that it was 1:00 A.M. She climbed the stairs with switch in hand and to her surprise found that every one of her children were sleeping just as she had found them earlier when she had made her nightly bed check. Not one child had moved from the place where she had last seen them. She went back down stairs and never gave this a serious thought as though this was a normal thing to do. She told me and the others of this experience and as children we were intrigued with the idea of ghosts. The ghostly children were making their presence known frequently. When you would go up stairs you often caught a glimpse of a shadow running in the hallway or into a room. There was one room that we would not stay in so the beds were moved into another room and this cold room stayed vacant. In the winter lines were strewn across it to hang clothes to dry. We didn't like to venture in this room because it felt as though you were being watched the entire time you were in there. Even in the summer it was a cold room.

A cousin visited one weekend with her small two year old child Jackie. Jackie seemed to be terrified during his entire visit. He wouldn't leave his mother's side and when it was time to go to bed he stiffened out, screamed and pointed at something. His mother couldn't calm him down and no one could see anything that he was pointing at. He just kept saying. "See? See?" He fell to sleep in his mother's arms but we never knew of what he had seen that frightened him to the point of such a fit. My cousin vowed that she would never visit us again as long as we lived in this house. Once again, we, for some reason, took it in stride. *The* winter winds were blowing and drifting snow was piling up around doorways. The kitchen door leading to the outside would not stay shut so Julia placed a knife in the woodwork to act as a lock. As we were sitting around the television we heard a loud ping and a door slam. Over the door to the kitchen was hung a heavy blanket and it was blowing with the wind. In the kitchen the outside door was open and there was no sign of the knife that had been holding it. This knife was never found and many times after that knifes would fly out of the door frame. It was a very busy house.

It was especially cold one day when we children had to go across the road to gather firewood. Frances had no heavy winter clothes so she had to wear Dad's pants, coat and boots. As she was complaining we walked out the door into the cold air. Frances offered up one more plea saying,"I don't feel right!" Julia's reply was "You don't look right either. God Dammit! Go get some fire wood!" This struck our funny bones and to this day we laugh as we think about four little children carrying huge fallen tree limbs across the cold snow. Our little hands and feet would be so cold but we could laugh.

Another incident we encountered was during one night in the winter. It was seldom that we felt fear from the strange happenings but we sometimes did. Elna and I had bundled in one bed to keep warm. I was awakened by a noise that sounded like a rocking chair just rocking away. I woke Elna for bravery but we were both afraid to venture into the empty room to see what the sound was. It rocked for a long time then it just stopped. We went back to sleep holding on to each other. When morning arrived we opened the door to the cold empty room and there sat an old rocking chair. We saw the rocking chair but we couldn't figure out how it had been rocking because there was an old mattress laying over it and pieces of a bed had been placed upon the mattress. We never figured out how that rocking chair had rocked so vigorously. We had a beautiful yellow cat that would hiss and arch his back at something each time he would venture into the house. On one occasion dad tried to remove the cat from the house as it had seemed as if the cat had lost its mind. It was running and screeching as it jumped on the hot cooking stove in order to escape something. As dad grabbed for the cat it leaped at dad with claws exposed and wrapped itself around dad's neck. It was quite a struggle removing the cat from the house without injury to dad or the cat. We never knew what frightened the cat.

Elna was a sleepwalker and many times when mom would try to enter our bedroom in the morning the door would be blocked with furniture. It was not just chairs but dressers placed on top of one another blocking the doorway. Mom just figured that it was Elna walking in her sleep. I wondered how in the hell Elna could lift huge dressers but you didn't question mom's word.

We thought this was a normal way to live so it seldom frightened us. In fact it intrigued us in the manner to seek out our own true mystical experiences. Monroe had quit visiting us and I didn't miss him nor ask where he had gone.

In the summer months each year I would stay a week and sometime two with my Aunt May and uncle Earl who lived in Southern Ohio. Each summer they would visit and take me back with them. I loved to stay with Aunt May but I had to be on my toes around Uncle Earl. He would always take the opportunity when we were alone to touch and kiss me. I would not allow him to go any further than touching me in the places where I was used to being touched by Monroe. As usual I took advantage of this and would use these times to put money in my bank. Aunt May never suspected him of this and I never told her. She was a devout Pentecostal and she lived her religion. I attended nightly revivals with her when I would visit. I loved the services and looked forward to each one. I would drink in the smell of the green grass under the musky smell of the tent each night as I would join others in song and prayer. The energy was so high in that you could see colors of energy around everyone. I asked, "Did you see the color around sister Avandale tonight?" My aunt would tell me that that probably was her halo that I was seeing. Sister Avondale was a singing prophet and I was intrigued with her gift. A singing prophet is one who sings Christian blue grass, in her case, and as she plays her guitar she tells others messages in song of upcoming events. I was eleven or twelve when I started seeing colors around some people especially at Aunt May's church. I loved it

When I was thirteen I quit spending weeks with Aunt May. She had gone to bed early and I was watching the late show on Television. Uncle Earl came in the room fully exposed and tried to rape me. I fought him off and vowed never again would I visit my dearly loved Aunt. I missed her as much as I missed her church.

It was this same year we moved from the big country house. We moved into the town of Urbana to a house that had indoor plumbing. It was tall two story house made of brick. Once again it was pretty worn down and shabby but it had a bath tub and a commode that even flushed. I was elated as we all were over indoor plumbing. Elna and I were allowed to obtain baby sitting jobs on weekends. When mom was home with her children we could watch other children and earn spending money. Mom's friend Beryle owned a restaurant which mom had worked in for many years. When I was thirteen I was allowed to work full time in the summer and after school during the winter. I now had money from an honest source, I thought. From this time on I would buy all my own clothes and school supplies. I was happy to do this as I felt it took a burden off mom. She was carrying burdens I knew nothing about but I knew they always were just under the surface. I never saw mom and dad fight but I knew there was a tension between them. Mom lived angry but we as children never knew the source of the rage. We walked on eggs with the fear that at any minute one of us would be the brunt of her anger. I needed to return a book that was due at the library. Mom said,

"Take back George's and Frances's books also." I tried to explain that their books were not due, and that they were still reading them. "Take them back," was her only response. "But mom they will get mad at me, they are still reading them, "I pleaded. At this response she leapt off the couch, grabbed me by the hair and slung me into the wall. I took the books back only to know I would have to face my sister and brother as the bad guy. They were not allowed to go to the library to retrieve their books to finish reading them. I knew I was not allowed to talk back but on many occasions. I tried to explain things without trying to sound as if I was arguing with her. Many times she would follow me when I left the house. She was behind me watching to make sure that I was not meeting boys or going some place that was different than where I was supposed to be going. This always upset me and it would end up in a fight with her winning.

Elna had a habit of scratching when she would find herself in a conflict with one of her siblings. She could grow beautiful nails that I envied. My nails and hair were always brittle and thin. Elna had thick hair and beautiful nails. Her nails were a pride and she took care of them as well as a professional manicurist would. I cringed when one of the younger children complained that Elna had scratched them. I knew that mom would become very angry and I would wish that she take it out on me rather than one of the other children. I felt so bad when I saw her clip off every one of Elna's beautiful nails because she had scratched her younger sibling. They grew back but this left a scratch on young Elna's heart.

When I was grown Mom told me that many times dad would say to her, "Well, I guess it's about time to tell these kids about that first baby. They should know what kind of slut their mother is." Julia would cry, fall to her knees and plead. "Please George don't tell them. I don't want my kids to know, they would not love me any more." He never knew the complete story, that baby Dovie was a black child. If he had known this, she felt that he could have done unspeakable things to her. This was a fear she held their entire twenty five years together

I worked summers at the restaurant as did Elna. On Sundays and Wednesday nights I attended church. We attended a Spiritualist church in Springfield Ohio. It was held in the basement of a medium's house. Mrs. Vansike was a large woman with an even larger gift of mediumship. It was at this church I first met Reverend Boyd. He was a small black man with a tremendous talent of mediumship and prophesy. He looked right at me and said, "You have the very same gift I have and with it you will reach many people in your life." I said to myself, "Oh sure, I could never demonstrate the gift of prophesy as he does." Later when Mrs. Vansike passed on Reverend Boyd acquired her church. He moved it to a small store front building on Main Street in Springfield Ohio. I was fifteen when I was put in front of a congregation and sure enough I heard my spirit guides giving me information that was as accurate as Reverend Boyd's. I became one of the mediums in his church and I loved each moment of it. I knew how to help others as well as being able to reach beyond the veil to bring messages from loved ones.

I was attending school, working at the restaurant, and writing sermons along side my home work.

I was a teenager, fifteen, living in the 60's and the strife of racial issues was running rampant was my sophomore year and my friend Pam and I had stayed after a fall school game in order to attend a Friday night dance. The tension was high as the black students gathered on one side of the gym and the white students on the other side. This seemed normal as they always gathered this way but for some reason the air held a friction. I saw nothing out of the order as I was used to seeing the students on opposite sides of the gym at such functions. Even the local theatre and the skating rink were segregated. I couldn't skate on some nights because it was designated "colored" night.

Pam and I were talking and enjoying ourselves. We tried to avoid standing in the stag line we stood close by to it, just in case. I said, "Do you see that tall black guy looking over here at me?" Pam looked and said, "I think he is trying to catch your eye just don't look over there." As she said this the tall handsome man walked toward us. He looked back at his friends and they urged him on. It appeared to me as if they were up to no good. "He held out his hand to me and said "May I have this dance?" My heart started beating like a jackhammer as I started to tell him no. As I held my head down I heard a wee small voice say. "Do it now!" I took his hand and walked toward the dance floor with him. Everyone became quiet but continued to dance as the music played. I couldn't look at him nor raise my head up to see if everyone was looking at us but I knew they were. I danced the entire dance with him without either one of us saying a word to each other. He escorted me back to my friends' side after the dance and he walked back over to his friends as they cheered. I was mortified as I said to Pam. "Lets get out of here I will never be able to show my face again in this school." At fifteen your life was based on what your peers expected from you, not from what was in your heart. I cried the entire walk home as Pam tried to comfort me.

Monday morning I dreaded going to school. To my surprise no one ever mentioned the incident to me and my school life went on as normal. Later in life I was told by my counsel of guides that this was a crucial moment. The group was not from the school and they were there to start a riot. If I had refused to dance with the young man all hell would have broken out.

Because I had listened to my guides and had responded as they requested I had prevented a riot that some would have been gravely hurt. I've often asked myself, "Why me? Why did he pick me?"

The house was quiet and it seemed as if the haunting had not followed us to our new house. Mom, Dad and I were attending classes with Reverend Boyd. We were learning how to develop our clairvoyant abilities as well as our own true spiritual selves. We would often set around the table and practice automatic writing and learn to communicate with our spirit guides. I always say when other children were playing board games we were practicing automatic writing. It was discovered at this early stage that every one of George and Julia's children had been born with a special spiritual gift of insight.

Elna graduated and soon after married Ed. The rest of the family once again moved. I was seventeen when this move took me to a new school and again to another busy house.

There was a lot of friction due to the fact that George had decided to join the Navy upon graduation. This news set George Senior into a rage. "No son of mine is joining the Navy," he shouted. George couldn't understand the anger his father was experiencing but this did not sway him from his decision. In fact this only made him more determined. George Senior was being reminded of the loss of his brother John, and he was dead set against his son going down the same path.

The brick house was in the country and it set back a long lane. It was heated by coal and everything was covered with coal dust. It seemed that there was no end to the black dust.

We, as a family, were still communicating with our spirit guides and would sit around a card table in meditation. We would ask our guides questions and the spirits would knock on or tip the table in response. One particular evening George made a comment in fun about how stupid this was. To our amazement the table immediately jerked and rapidly moved across the room pinning George against the wall. We learned though this experience that this was not an issue to be taken lightly nor anything to play with. It was serious business as we were in intensive training with our guides for our own spiritual development.

The house offered many strange experiences. On arriving home from school I discovered Dad was angry with me. "Don't come into my room in the morning before school and comb your hair in front of the dresser mirror," he was saying." And why did you have on a white uniform?" he asked. I tried to tell him that I was not in his room combing my hair and that I did not have on a white uniform" In fact I was on my way to school, 1 explained, why would I have on a white uniform?" He would not listen to me and mom entered the conversation. "George, think about it, she gets up before day light. If she did indeed stand before the dresser mirror how could she see to comb her hair in a dark bed room?" "Well, some one was combing their hair in front of the mirror this morning, she woke me up". Dad replied. We never knew who he saw and this happened on several dark mornings.

As we had retired to our beds we were startled to hear a loud noise coming from the downstairs area. It sounded like ripping cloth or the ripping of window blinds. Usually there was never fear with these experiences, but this time it frightened me as well as the others. Frances got up and went to the head of the stairs. As she arrived there she saw mom standing at the foot of the staircase. "What is that loud noise up there?" she called. Frances said. "It is coming from downstairs." and as she started down the stairs the noise grew louder and louder. By now was sounding as if it was projected through a microphone. As mom started up the stairs something ran past her brushed by her legs, as well as Frances's, and went into an empty room to the left of the stairwell. The noise ceased and we never knew what passed them on the stairs or what had made such a loud noise.

We lived in this house until I graduated from high school. The year I was seventeen I met Daniel. I was working in the restaurant when I looked up to see the most beautiful man that I had ever seen enter the restaurant. He was gorgeous and to top it off he wore a deputy sheriff's uniform. I will marry that man, 1 thought, but he is so beautiful he would never look at me. I was a trim petite young woman weighing only one hundred twelve pounds but I thought I was fat and homely. As he sat down I was all a flutter but I put on my brightest smile and took his order. He was shy and I didn't think he had even noticed me. Each evening Daniel would come in for supper and each evening I would flirt. I asked him if he could give me a ride home and from then on we became an item. Mom and dad had a big argument over the fact that Daniel was twenty seven and I was only seventeen. We were in love and to us age was not an issue. Graduation came and I was concerned that I needed a career but I saw no means to go to college. I wanted to teach but I saw no way to obtain an education. I was in Springfield riding around with my best friend Patty when I heard my spirit guide say, "Go to a beauty school and sign up for classes". I had never entertained thoughts of hair styling and as a matter of fact I was not the least bit interested in it. Never the less I entered the school and ask for information. I discovered that in order to begin classes I would need fifty dollars to sign up and then it required twenty dollars a week to attend. I didn't have fifty dollars saved so I told my spirit guide if I was handed fifty dollars I would start beauty school. As I arrived home I discovered a graduation card from my grandmother with a fifty dollar bill inside. Mom's friend Beryl told me that if I could work evenings at the restaurant after beauty school and on weekends I would be able to earn more than twenty dollars a week. I went back to Springfield and signed up for beauty school, I didn't want this as a career but it would do. At least it was a career. I put myself through beauty school and soon after completion of this nine month course Daniel and I were married in 1967. We had been dating for three years and we were both sure that this was a correct move.

I had obtained employment in The Beauty Nook a small salon in Urbana. I was talking to the owner and said," I will buy your salon within a year. "She replied, "Oh sure you will, I have no intentions of selling so how are you going to buy my salon?" "I don't know how I just know I will," I replied. I worked and enjoyed my new lifestyle of a married woman. I discovered that in a few short months after talking to my employer she decided to sell her salon. I made an appointment with my bank and shortly after I found myself a business owner with employees. I was twenty three years old and a business woman. I joined Business and Professional woman's club, a garden club and I was enjoying my life.

I was still working as a medium and by now I was teaching classes. I was teaching others how to get to know their spirit guides as well as awakening to their own spiritual potentials. As I was studying my Bible one evening Daniel noticed that I had written all over the pages. He said, "Why don't you get a loose leaf Bible or better yet write your own." These words hit me with a bang. Ever since then I have been working on a book called The Bible 2000. This is an esoteric interpretation of each scripture. I started to incorporate these teaching to my own understanding of scripture and it has been widely accepted by many students.

I discovered in the fall of 1969 I was going to have a baby. I was excited and started to buy baby items with a passion. In March of 1970 I gave birth to the most beautiful little girl that I had ever seen. We bonded immediately and became fast friends. Daniel wanted to name this pink, blue eyed bundle Natalee. I felt a sharp tinge in my heart when I thought of naming her Natalee. I couldn't do it so we settled on the name of Jennifer.

When Jennifer was three weeks old Daniel answered the phone and received bad news. My father George had died. He had been ill for several weeks but I thought that he would soon be just fine. He had turned the color of mustard and mom had persuaded him to enter the hospital. He had cancer of the liver and mom had been with him when he took his final breath. She told me that when he died he reached out his hand and closed it as if someone had received his grasp.

He died not knowing that his eldest son and namesake had joined the Navy. My brother George made the navy his career. It was a frightful experience for George during his first months as a seaman. He had a tremendous fear of drowning and often he would have to correct people when they called him John. People couldn't understand why they felt the urge to call him John they just did. George Sr. died never knowing that he had shared the remainder of his life loving the dear brother he had mourned for many years. He never discovered that his son was the reincarnation of his dear lost brother. George completed serving his country retiring as a chief with honors. He conquered his fear of the water early in his career and his father would have been so very proud of his dear son.

Julia found herself a widow at the age of forty six with two young children to provide for. George had no savings but he at least had enough insurance from his factory employment. Julia used the least amount of this money and paid for his funeral. She had just enough money left to put a down payment on a house. This was her first opportunity to own a home and she was proud of it. She continued to work at the restaurant but this took a toll on her health. She learned that she had diabetes and this made her extremely tired. Within a few short years she met and married Richard. Three years into the marriage she once again had to attend a funeral. This time for her second husband.

Jennifer was three when Daniel's father Frank gave us two acres of land to build our dream house on. We needed to tear down an old house on the land in order to build ours. In this old house I discovered an antique love seat. It was in much need of repair and the springs were tied with an old rope. I wanted to keep the love seat so I placed it in the barn for safe keeping. A few days later I enter the barn to find that the love seat was gone. Someone had claimed it for their very own, and had stolen it. The very next day as I am driving to work I hear a small voice that tells me to stop at a garage sale just ahead. I stop and walk straight to the love seat that bears a strong resemblance to the one that I had in my barn. "That love seat is not for sale," The lady barks at me. "Where did you get it, I asked." My husband got it somewhere, 1 am going to refinish it", she says. "Well", I reply," Can I have your husband's name? Perhaps I can call him and persuade him to sell it to me". She gave me her husbands name and I went straight to the sheriffs department to talk to Daniel, as he was already at work. I gave him the information and he took it from there. That evening he came home with the love seat hanging out of the trunk of the car. "Oh wow", I cried "how did you get it back?" Daniel said as he puffed out his chest, "I looked the man up, questioned him as to where he got the love seat and he told me that he had "found" it in an old barn. If no charges were pressed he would turn it back over. You can see that he turned it over to me and here it is." I was very excited. I was learning to listen to my spirit guides and was impressed that I had been directed to the garage sale.

Jennifer was having her own experiences with her guides. It was the year she was three when she called me into her bed room. "See up there on the ceiling mom? Do you see those people talking to me?" I looked and did not see anything. "No baby, what do you see describe the people to me" I said. "I see ideas." was her answer. "Ideas?" I asked. "Yes, you know when you read the funny papers and the people's words are in a little bubble?" She explained. "Well, that is what I see. But I don't see words, I see people talking to me". I then knew what she was seeing and I understood that my daughter had been blessed with the same abilities that I possessed. That night we had a long talk about guides, angels and her abilities. This was not new to her as she had been standing in front of the church with me from the time she was able to walk. She would hold on to my leg and peer out into the congregation while I presented my sermons and demonstrated my gift of prophecy with mediumship.

We had decided to build another beauty salon attached to our new home. This way I could work at home and be near the baby as well as still have the salon in town. I was so busy working with my business which now employed five hairstylists, building a house, and running after a very active toddler. I was helping to move furniture into our newly completed home when I told Daniel I needed to rest because I felt nauseous. "Eat a few soda crackers," Daniel replied. "This will settle you stomach." "I sure don't need the flu now, "I exclaimed. "I have so much work to do." Daniel smiled and said. "Oh I don't think it's the flu. If it is it should last about nine months." I sat down hard with my head spinning. "Oh my God," I said I never thought of that". I had been so busy that I hadn't even noticed that I had missed my period. Our second child was on the way and Daniel said, "This one is my boy."

June 12, 1973 I gave birth to our son. I wanted to name him Matthew. Daniel said, "Everytime I say his name, I will have a vision of 'OL Chester from the Matt Dillion T.V show, in which they called out Matthoo" We settled on Jeffery Daniel and he was perfect. As I was holding him after nursing one evening I told him that I was glad he had chosen me to be his mother. I would try my best to offer him the best that I could and that I would always be there. As he slept in my arms I just figured that I was just talking to a sleeping new born and I expected no response. As I had just completed my words of endearment he opened his big blue eyes looked straight into mine and broke into the biggest smile I had ever seen. He then closed his eyes and went back to sleep. Many say that this is just an expression of gas but I knew different. When Jeffery was four years old he would look longingly at an old grain mill each time we passed it. The grain mill was boarded up and had sat abandoned for many years. "Please mom can we stop and see the mill?" he would ask. I would tell him that it was all boarded up and we couldn't go in it. Each time we would drive past it he pleaded with me to stop. "O.K Jeff." I said, if you can tell me what is in there we will stop and look at it." In his little boy wisdom that seemed to go way beyond his years he said," Well, when you go inside you step up two steps. There is a hole in the floor and this is where the train pulls up and we load the grain down through the hole." I took his little hand and walked toward the old grain mill. I had to remove a few loose boards to enter. When we walked into the mill I was surprised to find that it was just as Jeff had described. As I looked at his small face I saw complete confusion. He looked around and said, "What happened?" I said, "Well honey, its just old and when things like this gets old it runs down." Jeff walked to the other side of the room stepping over boards and debris. He looked up at me and said, "But Mom, how did it get so old so fast?" Later that day I was sharing this experience with Daniel he looked shocked. "What's wrong?" I asked. "That's weird", he said. My grandfather and I used to ride the grain wagon to that mill and I would always watch as the train pulled under the shaft and the grain would be loaded on the train." I realized that my son had also been born as intuitive as his sister. He now as a young blond man of thirty has spent the last three years with his beautiful wife rebuilding his grandfather's house. It sets on the very land that Jeff, once clothed in the flesh as his great grandfather, bought and farmed nearly one hundred years ago.

I was a young mother with two successful businesses and a new home, and life was good. There was a song that was popular that read I am the happiest girl in the whole U.S.A. I adopted this as my song because this it how I felt. I was unaware that I was going to make a leap that would change it all.

I was attending and working at Reverend Boyd's church on a regular basis. I was attending classes under the assistant minister Reverend Mason. Reverend Mason was in my view the most spiritual man I had ever met. I looked in awe of this handsome black man. I had never heard nor thought I would ever again hear anyone with as much knowledge as he spewed forth. Each week as we prayed and worshipped together, I would often have to be careful as to not allow my true feelings to surface about him. I would just be all a flutter when he was near by and I would have to remind myself that this was foolish. He after all was a man of God and I could not understand my feelings. I came to the conclusion that I knew that I was in love with Daniel so this had to be a God felt love that was very spiritual.

I was to be baptized on Easter Sunday. I was looking forward to this as I had decided that my life was to be a spiritual teacher and a minister. When I stood with Elna and Mom waiting for my turn to be led into the baptismal pool I watched Reverend Boyd and Reverend Mason baptize those before me. As I looked at Reverend Mason's feet in the water I drew in a breath in shock and surprise. I had never seen such beautiful feet on any one before. His dark skin seemed to glisten as if there was a glowing light emitting from them. "Do you see a light coming from Reverend Mason's feet?" I asked mom and Elna? "No", they answered. "Well' I do", I said. As he approached me and led me into the water I never knew at this time as I surrender to God, I was also at the same time surrending to this beautiful black man holding me under the water.

Later that summer when the phone rang it was Reverend Mason. "You have to go," he said. "If you don't go now the door will close and you will miss opportunities that you need to grow from." We were talking about a spiritualist camp in Indiana. This camp offers week long seminars which afford the student credits. These credits can be put toward certificates of mediumship as well as ordination. "I don't know. Rev. Mason, I am not sure if Elna can watch the children," I said. "I will ask. A week is an awful long time though. We'll see". I hung up the phone and felt sure that I needed to go to Camp. I called Elna right away and she agreed to watch Jennifer and Jeff. Daniel agreed to the idea that I needed classes and he was not opposed to me going.

The week I was to leave for camp arrived and I was really excited. I dropped the children off at Elna's and I was off. It was a two hour drive from home and I thoroughly enjoyed the little trip. I had been to this camp before but not to attend classes. In fact mom's family often visited this camp in the nineteen twenties and thirties. This was not a new place for me to go but it was new to me to leave home for an entire week since my marriage.

When I arrived I registered for classes and got settled into my hotel room. I wasn't there long until I saw Reverend Mason. He was himself attending classes but he also was teaching one. I was flattered that he had selected me from his class as the only one that he thought needed classes. I walked around the lush spiritual grounds and felt as if I had found the perfect place on God's green earth. I felt as though I had been elevated several levels above the material plane. I was on a natural high and I hoped that I would never come down.

The next morning I was eager to attend my class about numerology, and then the second class about Dreams. I was learning what I had known for many years but this time I was learning new angles to these arts plus I was earning credits. At noon as the students shared around their lunch in the cafeteria I was thrilled to meet many new friends of like mind. Reverend Mason came in and walked up to me. "I see you haven't bought your lunch yet", he said. "Would you like to go into town and have lunch with me? Of course I would I answered. We went into town and enjoyed our meal together. We talked about the classes, church and how someday I would be a minister and maybe be able to teach at Camp." This seemed like a dream that I could never obtain but I could hope.

"I have to pick up a book at my hotel room before we go back to camp", he said. "Oh, I thought you had a room on the camp. Where do you stay when you come here? I asked. "I get a room in a motel", he replied. "It's a more comfortable place than the primitive hotel at the camp". We laughed. "Yes I have to admit going down the hall to the bathroom wasn't very convenient but the other things the camp offered made up the difference." I explained. "Here we are". Reverend Mason said as we pulled into the motel parking lot. "I will wait in the car for you," I said. "No,come on inside it will only take me a minute and further more it's hot out here," he said. I followed him into the room and sat down on a chair by the front door. He flipped on the television and plopped on the bed. I drew my legs up under me in an Indian fashion and wondered how long we were going to watch television. I had no clue that this man of God could think in ungodly ways toward me so I felt safe with him in a motel room. I heard him whistle a low whistle and I looked over at him lying on the bed. He was smiling and beckoning with his finger to join him on the bed. I noticed that he had kicked his shoes off and I thought of his beautiful feet under his socks. When I looked at him again it looked like he blended with the rich mahogany of the bed. My heart thumped, he is so beautiful, I thought, I shook my head no and continued to stay in my chair with my feet drawn up under me. Feeling like a little girl and now unsure of Reverend Mason, he said "Come over here and rest with me". I felt like a zombie when I rose from my chair and joined him on the bed. I was now feeling a little uneasy but I trusted him. After all he was my minister. He kissed me. It was a light kiss and I still was clueless as to his intentions. I was so naive and trustful of him. He kissed me again, this time with a little bit more determination and then I understood his motives. "I can't do this, 1 am married", I told him. I had always tried to live by the Ten Commandments and this was a big no no in my book. Again I said "No, Reverend Mason I can't do this". He pinned me down on the bed and even before I could stop him it was over. I had sinned. "Oh my God I thought I have to tell Daniel and he will be mad, I am not worthy of him as a wife I have slept with another man. When Reverend Mason took me back to the camp he explained to me that because I was white and he was black this could never go any further than us. He had a congregation to think of and they wouldn't accept us. I was so confused. How could a man of God with all the answers do this? I felt as if my world had ended and I wanted to go home. I stayed the remainder of the week and enjoyed my classes. Whenever I would see Reverend Mason he would smile but seemed to stay away from me the rest of the week. I just thought it was because he needed to keep a certain image. He was going with Joan a very beautiful black woman and I figured he didn't want the news to reach her that he was in love with another woman. Me.

I arrived home after one full week of classes. Daniel was in the basement ironing a shirt when I approached him. I held up my certificate of completion that I had been awarded upon attending all six classes. I said," This is my new life." He looked up at me and said," But what if I can't go along with it with you?" I replied. Well then I have to go alone." This started the drift between him and me and soon, after twelve years of marriage we were talking divorce. I told him what I had done and that I was not worthy of him any more. We both shared many tears over this and to this day I love him dearly.

I went to Julia, and told her that I was in love with Rev. Mason. "You must follow your heart," she said to me. "The heart sees no color." She then sat me down and told me of her love she had shared with a black man many years ago. She also told me of a beautiful little girl that she prayed for daily. "Now don't tell anyone else", she said. "Let this be our secret." I was unaware that this very same conversation had taken place years ago in a tiny little birthing cabin. I couldn't keep her precious secret. I told Elna. I didn't know why I needed to share this with her but I did. The next morning I woke early, drove to her house' and revealed to her that I had betrayed her trust and had told her secret. "Well, maybe it's for the best. Now you girls will know that I am no good." We assured her that we loved her just the same but we were a little hurt that she had not confided in us earlier.

Reverend Mason, I learned later that he did not love me as I thought. In fact I soon learned that several other women and I had almost identical notes of comparison. He had a habit of seducing his students and leaving behind many broken souls.

I was determined that this was not going to break me; it was going to make me strong. I was still going to be a minister and a teacher and no person could detour me from it. I continued to teach classes of my own and work at the church right along side of him. He made many attempts to seduce me over and over again. I fell for it a couple of times in the beginning but I soon realized that he was a snake.

Daniel and I tried to work through this but I couldn't live with the guilt. I wanted to be faithful to my husband but I knew that I had failed in this area. I needed to live on my own with my two young children. I was at a cross roads in my life without a direction. Daniel said I could stay with him and I wondered if I should for the sake of the children. I was praying for a direction as I was sitting on my front step in the cold winter month of January when out of the sky I received my answer.

As I was sitting on my front porch wondering what direction I should take my life into I noticed something blowing in the wind. As I watched, this object float to the ground I discovered that it was a piece of paper. As I watched it slowly drifted toward me and landed lightly at my feet. I saw that it was a page from a book, a Bible in fact. As I examined this old tattered page I could only read the wording at the top of the page. It read Daniel 8, 9. I could not read the other words as they were written in German. This immediately caught my attention because my husband's name was Daniel. I knew that in the art of numerology my life path is eight. To make it even more intriguing my last name with this marriage was of German descent.

The page was yellowed and the edges were torn but it still was in very good condition. I immediately took it inside to compare it with my King James Bible.

In chapter eight verses 1 through 10 it tells of a vision. It speaks of a goat which had a notable horn between its eyes. The goat charged the ram and broke off the two horns. In chapter eight it tells of the goat waxing very great and the horn dividing into great ones which also waxed exceeding great. This old tattered page from a German Bible had provided me with an answer to my dilemma. My husband Daniel was born under the sun sign of Aries, the sign of the ram. My sun sign is Capricorn, the goat. The two horns that were broke off the ram represented to me, our children that I was so concerned about. The vision that the page told of was an answer to me in my time of questioning. The Bible page assured me that the children would be fine if I were to venture into a new beginning. This was the interpretation that I understood at this time. I understand that there are other ways of interpreting this scripture, but at this time in my life this was what it meant to me.

I understood the concept of Apports. An apport is an object that appear from out of nowhere from a spirit helper or guide. The word apport is from the French word apporter meaning, "To bring". I knew that I had received an apport as an answer to my question. This was only the first of several that I would receive through out my life. I had no idea that I was about to enter a test period of my faith and through out it all I was protected and guided from many on the other side of life.

I sold my antique doll collection, my beauty salon and started out on my own with two small children. I did not ask Daniel to sell our home nor did I ask him to leave it. His father had provided the land and I understood that it was still family land. Instead I purchased a mobile home and me and my children moved away.

It was a difficult task to establish my self as a single parent but I soon adjusted. Daniel and I remained friends. He often visited the children as well as took them on most weekends.

I was still attending Camp on my own and attending as many classes as I could. There I met Dave and Barb Carter a couple that lived and worked in the camp. The camp is set up so that individuals can purchase houses, but not the land and become staff while they lived there. Dave and Barb owned and operated a beauty salon in Anderson Indiana. In speaking with them I learned that they wanted to sell their business and I was interested. This would afford me the opportunity to be close to the camp as well as be able to have a means of support. They would sell me their business on land contract. With two thousand dollars I could take over the business and have enough money left over to rent an apartment. I was excited as I signed the contract and started the proceedings to move to Anderson Indiana.

Elna decided she wanted the mobile home and I had all my ducks in a row, or so I thought. I wanted to be near the Camp and had hopes of eventually living on the grounds. On the day I was packed and ready to go I thought that I should call Daniel and tell him that the children and I were starting out with our last truck load. As I dialed his number I thought I had dialed a wrong number. I received a dial- a- prayer service, or so I thought. I hung up and redialed to my listened. The prayer was spoken with a very soft angelic voice. I listened to this soft voice tell me that I was about to venture into rough seas. I was always to remember that God was at the stem of my ship. I listened to the entire prayer and then heard silence when it disconnected. I didn't think too much of this as I dialed Daniel's number. I put each child on the phone to talk to him. After we hung up I started out on the highway into the unknown wilderness with my possessions and my two young children.

I settled into a nice apartment, enrolled Jennifer and Jeffery into school, and started working with my familiar trade as a business owner and stylist. Every other weekend I would take the children to Ohio to spend time with their father. We had successfully made the transition and I thought all would work out just fine. At least it started out that way.

Dave remained working at the salon. I named the business The Zodiac and he would answer the phone with Carter's Zodiac. He told me he would remain at the salon and offered to pay me fifty dollars a week. I was unaware of the fact that this year Anderson In. was economically distressed and I was attempting to start a business. Needless to say I lost money each day that I was in operation. I would watch as Dave counted his weekly earnings of five to six hundred dollars and then hand me fifty. I soon realized that I had helped him out of his financial dilemma as I took on taxes, utilities, insurance while the same time needing living expenses for myself and two children. The children went to Ohio to spend the entire summer with their father and I had to give up my apartment in order to support the business. I rented a shabby little three room fixer upper and I was struggling to keep my head above water.

I was determined to make the most of the salon even though it was failing. I was attending the spiritualist Camp classes and holding on to the faith that God will provide. Things progressively got worse but I was not willing to give up. It only seem to make me even more determined to succeed. Each day, it seemed, I would receive another blow. I received a letter stating that Daniel had obtained custody of both children due to the fact that I was not able to support them. I thought the world had ended. I had nothing to live for, or so I felt, without being able to see the sunshine of my children. The light of my life was removed and I could only see darkness. I didn't know at this time that I was surrounded by intense levels of darkness just by my associations, seen and unseen.

There was at this time a book published about the camp called *The Psychic Mafia.* The students as well as residents were all a buzz about this book. The students were discussing the the book's contents and held many questions about the proceedings of the camp. The camp holds séances and demonstrates various acts of spiritual phenomena. The acts of blind fold billets, materialization, and channeling loved ones to seekers are their forte. This book tells of fraud that is practiced there and gives away many secrets held by the "Open mediums". Open mediums is a term used to describe those in the club. The club consists of the main mediums which exchanges information on each seeking person that visits the camp. I could not believe that such practices were prevalent at a spiritual place of love and light. I was talking with a fellow student when I felt the presence of the president of the camp (Elizabeth now reincarnated) standing next to me. She drew me aside and said, "If you continue to discuss this book I will see to it that you will be thrown off these grounds." I was stunned; I had no idea that the book *The Psychic Mafia* was such a hot issue. Later on when the book was brought up I was told to respond by saying that that it was written by a disgruntled ex-resident that held anger against the camp and that it was all a lie. I really believed this statement. I couldn't see that any one who had earned the privilege of living on this sacred camp would lie to me. After all we were all there to do God's work or so I thought. I was convinced that this camp was a spiritual place on earth. I was to later find out in my life that the disgruntled ex-resident was right but the book in no way described the evil that lurked behind the scenes of these beautiful grounds.

I was trying to make a success of the beauty salon even though my world felt empty without Jennifer and Jeffery. Soon after loosing custody of my babies I faced the issue of not having money to live on. I had even sold all my belongings to support the business. I gave up my little shabby three room house and started living in my car. I would park around the salon at night, clean up in the salon and on some occasions sleep on the floor. I was determined to regain control of my finances not realizing that Dave Carter was draining funds as fast as I could build them. I believed in him and his wife because they lived and worked at the camp so how could these two people not be spiritual. I went to the president of the camp and explained my plight to her. I asked if I might be able to stay in a room at one of the hotels until I regrouped. Her answer to me was, "Madgelyn, do you want me to give you a lantern so you can walk the halls and play martyr?" No was her answer. I was surprised because I thought we were a spiritual caring family that would help one another. I hung around the camp when I was not working at the salon. I could not build a clientele due to the fact that Dave needed to survive more than me, or so he thought. He would take each new customer that came in, and me building a clientele was futile. I felt like ending it all when once again I received a gift from my spirit guides. The apport was different than the Bible page. I found this one at my feet while standing in the salon. It was dark and I had just completed cleaning and sweeping. I knew the floor was clean but I discovered a rock at my feet. I still hold this token when I need strength- The rock has smoothness unlike any other that I had seen before. It is in the shape of a heart with a K carved in it. I knew at once that this was a gift and that I was protected and loved by my spirit helpers. I understood that my teacher is Krymel from the spirit realm and I understood the K carved in in the rock. I felt strength and a renewed since of faith and I understood what I was to do about my life at this time.

The next day I told Dave that I was giving him back his salon and I was not going to work with him any more. He called me a f——— c——— and other names that I had never heard before but I handed him his keys and walked out. I was not going to let him use me again. I had no place to go so I drove to the camp.

I walked to the old rickety hotel and sat on a porch swing to ponder my next move. Now what, I did not have a dime in my pocket and no means of support but I knew that I would receive an answer if I listened within.

A white haired man of about sixty or older approached me and said, "Hey kid, we need to talk." I followed him to the lush green prayer garden and sat down on a stone bench. He told me his name was Michael and that I had passed my test. "Passed my test? I don't understand", I replied. He answered," you have been watched by a counsel ever since you were a small child; you are a person with a mission to teach many souls. You have been placed through a learning experience and you have passed into the next phase of your education. Consider this an initiation, the first of several to come. When a person has such a mission he or she will pass through many tests of learning to prepare for his or her service to mankind. When you were taken aboard the craft when you were a small child you was made aware of your task. You agreed to the lessons as well as the mission." I was in awe of this silver haired blue eyed man. I was held spell bound by his soft velvet voice. I asked." When was I aboard a craft?" I knew that I had never been in a plane or any type of aircraft for that matter. Michael smiled and spoke of a little girl that was frightened long ago when her hands seemed to be falling into holes. I understood. He then handed me an envelope and said, "What is in this envelope is charged. You will never have less than this the rest of your life. Don't look into the envelope until I have gone." "Michael," I said, "I have a question. What was the test that I have just passed?" He replied, "Learning that all there is a God, and you allowing each dear and cherished thing to be taken from you, and not losing your faith."

171

"You mean something like Job," I asked. "Ah, you do understand my child, he said. I must go now, but always remember you are never alone."

Michael walked away. I didn't see where he went as I turned the envelope over in my shaking hands.

I sat for the longest time just holding the long white envelope. I couldn't bring myself to the point of opening it. I was so tired after a whole year of trying, that I just figured it was some sort of advertising that would offer me a self help magazine or a saying to bring me luck. I was not sure of Michael, but he did know about my vision when I was a child. What the heck go for it, I thought as I opened the envelope. As I looked into it I saw a crisp new one hundred dollar bill. This would get me home, I thought, back to my babies. Without hesitation, I filled up my little A.M.C. Hornet with gas and hit the highway to Ohio.

When I arrived at my sister Elna's door she was glad to see me. Her face could always bring a light in my eyes. I knew she was always there and I was glad to see her. I wanted to see Jennifer and Jeffery right away. I picked up the phone dialed Daniel's number and once again. "Dial -a-prayer?" I said. "Elna, listen to this lady as she prays. Doesn't this sound weird?" Elna took the phone and jokingly said, "O.K. lady this isn't Sunday quit praying". Dial-a -Prayer in a sweet low voice," Bless you dear Child, Now may I speak with Madgelyn?" Elna held out the phone to me and said, "Dial -a-Prayer wants to talk to you. "As I listened wide eyed she told me that I had passed a test and to see my problems as large flaming ball of fire. She continued," Take this flaming energy and throw it out into the universe and watch as it illuminates many areas of the world." After her prayer the phone went silent and I hung it up. "I have had so many strange experiences". I told Elna. Let me call the kids and then let's talk.

That very same day I had in my arms my two main reasons to live. Daniel agreed to give me back custody and I now needed to get about the business of rearing my little ones.

Another hard task was yet to come, I needed funds to survive and working as a hair dresser wouldn't' provide enough income to support two children. My license had even expired because I could not even afford the fee to keep them up. I didn't think I would want to practice this trade any way so I never had them reinstated again. Elna helped me to obtain an apartment and I now needed an income. I had friends who worked in the Welfare department, so I was reluctant to apply for public assistance. I knew though, that this was an opportunity to go to college. I made an appointment at the welfare and was very embarrassed to see many ladies that I had laughed and shared with when I was a member of Business and Professional Woman's organization. I held my head up and filled out my paper work. I started receiving my monthly check, medical benefits and stood in long lines for my food stamps each month. I felt humble and grateful. I applied to Urbana University and was delighted to receive admittance. My major was psychology and I attended school while my children attended theirs.

I was now discouraged about being a minister and answering my call to do God's work. I decided to obtain my degree and become a social worker and forget that I had ever seen a church. I was going to depend on myself and not God nor any one else. I was soon to discover that this was not a wise choice.

I found a nice big house on Rice Street in Springfield Ohio. It was so much bigger than the mobile home and I was so excited to find that the rent would fit my tight budget. The children and I moved and settled in our big roomy house. I loved it and we were together. I would watch these two gifts from God and just smile from deep in my soul.

Julia's two youngest children Mark and Crystal were now grown and were successfully on their own. Julia had been introduced to a widowed man in Anderson, Indiana through a friend of my sister Frances. She and Herb fell in love at once and within two months Julia was married for the third time. She moved to Anderson, and for the first time in her life she was happy. She sold her house in Ohio and settled into Herb's home. It was the first time that I had ever seen her entire face smile. She and Herb were like soul mates. They enjoyed each other in all ways. Julia's happiness was short lived. After only six months of a pure bliss. Herb had a fatal heart attack. His sister claimed possession of the home and once again Julia was thrown into a state of complete destitution.

Frances, now a single parent, had moved to Minnesota with her family of three. Julia moved there to be close to her. She attended classes to obtain her high school diploma. She was so proud of this diploma as she felt a since of accomplishment. She then proceeded to take classes to receive a certificate for nurse's aid. She felt important and proud of herself because of her ability to help others. She now felt as though she had a trade other than waitress. A few short months into her new career she suffered a major heart attack that required open heart surgery. She was grateful for the insurance Herb's death had provided for her otherwise she would have had no means to pay for her health care and medicine. It was going to be a real long process back to the road to health but she would never make it. Julia still would not watch her diet and her diabetes was out of control.

She came back to Ohio and moved in with me just until she was old enough to apply for her social security check. She found a low income senior citizen apartment and settled there. She wasn't happy but she was so used to being miserable that she soon adjusted. I felt so bad for her but I could only offer my love and support and I never felt that it was enough.

I was attending school and had taken a part time job on weekend when the children were at their fathers. I had applied for a position as child care worker at a group home for residential treatment of incorrigible girls. Mr. Richers paid me under the table and the extra income helped but not enough. It was a rough place to work but I needed the money.

I was working and attending school and rearing my two children. Life was a task. I was standing in the hallway at school when a dark complexioned man approached me. "I have had my eye on you for several days now." He said with a smile. I smiled back and we struck up a conversation. I saw him each day as we shared one class together. He asked me as we were waiting to enter the class room. "Do you have a boyfriend?" "No" I laughed. "I don't have the time. He wrapped one of my curls around his finger and placing his face near mine said in the lowest tone, "You do now." I didn't answer I walked into the room and took my seat. I was relaxing in my home one evening when I saw a dark figure of a man standing in my back yard. I looked again and he was gone. Throughout the months to come I soon understood that I was being stalked. I approached him at school and his reply was, "Just go out with me that's all I want." I decided to go to dinner with him and this was all it took. He was in love. I didn't want him in my life and even more so after he had told me he was in college due to a prison program upon his release. I asked, "Why?" his answer was for killing my wife, but it was an accident."

I knew then that I really didn't want this man in my life. I told Mr. Richers at the group home about this stalker. "Go to the police and get a restraining order." He said. "I can't" I said, "He told me that if I should cause him to go back to prison he would see to it that my children were harmed, and I would regret it." I felt as if I had no where to turn.

One night when the children were at their father's I heard a knock on the door. I saw that it was the stalker and I refused to open the door to him. "Let me in!" he bellowed. "No! Go away I don't want anything to do with you!" I screamed. I ducked in time to miss the flying glass as he banged his fist through the glass. I grabbed the phone and dialed 911 only to have him yank the phone out of the wall and hit me with it. I heard the upstairs phone ring and I headed for the stairs. I screamed 230 Rice into it just before he jerked it out of the wall as well. He was sitting on top of me strangling me and spitting in my face as he heard the sirens. He bolted out the door before the police arrived and I was afraid to press charges for fear he would be placed back in jail. I was afraid that he could do more harm to me and the children as he had promised upon his release.

The police left and Mr. Richers drove by just as they were leaving. He stopped and came into the house. "I was really worried about you, and I just was driving by to see if you were alright," he said. He held me and as I looked into his dark eyes and handsome black face I knew that I was in the arms of a safe and caring man. He took me to his home and I slept on the couch He told me that he would see to it that the stalker would be taken care of. I was assured that I would be protected from him, and not to worry. I later heard that he was placed back into prison but I have not seen him since.

It was a warm day when I noticed a portly man standing in front of the neighbor's house. He wore a white shirt with white pants and was looking up one end of the sidewalk to the other. My first thought was, I wonder who that could be, and he looks like a fat plantation owner surveying his land. I paid him no further attention and went back into my house. Later that week I saw him again and he introduced himself to me.

"Hi my name is Tad, "he said. "I was noticing you the other day and I thought you were Jennifer and Jeffery's older sister." "Oh sure you did", was my response. I wonder what he wants, I found myself thinking. I saw a lot of Tad that summer. In fact, we even dated a few times. I didn't like his selfish arrogant manner and I was quick to tell him so. I just didn't like him for a number of reasons, but he thought I was a conquest. Each date I would have with him would end up in a power struggle. He just knew that he was just what I needed to make my life complete.

I was still attending school and working part time at the group home. My welfare check and my part time income were not stretching enough, and by the end of summer I received a notice that the gas had been turned off. Fall was approaching and I had two children to keep warm. When Tad offered to pay my gas bill if he could move in with us, I felt as if I had no choice. Tad moved in and the gas was turned on, but the house wasn't the only thing that was heating up in my life.

I was miserable with Tad in my house. I liked him less each day and the feeling was mutual. He had won, I thought, by him moving in with me. I was not going to marry him although he constantly pleaded for my hand.

The fights and abuse went on for a year. My college professor and I were discussing Tad's and my situation. "You must love him unconditionally, if you are waiting for him to change you will be waiting forever", he said. I realized that I indeed was waiting for him to change; I understood that I was the one who needed to change. If I was not happy it was up to me to find happiness. I was looking for the relationship to become happy when he changed. Wasn't going to happen.

I tried a different approach and it didn't change I still felt a deep sense of hate for Tad. I couldn't understand it but it was definitely hate. On the other hand I thought, at times that I loved him. I was becoming more and more confused over this relationship.

Tad said to me one day. The reason I don't get along with you is because you won't marry me." I still didn't want to marry Tad but I thought that he might be right. If I was to marry him perhaps he would feel more secure and would not be so mean to me and the kids. I told him I would think about it.

I had also applied for license as a foster parent through the group home and was accepted. It wasn't long after the application was approved that we had a new house resident. The first of many to come. I could now get off welfare and hold my head up. I had decided to marry Tad. I asked my spirit guides to block me if this wasn't the right move. I prepared for the wedding without thinking about it. Both children were upset over the idea as they saw the abuse and knew of my feelings about Tad. I allowed him to over power me and I gave in to his pleas of marriage. I didn't realize that he again wanted to make me a conquest.

The day of the wedding arrived and I figured I would just get through it. My family was opposed to the marriage but we support each other in our choices. The rain was pouring as I prepared to leave for the church. I was to drive the fifteen miles to the church by myself as the children had stayed the night with their father and was to be picked up by Elna and taken to the church. Tad had stayed the night with his sister because we were not supposed to see each other on the day of the wedding before the service. I put on my ivory colored suit, ivory heels and started out in the rain. About five miles out of town, on a country highway the car sputtered. I coaxed it a few more miles and to my dismay the car stopped dead in its tracks. The rain was pouring and I was sitting in a car that would not start. I knew everyone was waiting at the church and I needed to get there. I decided the only solution I had was to walk to get to a phone. I walked to the nearest house about a mile down the road. By the time I arrived at the house I looked like a drowned rat. I called the church and my brother in law came after me. I arrived at the church late with wet hair, shoes, and clothes. I had received my block I asked for but I didn't heed it. I married Tad any way and two weeks later we were separated. Tad wouldn't give up. He wanted to come back in the house. He promised to change and once again, like any other co-dependent person would do I tried once again.

A month passed and by now I had been hired at the Human service department as a child care worker, and we had two foster girls, Laurie and Tammy, under our roof. Tad stayed with the foster girls and I worked third shift.

The children attended a Swendenborg church camp in Almont Michigan each year. I took off a week and Elna and I worked as dorm moms for the week. I didn't take the foster girls and left them with Tad where I thought they would be fine. The girls were sixteen and seventeen and I knew Tad would be a stem parent figure whom I could trust. WRONG! When I returned home I was told by the younger child Laurie, that Tad and Tammy had gotten married. "What?" I asked with a look of total shock on my face. "Why would you tell me stupid stuff like that Laurie?" I asked. "Well, they did, they went to Tennessee and got married. Tammy told me so." she said. I asked Tammy and Tad and they both looked sheepish but denied it. I felt as if I had been lied to and betrayed even though they denied it.

I watched Tammy's behavior around Tad and I knew for sure that something was going on. I approached Tad again and he confessed. Yes they had gotten married but he was taking care of it. "Taking care of it! How?" I screamed. "What are you thinking?" I knew that he was abusive but I thought he loved me. My sense of reality was upside down, sideways and scrambled. His answer was that he had gotten high with the girls and didn't realize that he had done this. "Sure." I answered. I reported him to the license bureau and both girls were removed immediately from the house. I also lost my license as a foster parent. Tad refused to leave the house he wanted to stay with me and work things out. I called an organization that dealt with abused women and made an appointment.

The counselor Rose was a marvelous woman. I took a lengthy test to determine my state of mind. When we reviewed the results she said to me. "This test indicates to me that you are just fine. Now if you can get that man out of your house and life you don't need to come back again." I went home with fire in my eyes and told Tad he had to leave. "I have no place to go, so I am staying here." I grabbed a butcher knife and as I stabbed the wall in rhythm he saw that I was serious and had found self strength. I had never before felt the ability to take control and I liked it. I had no intention to harm Tad but he was unsure of my next move. He had never seen this type of control from me before and he was frightened. He packed his belongings and left. Soon after we were divorced. I don't know what he did about the marriage to Tammy and I really didn't care to find out. I was still not interested in church although I was giving readings to many that were coming to my home.

I maintained my position at Human Services and was still attending college part time. I purchased a house on Clifton Ave and I enjoyed my single status. I was able to obtain credit and shouted as I drove my new car off the lot. I had climbed out of my hole of poverty and was back on top. Jennifer was in high school and was a 4 point, student Jeffery was doing just as well and they were both well balanced much to my surprise.

I was awakened one night from having a strange dream. I dreamed that I was going into different houses and asking where their small door was. The small three foot door led into the walls of the different houses. As I approached the little door I would hear a shrill scream and would recoil in fear. I told myself that fear was a negative emotion and that I needed to enter the door. The door led between the walls and in there I would find a mean spirited little girl. I would take her by the hand gently and lead her to the next doorway which led into another house. She would fight me all the way and on many occasions I would lose her in the maze between the walls. I took her through many houses and in the last house I encountered a red headed family. I had never seen such red hair on the entire family. I asked. "Where is the little door? I must go through it." The red headed family told me that the door boarded up due to the fact that it was to scary to enter and that loud screams would come out of it. I removed the boards from the door and entered only to lose the little girl again. I soon found her and took her through the next door. I said to her, "This is the last house and I must leave you here."

In this house was a pregnant woman rolling dough on a long t
her feet sat many small children at play. One side of the room was furnished
in antiques while the opposite end was done in modem furniture. The mean
little girl sat an antique rocking chair which was on fire, and I drew back my
hand with flair and put out the flame. I kissed her good by and woke from
my dream. strange, I thought upon my awakening. I wonder what that dream
could mean? I would find out what it intended to tell me about ten years
later.

Jennifer had spent the weekend with her father and I had the night off. I
decided to go to a night club not far from the house. I don't drink but I
would sometimes sit and enjoy the music while sipping a soft drink. I had
taken Julia to the doctor that day and I needed time alone. Julia had a sore
on her foot that was not healing and the news that she would lose her foot
had me very upset.

I was sipping my soda when I noticed a cute man walk by and smile at
me. I thought well isn't he a cutie but I gave him no more thought. As I was
preparing to leave I looked and noticed that this cute man had returned. He
walked straight to me and said, "can I buy you a drink?" "I don't drink and I
was just leaving was my reply." "Well then can I buy you a soda?" he asked.
I couldn't help but notice his blue eyes and silver hair. I allowed him to buy
me a soda and we became acquainted. "My name is Dale. What is yours?"
he asked. I told him my name and once again I told him I needed to go. I
was not interested in another relationship after Tad. Dale asked me to stay a
little longer and I agreed to for a short while. He told me he worked for the
rail road and that he was doing work in the Springfield area. "My home is in
Pennsylvania". He said. I asked, "Do you have a wife in Pennsylvania also?"
He answered, "Yes I have." I was more at ease because of this. I felt as if he
was safe just to talk to and that he would not pursue me for a relationship.
We talked and I asked him about his interests. "You will think I am strange
if I tell you what I read "he said. I said with a smile, "No, I wouldn't think
you were strange at all." He asked, "Have you ever heard of Edgar Cayce
and his ideas?" I knew that Edgar Cayce was a man referred to as the
sleeping prophet that had many insights about psychic development. I
replied." I am very familiar with that author, and no I didn't think you you're
strange, because I am just as strange. I said, "I am a certified medium. I
received my certification several years ago". He was intrigued and said, "I
knew your kind of people existed I just didn't know how to connect with
them." We shared ideas about spirituality for a long time and when I was
about to leave he asked me for my phone number and address. "Why do you
want them?" I asked. "I am not interested in married men," I explained. Dale
said," I would like to have it in order to talk more about these beliefs." I felt

confident that this would be all there was to it. I did not give him my address but I did relinquish my phone number.

The next evening Dale called and asked, "Would you like to meet me tonight at the same place to talk?" I told him. "I can't. I am due at work in a few hours and that I wouldn't have time this evening". He persuaded me to join him for a soda before work and once again I obliged. We became fast friends and it was soon time for him to return to Pennsylvania. He asked if we could start a relationship and my answer to that was. "If you want me you have to leave the wife." I was sure that this would detour him and he would remain with his wife. I was stunned when he, out of the blue, called her and told her that he wasn't returning to Pennsylvania. I did not expect this and I then felt as if I had no choice in the matter from here on. We both felt bad about hurting her but by this time we were experiencing a connection that puzzled us both. We were not in an emotional love but we shared a love that felt as if we were one soul. It ran very deep and was very spiritual. We neither one at this time knew that we were William and Maggie once again reunited.

After we had settled into each others lives Dale wanted to experience the Camp where I had received my papers. I had left the church as well as having anything to do with the Camp." I had left my religion in fact I had even denounced God. I just couldn't bear the responsibilities of disciplining myself nor did I want to teach others any more.

Dale would not give up and we soon were on our way to Camp. I was welcomed back by many of the residents with open arms. The only person who seemed to be perturbed was the President. This was the same woman who had told me she would kick me off the camp and had later denied me shelter. I didn't understand why she didn't like me as I had always respected and admired her. We attended seminar and Dale was delighted that he could take classes for his own spiritual development.

O.K. God maybe I have been wrong, I prayed. I surrender my life to your guidance and love. I had always lived my religion but after wandering in the wilderness I once again dedicated my life to God. I thought about the little girl on her knees at the alter surrendering her life many years ago.

It wasn't long after we returned home that we purchased a huge house and started our center. We charted and incorporated it as a church and opening services we had a full house. I received my ordination from the camp and I was back teaching and serving. On the premises we opened a book store and the church and business was going well enough that I quit my job as a child care worker. I put my entire energy into the center and was glad that it was progressing along quite well.

I received a phone call from a local radio station and was offered my own talk show. I couldn't believe it. I was allowed to advertise my center and classes over the air, and it was all for free. The guides were really working hard to promote the word through me. I had a different guest each week to present a spiritual topic for the first half hour, and then we would open up the phones for the last half hour of the show. I had also planned a seminar and was promoting it over the air. All was going smoothly and I was doing my work with love.

I was surprised to receive a call from a Camp board member. "We would like if you would move here and become staff on the camp." she said. I couldn't believe my ears. I had given up on this goal several years before but not entirely. I answered that we couldn't buy a house because we had put all our funds into restoring the center. She said, "We will rent you a house. We want you here." I was so amazed that this could become a reality, and Dale and I packed up our belongings, closed the center, and allowed the previous owner to have it back, as it was a land contract. We then set forth on an adventure that would almost take my life

I did not realize what lay ahead for me when I moved into a place that I had always held in my mind to be a loving, truthful, caring group of "spiritual "people. We moved into our little house and I thought that this was one of the most beautiful spiritual places on God's green earth. I soon learned that this spiritual society is compromised of many that lack formal education other than a few classes at random. The majority of the residents could be classified as co-dependent and live in fear of exposure of their fraudulent activities. There have been many books written that try to enlighten the public on their practices. A book titled *Doors to other worlds* by Raymond Buckland and *Zolar's Book of the Spirits* by Zolar are two that have mentioned the fraudulent practices of this camp and I have mentioned *The Psychic Mafia* by Alien Spraggett earlier in this book.

In the nineteen sixties a gentleman by the name of Tom O'neil entered one of the very popular séances with an infrared camera. He captured on film various mediums dressed as spirit supposedly communicating from the other side to their loved ones. This video is titled, *Arthur C. Clark's World of strange Power, Messages from the Dead*, and can still be purchased.

Although this camp has been in operation for over one hundred years and many in the past have tried to expose it as the cult that it is, it still continues to operate under the guise as religious truth. Many people experience grief at the loss of a loved one and I soon witnessed many take advantage of their loss and put money in their pocket from so called contact with the departed loved one.

I learned almost too late why we were asked to move on the grounds. I was a member of their organization and in their view, I needed to be controlled and the center in Ohio needed to stop. I at this time did not realize that this was an active cult under the influence of the dark side and they needed my light. The dark side needs s lights to gain strength in order to survive. There are some living in this camp who are totally unaware of how it is operated. Unbeknownst to them their energy is being used. When I would lie down at night I would have visions of many piranha fish holding on and biting me with steel like grips. I later realized that I would have to leave in order to keep my sanity as well as my soul.

Dale and I were unaware of the hidden practices at the camp and we settled into our house in the month of October. One of the first things I was met with was one resident saying to another. "This one is going to give us a run for our money." I tried to explain that I had no desire to give any one a run for anything but was met with sarcasm. I didn't understand this but I felt intimidated.

It was nearing Christmas and our first year there I thought it would be nice if the residents would all pitch in to buy the president a nice gift. The previous president had been voted out and the camp after ten years had a new president in the office. I was more comfortable with her and I had a high regard for her as a person. I went door to door with my collection basket expecting to be met with loving, kind hearted, spiritual people. To my surprise I was met with some who opposed the idea but gave anyway. One resident who taught and practiced yoga was particularly nasty. I looked at him with amazement when he said, "No, I won't give anything to that bitch. Oh on second thought yes I will, here is a dollar maybe it will melt her f——— heart." I walked away sick to my stomach thinking that this person could harbor such hateful thoughts and live on these grounds.

In the attic of our house I discovered a trumpet that once belonged to a Mable Riffle. The trumpet had her signature on it so it was definitely Mable's. Mable was once a very powerful figure that lived on the grounds. In fact when Mable told the board to jump they ask how high. If a medium got out of line Mable was the one they had to stand before in judgment. She held a very powerful position in the camp in the nineteen thirties and forties.

This was not a musical trumpet but one that a medium uses in a séance. The voice of the departed loved one is amplified through the trumpet as it supposedly floats around the room over the heads of the sitters. There is a museum on the grounds and I told Dale that this should be in the museum. I immediately took the trumpet to those in authority and tried to have it placed in the museum. I was told that the trumpet was meant for me and I was to keep it. If I was to leave the grounds it should be placed in the museum. I felt honored that I was in possession of such an object that was once owned by such a strong woman. I was told that the trumpet was in my possession because I was to be the next "head bitch". A job, whose duties I wasn't eager to fulfill

It was difficult living at the camp because of the jealous residents but I and my husband were surviving. The backbiting and fears amongst the residents was something I couldn't help but to get caught up in. On top of everything else I was even being accused of having an affair with a friend that had visited our home. This friend was a person that had discovered their "secrets" and was watched each time he entered the camp's gates.

I was also told of a secret club that is the backbone of the camp. It seems that only a few are invited into the club. This club was the main topic of the book *The psychic Mafia* and I was shocked that this book was in fact true after all. The club consists of star mediums that have a tremendous ego that needs fed daily. The main function of the club members is to cheat the public in the name of religion. How this is accomplished is by the trick of the billets. Let me explain. When a person attends a church service he or she is handed a small piece of paper with the instructions to address the billet to one or more spirit guides and one or more loved ones in the spirit realm. Also one is instructed to ask a question and to sign their name. These papers are collected and the medium is then blindfolded for effect, and proceeds to answer the question on the paper and call out the name of departed spirits. When one is presenting the act of blindfold billets the congregation sits in awe as their billet is read by a medium that they are led to believe cannot see. It is explained that the tape and blindfold is used to form a dark cabinet around the medium's consciousness in order to concentrate better. What the congregation is not aware of is the technique that is used to pull off this unique parlor trick. After the billets are collected and have been presented to the medium he or she then shuffles through them while the congregation sings hymns. At the flip of a wrist one billet is opened and placed to the side under the downward view that the medium has provided for him or her self from under the blindfold. The medium shuffles the billets and pretends to be reading the one held in hand while in actuality the one lying on the pulpit is the one being read. Some will call for a silent meditation while he or she reads the opened billet. This depends on the medium's technique and it varies. The one that the medium holds is then opened and placed on top of the already opened one. The next one is picked up and the medium reads the previously held one. It is the trick of reading one ahead. The trick is quite effective as the sitters are led to believe that their loved ones are communicating with the medium. Sometimes this is done without blindfold but the main object is that this trick is performed daily during camp programs. Some mediums will not use a blindfold and can effectively see through the thin paper. I have seen one medium pick up the billets and never look at them or open them. This is very convincing to those that is not aware of the medium's club and do not expect fraudulent activity. This medium has done her homework and knows who is on the grounds. Her information does not come from a billet it comes from names memorized of those who is expected to be in the congregation. She holds the billets and the crowd thinks that she has theirs in her hand as she calls out names. This medium can be seen running and bustling around the grounds all day checking who is on the grounds and relaying this information to others so their files can be pulled. I was told personally by this particular medium that this was one of her duties as a member of the club.

When the medium goes home after services he or she is expected to call the other members of the club and inquire if they need information from the billets for the upcoming séances or readings.

I was told that I was to do billets even though I did not request to do so. I wasn't pleased with the task of cheating the people but I was told to kiss ass and do as expected if I wanted to survive living at the camp. So I was instructed to have training sessions with a senior medium to learn the art of fraud. I performed my feat of blindfold billet reading and was told I presented it quite well. I was told soon after by a resident that once held the office of president that I was lousy at presenting my trick. This medium holds extreme jealousy and hate toward others. This medium also has an active guide that presents himself as fire devil. Before a church service this medium calls upon this guide. Any benevolent entity will not refer to itself as a devil of any kind. I found this camp to be the dark side of the light. Many who come through the gates think that they are practicing their religion in the light of God. The false entities hide themselves under the disguise of the light and many souls find themselves trapped and enthralled with this dark vortex of a place.

One who is in the club referred to as an "open medium". One who is not a member of this club is referred to as working closed. I was told to get in the club or get the f— out of the camp. This was something that I just knew in my heart that couldn't be true, but it was. I was so upset and I went to a resident whom I had trusted to be of the spiritual light and was reassured that our little talk would be confidential. I ask why was this club in operation and was concerned as to why many relied on fraud and appeared to the public as the real thing. I was told that many of the mediums could not work any other way. We talked for several hours and I felt a little better having someone I could talk to about my uncertainties. I no sooner got into my house when the phone rang. "Get over to my house now!" I was told. It was Dave and another resident. Yes Dave was still on the grounds and he was an active member in the club. When I ran to his house I was confronted by him and another club member. I was screamed and yelled at by these two members. I received a viscous tongue lashing. It became apparent to me that

I was inside an evil cult that all worked together. I understood that our private conversation was broadcast among the club members. I learned that because I was asking questions I was to be watched and was considered dangerous. I also learned that this resident that I had shared my concerns with was the head leader in the practice of full moon rituals. I was not permitted to attend a ritual even though I have often looked at a picture that was taken when Dale and I moved on the grounds. In this picture we are holding lanterns by the fountain and we were asked to put on black hooded robes. I never saw these robes again but I have the newspaper picture with us wearing them.

Now I realize of course that many religions hold rituals such as the Catholics, but these were held to control another that the group did not want to run for president.

I had the opportunity to witness a very evil entity that exercises control over one of the male mediums. This entity works through the medium that I had shared my fears with. I was attending one of his full moon festivals known as Wesak. The church alter had been prepared by the lighting of several candles. The congregation was sitting in a quiet meditation. The church doors had been locked so one could enter nor leave. One woman from the pews noticed that one of the candle flames was burning noticeably high and took it upon herself to extinguish it. As the woman approached the alter, the medium leaped to his feet with a look of pure hate and anger, and with a loud deep voice bellowed, "Don't touch that candle!" The medium took on an entirely different look that was not like him, and he was even foaming around the comers of his mouth. I felt as though I had been hit in the stomach. My first impulse was to leave but I knew the doors had been locked so I had to stay. I was informed later that I made the right decision to stay as if I had tried to leave it would have made a statement. I knew that I had seen an evil entity that works through this medium. The problem is that this medium has no idea that he is being controlled by this dark entity. This is what I refer to as working in the dark side of the light. Many residents living on this camp are unaware that they are under the control of the dark side. If this had been a loving entity this spirit would have been tolerant of the ones gathering as students.

While I was struggling to get along with the camp residents I was faced with the knowledge that I was the one daughter Julia had decided on to move in with. She had lost part of her foot due to her illness of diabetes. She entered the hospital not long after moving in with me to undergo open heart surgery. Due to this surgery straining her system she was placed on dialyses for kidney failure. I was caring for her as well as trying to perform my expected duties as a camp resident and staff. I was also suffering empty nest syndrome as Jennifer had married and was in Germany with her new solder husband Rob and Jeff stayed in Ohio with his father.

As I cared for Julia and performed my duties I soon learned many tricks of the trade of the open medium's club. As each day wore on I was becoming more and more frightened and concerned for my own health. I was a battery of light for the dark vortex and its residents. I lived there for a year before I was told after testing that I had a blockage in the heart. I was to undergo a catheter and was very concerned. I decided that I was not going to accept this and started praying for healing. When I underwent the procedure no blockage was found. I knew then that I must leave the camp as I put two and two together. Many residents had died due to heart problems and I soon understood that the heart area or chakra, a point of energy in the physical body, was under attack by what is known as psychic vampires. This dark energy had attacked my own being.

I was given the opportunity to start a newspaper column in the Anderson Indiana newspaper. The column is a metaphysical advice column and is received by the public with much enthusiasm. The president of the camp called me once again to the office and told me that as

long as I lived on the grounds I was not permitted to write a newspaper column. Her answer to my why was that there was too many jealous residents that did not like it.

Dale and I made the decision to leave my beloved camp I was devastated to learn of their practices and learn of the hate and anger the residents harbored against each other. One early morning as I was walking the beautiful grounds I was crying and wondering about my next move. I had thought that when I moved on the grounds that I would stay there for the remainder of my life. The camp had been a goal of mine from my early teen years and now I learned that it was not a spiritual place but a dark and nasty vortex. I cried out through my tears, "God what am I supposed to do, will I be alright if I leave? And God where do you want me, as I have dedicated my life to teaching? Now where am I to teach from? I no sooner spoke my prayer when I once again heard my still small voice tell me to look down. When I did I saw a swirling energy that looked like blowing sand. As I watched in wonder the sand took on the form of a rock and became still. I stooped down to examine the rock closer and was amazed to find that it was in the form of a Madonna. The base was flat so it could sit and I noticed that it was very lightweight. I had once again received an apport from my council of guides and I knew of my direction.

By now Julia's badly diseased leg had been amputated and she was placed in a nursing home to recover. Dale and I found a home in Indianapolis and we proceeded to move.

The open mediums were angry to hear that I was leaving. I had been given the knowledge of the secrets and now I was leaving. I was not afraid of them even though I had seen them try to do harm to others that they considered enemies. In their eyes I was now a threat that could not be controlled and this concerned them. I had no idea that I had become involved in a cult but I knew that I had to get out. As I was silently praying I asked once again, God if this place is so beautiful how can it be so evil? I then heard a still calm voice that said, my child, who was the prettiest angel in heaven?

Dale and I moved to Indianapolis close to Beech Grove. Dale had three years left to work before retirement and his place of employment at Amtrak was located in Beech Grove.

Jennifer was now in North Carolina and was due to give birth to my first grandchild. I was able to visit her often by train and was so glad to share in her pregnancy.

Julia was in the nursing home for her recovery but her health was failing fast. I spent a lot of time with her and tried to help her as much as I could. I would still cringe when she gave me that look. The look came if her laundry that I had taken home to wash was not white enough, but I was there for her. I had to go to Ohio to spend time with Jeff and I explained to Julia that I would be back on Sunday evening. She looked into my eyes with her crystal blue ones and said, "I am bored here." I replied," I know, but when I get back maybe we can go to a movie or something." She fixed her gaze strongly into my eyes and said, "You don't understand, I am bored here." Once again I reassured her that I would be back and we could do something even if it was a trip to the mall just to window shop. I left and that was the last words I ever heard from my mother. She died the next day by simply closing her eyes as if to take a nap. Julia was gone after a life of pain and concern for her life long love of two people, her loved Sug and their beautiful baby girl.

At her funeral I thought of her once spoken words to me concerning her death. She strongly believed that once she was departed from the physical plane she would be able to contact me. "I will contact you in a way that will not be mistakable", she said. Now I must watch for any sign that she lives on, 1 thought as I looked at her calm face that did not show her sixty nine years of pain. My thoughts went out to my brothers and sisters at this time of grief but I knew that we would all be just fine because Julia had raised six very strong deeply spiritual people.

I went through the normal grieving process but it was made easier preparing for the birth of my new granddaughter. Julia had been gone for four months when I received a call from Jennifer telling me that I was needed in North Carolina. The baby was due in a few days and the doctor was placing Jennifer in the hospital to induce labor. I took a train and arrived with a happy heart knowing that I was soon to see the face of my beautiful granddaughter. The labor went smoothly and Jessica was soon born into the world. I walked to the nursery and was so surprised to see that she looked exactly like Jennifer looked when I first saw her tiny face. Jessica was crying loudly when I first approached her. I said. "Jessica". When this tiny little girl heard my voice she stopped crying immediately and tried to focus her tiny crystal blue eyes. When I looked into her frightened eyes I stepped back and said, 0h my God, You said you would send me a sign". I was unprepared to see Julia's eyes looking into mine but the look was unmistakable. I knew at once that she had come right back. I reached for her tiny hand with tears in my eyes and said," Hi lady welcome home," Jessica's little bow mouth turned up in a smile as she held my finger and drew strength from my hand.

Everything had gone well with the birth and mother and baby were doing fine. I went home knowing that Jennifer and Rob were doing great in their new role as mom and dad.

I had started teaching a new group of students and was writing my books on a daily basis. All was going smooth. On occasions I would still hear from a couple of open mediums showing concern about me talking about the secret practices at the camp. I still wasn't worried about them being able to cause me any harm until one day I received a desperate call from Jennifer. "Mom, I need you," she cried. "Rob has been shot". "What are you saying?"I asked." Rob has been shot', she once again cried, "Can you get here?" Rob had decided to go to the store for some ice cream and on his arrival at the store a man in a van accused rob of taking his parking place. A few words were spoken and the man in the van shot Rob in the lower half of his heart. The bullet lodged in his lungs behind the heart and he was on his way to the hospital. I hung up the phone in shock and called for the next flight to North Carolina.

I arrived to find that Rob had undergone surgery to repair the heart but the bullet was lodged in the lung and could not be removed. When Rob woke from surgery his first comment was, "Whew I must have done something to that man in my last life."

I was always placing the white light of protection around myself as I meditated. I failed to envelope the children in this type of protection and I was certain that the dark psychic vampires, directed from the camp members, had found their target. Of course I had some doubt about this practice but when a dear friend's daughter was involved in a near fatal car accident I was certain that mere was certainly dark forces at work. My friend had decided to run against an open medium for her seat on the board and had won. This act angered many of the open mediums and shortly after she nearly lost her daughter. I was convinced that I now needed to protect not only myself but my loved ones as well. The act of karma was carried out here most likely on both accounts. It was the act of karma along with the act of hateful revenge that activated such severe actions. Rob was going to have to collect from his past deeds but perhaps not so severely. Rob survived as did my friend's daughter and both are doing well. Rob will always have the bullet lodged in his lung but he is living a normal healthy life otherwise. Rob now understands the laws of cause and effect. He holds no resentment in his heart for the man who shot him. He often feels the scar and now understands that many years ago he as Matt, a caring young, man had to shoot another in order to save himself. With this healing knowledge he has grown into a thoughtful, forgiving person.

I remained with them for several weeks. I was assured that he was healing fine before I started my journey home.

After I arrived home I wanted to rent a building for a seminar that was owned by a Baptist church. I was unaware that the church owned it and I arranged a meeting with the owner. As we sat and talked I soon learned that he was a minister. Rev. Robb was very interested in my views. We talked for three hours and his first intention was to convert me to his religion. I was unable to rent his building but his talk with me opened my eyes to truths that I had not entertained before. I was under the understanding that all was good and was as naive as a new baby. I was so surprised that the so called spiritual people could do such dastardly deeds to their fellow man. He said, "If you hear that you have rats in your house, and you don't believe in them they will increase in number. Again you are told you have rats in your house and you deny them again. Soon the rats will increase and will overtake you and certainly destroy you." I was confused by his allegory and he explained further. If you go through life not recognizing the strong force of Satan, soon you will be so involved in his energy that it will destroy you. I was not yet a believer in his concept of Satan but I understood his message. It was the dark force that I was thrust into and I and my family was nearly destroyed. He explained to me that I was not a psychic but a prophetess When the Prophets are sent to do work on the earth they will meet many times with situations that will set out to destroy their true mission. I thanked Rev. Robb and was so surprised to receive a letter from him that helped to change my life and my views. He stated in his letter," *Thank you for your visit this morning. I enjoyed it immensely and I learned a lot from you, but as you know that is the way the Holy Spirit teaches. So I believe you were sent here and I thank him for that. Ask the Lord to teach you and develop those tremendous gifts he has given you. Tell him that your whole life is dedicated to glorifying his Son here in the earth and thank him for leading and guiding you unto all truth. Seldom do I have the opportunity to meet someone such as you who radiates such gifts which are certainly from the Lord for he has surely called you as his instrument."*

I was so impressed with his letter and it opened an entire new viewpoint into my life. I had thought because I possessed these gifts that it had to be practices of Spiritualism and this was the direction I had taken. I did not understand the entire picture and this man had opened my eyes. I held to the idea that Spiritualism was the only religion that one who had the gifts that I have could practice. I knew that I was a Christian and had been from early childhood but with the gifts I had I was unaware that I was not just a medium but that I was a Christian Mystic and prophetess. I had experienced many encounters that nearly took my faith. When I had denounced God I was thrown into a life path that created much pain. I know knew what my calling was and I was determined that nothing could ever again separate me from my faith and God I hold this letter dear to my heart and when I get down I read his words and I feel as if God is speaking directly to me through this man of God.

I watched in awe as the new neighbors moved in next door and I was reminded of the dream which had involved a red haired family. This entire family was bright red headed. Not only the five children but the parents possessed the same red hair. I watched and thought of the dream that I had many years ago about the little girl finally being left with the older woman in the last house. This must be the last house, I thought. The dream revealed itself to me as I watched this family move in their belongings. The little girl was me in the dream as well as the older woman was. I had completed my many lessons along my life path and I was now about to enter the part of my life where I was to have no more harsh trials that could overwhelm me again. I now knew that I was to reopen a center and make a place for others to come to and learn about their own spirituality. This was my "last house". I now completely knew self and was about to embark on a teaching quest for others.

I understood that my life had been in danger far more than I could have imagined. When I had left God to take my life into my own hands I had created a life of hell on Earth for myself. I was under the impression that I was a psychic and that was all. I know understand that all the gifts that I have are in fact true gifts direct from God and are not to be taken lightly. I now understand my mission and my true purpose of life. I am here to teach and to help others grow spiritually by allowing God to use me to express his will through me. I am a Christian mystic and an evangelist for the new age or era.

A dear friend once said to me. "Your understanding is like a candle. The brighter your flame becomes the more bugs it will attract." I know this to be true,

Jennifer and Rob had made the decision to move back to Ohio. The Army has honorably dismissed Rob due to his health condition. I traveled to their home to spend their last thanksgiving with them in North Carolina. Jessica was learning to talk and called herself Gotika. This was as close as she could come to saying Jessica. She was now eleven months old and was talking fluently with a few mispronunciations. As I asked her her name she looked at me with an intense stare and said. "Judy". I asked her once again and got the same response. I said, Jennifer does she have a friend at day care by the name of Judy?" Jennifer replied, "No, not that I know of and besides she can't say the letter J." "Well, she just did", I said. Jennifer asked her her name and Jessica laughed her baby laugh and said, "Gotika". I thought I had seen my mothers look in her eyes at birth and now she tells me her name is Judy. I knew then that Julia had come right back.

In the spring of the year I went to visit a dear friend Glenn, who lives in Nashville Tennessee. Glen has a job of tour guide for the tourists that visit Tennessee. One afternoon she and I were talking and she decided to take me on my own private tour of the city. She wanted to show me homes of country singers and the grand 'ol opery building. I was intrigued with all that I saw and enjoyed my private tour. Glen wanted to show me a place that was not on the tour because she felt as if I would enjoy seeing an old plantation. As we approached the beautiful mansion I felt a rush of emotions that I could not explain. I couldn't see enough of the beautiful house as well as the spacious grounds. I started crying without explanation and felt a sense of helplessness as well as hopelessness. I felt as if I could throw myself down on the dusty ground and cry. I could not understand my feelings and was at the same time flooded with memories that I had no idea of where they stemmed from. I at the time did not realize that I had walked through a time hole that revealed my past life as a slave living on this very same plantation. I looked at my hands and they appeared brown, I looked at my feet and they too were dusty and brown. My clothes seemed to appear to be a long brown skirt and I was Maggie once again. I told Glenn that I needed to go over by a tree and rest awhile and when I did I was reeling with memories and emotions. We talked to the curator and I asked information about the resident slaves. She informed me that there was no information available to the public but there was a limited amount that could be made available. Glenn and I left and I had so much information in my head that I needed to go home to sort it all out.

Throughout the next year I made many notes of my surfacing memories and once again wanted to visit the plantation. On arrival I was delighted to find that information on the resident slaves was now available and on display. As I read what information was there I was not too surprised to see that the overseer was named Tad. This just confirmed my flood of memories and I knew for sure that I had experienced unlocking my past life. All that I have done in this life was and is a continuation of many lifetimes. The life of Madgelyn is merely a chapter in a large book called life. I had the key and by writing this book I share it with you. All that one does is set into motion from a past act. One can learn from it, collect deeds either good or bad, make amends, and grow spiritually. The purpose to life is to grow spiritually and to share it with others.

I now understood Rob's near fatal shooting that held a dual message which was one of a past deed, and another of learning to protect oneself. I knew of the reason for Julia losing her small baby, my marriage to Tad and many more issues that I have experienced. As Dale approaches the date of retirement we were delighted to be able to purchase a beautiful home in Ohio near my family. As we were settling into our new home I received a phone call from Tad's (my second husband) sister. Tad, at the age of 44 had undergone a stroke and is presently in a nursing home to recover. He spent a few weeks in a coma and upon awakening he asked for me. Tad and I have not seen each other for at least twelve years and I am the first person he asked for. I made the trip to see him and his response to me was that I make him feel so much better and that he loves me. As he was injured in the civil war period he lost use of his left arm. Tad will spend the remainder of his life now without the use of his left arm due to the stroke. Tad and I span many lifetimes together and will always share a deep spiritual connection.

As I read about the history of Belle Meade Plantation I notice that in the chronology of the family many names have been repeated in my lifetime. Coincidence? I don't think so. In the Plantation's family's history there can be found names such as George, John, Francis who had a daughter named Amanda. In My life my father's name was George as well as my brother's name. My father's brother was John. I knew now that George my brother is the reincarnation of his uncle John. My sister Frances has a daughter Amanda. This is just an example as there are many other family names that have repeated. Through out the history there are name vibrations that repeat. When one needs the experiences the vibrations often remain the same throughout time As I was taking my beautiful 6 year old granddaughter, Julie/Julia disguised as Jessica, to visit a friend the other day she turned her crystal blue eyes up to me and ask, "Nammy, is 2000 the year or is that the address we need to find?"

About the Author

Madgelyn was born with the gift of prophecy. She is an ordained minister and certified medium missionary. She has six years of college with a major in psychology. For three years Madgelyn had a metaphysical advise column in Indiana and a raido talk show in Ohio. She has made several guest appearances on television in the Dayton Ohio area. Madgelyn has worked with local universities and their religious departments, visiting prisons and lecturing to students about their concerns of the expanding Beleif system on the planet. She and her husband Dale reside in Springfield Ohio and is presently working on another book.

LaVergne, TN USA
01 December 2010
206835LV00005B/197/A